Penn took his time discovering the contours of her hips and thighs. Her body was pleasantly curved and he could feel the outline of a suspender belt. His fingers traced the straps that ran down her outer thighs.

'My wish is your command?' he said, breathing in her perfume.

'Yes.'

Slowly, he began to move the skirt up her thighs. She gasped and he watched her reflection in the mirror; she closed her eyes, but said nothing and did not change her position. He slid the material higher and she still did not object. Then, with a final slither, the tight skirt slid completely over her hips and remained bunched at her waist.

His hands descended again . . .

The Voyeur

Phillip Mason

NEW ENGLISH LIBRARY
Hodder and Stoughton

First published in Great Britain in 1998
by Hodder and Stoughton
A division of Hodder Headline PLC
First published in paperback in 1998
by Hodder and Stoughton

A New English Library Paperback

10 9 8 7 6 5 4 3 2

A CIP Catalogue Record for this title
is available from the British Library.

Mason, Philip
The voyeur
1.Erotic stories
I.Title
823.9'14 [F]

ISBN 0 340 69501 3

Typeset by Hewer Text Ltd, Edinburgh
Printed and bound in Great Britain by
Clays Ltd, St Ives PLC

Hodder and Stoughton
A division of Hodder Headline PLC
338 Euston Road
London NW1 3BH

Chapter 1

Charles Penn could not get Tamara Fenwick out of his mind. He had met her only once and was in danger of being smitten. This was not the way for an icon of the publishing world to behave. Especially a middle-aged icon with a reputation for playing the field.

He had welcomed the business trip as a way to take his mind off the girl who was half his age. If he was honest, at twenty-three she was less than half his age, but he had rarely been honest in the last twenty years while he had been building an empire that included magazines, a television franchise, an independent film company and a book publisher.

Penn was wealthy but had no intention of sitting back and letting others run his businesses. He was a man who liked to be involved and who enjoyed the attendant publicity, which was why he was flying to Majorca for the final two days of the sales conference of Pennworld Publishing.

He would be required to mingle with his staff, shake hands, pat backs, deliver a keynote speech and accept the thanks of his workforce for giving them a five days' out-of-season business holiday in the sun.

The speech was written and in his briefcase. Not too long to be boring, not too short to be dismissed, and with the right balance of jokes poking fun at the different heads of department. Keep them laughing and keep them loyal. Enthuse them with the aura of a special team.

They *were* a special team, and this time he was being honest. The best at what they did, which was why they were successful and which was why he employed them. He looked out of the window at the white blanket of cloud below and wondered what Tamara would be doing?

An attractive female flight attendant brought him another half-bottle of champagne without being asked and he nodded his thanks. She opened it with a napkin around the cork and poured the wine. He was used to attractive young women doing his bidding and he had no illusions about the reasons.

Penn realized he was reasonably attractive, even at fifty. He exercised and watched his diet and he could afford to dress with style. But he knew that his power and wealth enhanced his charm for girls who were half his age ... which was part of his dilemma.

He was hardly in the right emotional shape to fall in love, anyway. His track record was disastrous. Perhaps both he and the girl would be better off if he forgot about her, but that was easier said than done.

Perhaps Majorca would take his mind off the problem?

Palma Airport was busy as always. Penn had only his briefcase and did not have to wait for the baggage handlers to unload, nor did he have to fight for a suitcase at the carousel. He went through the disembarkation formalities and strode onto the arrivals concourse.

A blonde girl in her twenties, whom he vaguely recognized, stepped forward to greet him. She had an intelligent face, blue eyes and the beginnings of a tan, and wore a navy blue business suit with tight skirt and high heels.

'Mr Penn. I'm Caroline Lee.'

They shook hands and he remembered she was part of Pennworld public relations.

'Hi, Caroline. Call me Charles.'

She flushed with pleasure at the offered intimacy.

'I have a car waiting, Charles.'

They left the air-conditioned building for the heat outside and a stretch limousine that had a black driver. He wore a white T-shirt, white canvas trousers and a white peaked cap that might have been more appropriate on a yacht in Palma Marina.

'This is Roy,' Caroline introduced the chauffeur.

Roy opened the rear door for them and they climbed back into air-conditioning.

'How has the conference been?' he asked.

'First-rate. Objectives identified, strategies planned. Being away like this has brought a lot of people closer.' She smiled pleasantly. 'A sort of encounter group in the sun.'

'It's good internal PR. I'm glad you recognize the fact.' He glanced at her attire and the sheen of her stockings. 'You also seem to be taking it seriously. I half expected to be met by someone in a bikini.'

Caroline said, 'That is the last thing you expected. There's a time and place for fun as well as business, and this part is business.'

'Strictly business?' he said.

The girl blushed prettily and her smile changed. Already they were flirting. It invariably worked, especially when the attractive young woman concerned thought he might be able to further her career. Or was he just being cynical?

They were deposited at a five-star hotel on the road around the bay and Caroline escorted him to his top floor suite. In the lift, he said, 'Gio by Giorgio Armani.'

'That's right,' she said. 'Do you like it?'

He leaned down and sniffed her neck and saw a nerve twitching.

'It's exactly right.'

Caroline opened the door of the suite and he followed her inside. The living room and bedroom had a connecting balcony but the blinds were drawn against the sun. His clothes, which had been brought out earlier by a member of staff, had been unpacked and were either hanging in the wardrobe or put away in a chest of drawers.

'Would you open the blinds?' he asked, and the girl obliged.

The living room had a bar and he went behind it to check the contents of the refrigerator.

'Did I miss anything?' she said.

'Bollinger.'

'I'm sorry. I'll have some sent up.'

She called room service and ordered the champagne while he went onto the balcony and looked at the view of Palma Bay. He turned and saw that she was waiting in the living room by the desk upon which was the telephone. He sensed that she was intimidated by him. He re-entered the room.

'Anything else?' she said.

'I'm not sure.'

He looked at her speculatively and she smiled hesitantly and shrugged.

'Your wish is my command,' she said.

'Really?'

Caroline licked her lips.

'Yes,' she said, the word almost a whisper.

'You are a very beautiful woman, Caroline.' He touched her chin with a finger. 'Intelligent. Ambitious.' He dropped the finger to the top of her suit jacket. 'You could go far.'

'I hope to.'

'But in this weather, you appear to be a little over-dressed.' He unfastened the top button of the jacket and parted it with both hands so that he could see her breasts in the lace cups of a black brassiere. Beads of sweat like tiny tears nestled in the curves. 'Perspiration,' he said.

'I need a shower.'

He continued to look into the folds of the jacket and reached with one finger to move one of the cups from her breast so that he could see the nipple, small and vulnerable, and the line of her tan.

'I see you keep your breasts covered,'

'Pardon?'

'When you sunbathe?'

'Oh. Yes.' She forced a smile. 'I wouldn't dare go topless with the rest of the office watching.'

'Of course not.'

He released the jacket and said, 'What's the schedule?'

Caroline took a deep breath and turned to the desk. Upon it was a piece of paper with a typed itinerary. Above it was a mirror.

'It's all here.' She rested her hands on the desk. 'Seven, drinks in the piano bar. Dinner at eight . . .'

He stepped close behind her and placed his hands on her hips; she ran out of words, staring at the piece of paper in silence.

Penn took his time discovering the contours of her hips and thighs. Her body was pleasantly curved and he could feel the outline of a suspender belt. His fingers traced the straps that ran down her outer thighs.

'My wish is your command?' he said, breathing in her perfume.

'Yes.'

Slowly, he began to move the skirt up her thighs. She gasped and he watched her reflection in the mirror: she closed her eyes, but she said nothing and did not change her position. He slid the material higher and still she did not object. Then, with a final slither, the tight skirt slid completely over her hips and remained bunched at her waist.

His hands descended again, and he looked down at the golden flesh they were touching, golden flesh that was covered by black French panties, and across which the ruched black satin of suspender straps stretched to hold taut her tan stockings.

Her flesh was warm and soft and he felt her shudder at his touch. Not a shudder of repulsion but of apprehension of the unknown. His right hand went down over the curve of her bottom and between her legs from behind. His fingers brushed aside the panties and stroked her vagina.

'O-oh,' she murmured, her eyes still tightly closed.

He held her hip gently with his left hand whilst his right worked between her legs. His fingers parted the lips of her vagina and pushed between the folds. She was dry but his index finger dipped deeper and found her moisture. He stirred it and she shuddered again as he lubricated her.

Now he was able to insert two fingers inside her and she made small noises in her throat. He watched her reflection, gazing at the eyes tight closed and the mouth that was now partly open. Delightful pink lips, the bottom lip pouting. He removed the fingers and ran his middle one forward into the cave at the front of her vagina and found her clitoris.

He rolled it: she moaned and that delightful bottom lip shook and her body shuddered. He inserted his thumb into her vagina and used his index finger to rub that sensitive bud.

Her hips moved around his hand, her buttocks clenched and unclenched and she squirmed upon his fingers.

The knock at the door caused her to tense and her eyes to open. He held her gaze in the mirror.

'Close your eyes,' he said.

They were big and blue and full of uncertainty but she closed them and his fingers continued their work.

Charles Penn shouted, 'Enter.'

The door opened and a waiter came in carrying an ice bucket in which was a bottle of Bollinger. He stopped halfway across the room at the sight of the young woman leaning forward against the desk with her skirt around her waist while the man behind her moved his hand between her legs.

Caroline could not believe this was happening. She could not believe she was *allowing* this to happen. She had known of Charles Penn's reputation and had been prepared to indulge his sexual advances but this was unexpected.

'Please open the champagne,' Penn said.

The ice bucket clinked as the waiter put it down. With her eyes closed, she had become extra-sensitive to sound. She could hear the noise of Penn's fingers as they stirred her vaginal juices. She could smell herself.

How long would the waiter take? What would he think?

The fingers continued to slurp and rub and she could not stop herself from reacting. The attention he was lavishing upon her clitoris was insistent and caused her to gasp.

'Time to come, Caroline,' he whispered in her ear. 'Can you do that for me?'

His finger increased its speed upon her clitoris and her body quivered as she whimpered and shook. Her knuckles went white as she gripped the edge of the desk and she tried to bite back the cry as she orgasmed.

Penn slipped his left arm around her waist for support as he felt her climax, her body twitching upon his right hand. As she subsided he kissed her ear and the waiter finally popped the champagne cork.

'Leave it,' said Penn, and the waiter, still stunned, left the room.

Penn removed his right hand from between her legs and eased the skirt down over her hips. He smoothed it back into place and then stepped away and went to the bar.

Caroline opened her eyes but remained holding the desk and staring down at the sheet of paper for long seconds.

'Champagne?' he said.

She licked her lips, attempting to gather what composure she could, and turned to face him. He poured wine into a fluted glass and held it out to her. She stepped forward and took it. He put down the bottle, picked up the other glass in his left hand and ran the first two fingers and thumb of his right hand around its rim. Only then did he pour the wine.

He raised this glass to his nose and inhaled the aroma before raising it further in a toast.

'To you, Caroline. And an interesting two days.'

Inside, she was still quivering, but she raised her glass in response and they drank. He had given her an orgasm while a waiter watched but he had not climaxed himself. He still looked calm and unruffled.

Did he run his sex life the same way as he ran his businesses? With total control?

'Will there be anything else?' she said.

'Not at the moment. But I'm very impressed with you, so far. Tell me, honestly, do you always wear stockings?'

She hesitated and said, 'No. Not always.'

'Why today? In this climate?'

'Because you prefer women to wear stockings.'

He smiled, and said, 'You've been reading my Press cuttings.'

'Of course.'

Now he laughed.

'Of course, of course. It's what a good PRO would do.' He sipped champagne. 'You wore them for me?'

'Yes.'

'Thank you. The gesture is appreciated. Is your room nearby?'

'I'm on the next floor down. My number is on your itinerary.'

'How thoughtful. I shall call for you at seven, Caroline, and we shall make an entrance together. Set a few tongues wagging, perhaps?'

'Without a doubt.'

'And now, you probably need that shower.'

'Yes.' She finished the wine and put the glass on the top of the bar. 'I'll see you at seven . . . Charles.'

'At seven, Caroline. Be pretty.'

The young woman left the room and Penn exhaled with quiet satisfaction. His body was alive with sexual tension and, for a short time, he had forgotten Tamara Fenwick. But now Tamara came back to fill his thoughts, slim and fluid in a long silk dress of the palest blue.

He remembered their introduction. She was sitting at a table in the Café de Paris in London, he was standing awkwardly. He was caught by her Amazon-green eyes and husky voice, her raven hair in an elfin cut that emphasized the bone structure of her face.

She stretched her arms to shake hands and leaned

forward. The dress gaped and he saw her breasts, free within the silk, small and pertly pink-tipped, her nipples giving the impression of being permanently aroused.

Afterwards, he was sure she must have known he was staring into her dress, for the smile changed with understanding at his desire and she invited him to sit next to her and join her party. They had talked for two hours and he had been captivated.

Could this be different?

Chapter 2

The evening was a success, although at one point Charles Penn became detached enough to wonder if he would be enjoying it quite so much if he were not the centre of attention.

Caroline Lee was pretty in an informal blue and white dress in crêpe de Chine with a scoop neckline and a short floating skirt that was extremely enticing. Penn noticed most of the other men present thought so too, and he took pleasure in placing a hand upon her waist from time to time to let them see he had seigneurial rights.

A bonus was the presence of Dr Tess Flanders, the American sex guru, for whose work Pennworld Publishing had the UK rights. She was a best-seller on both sides of the Atlantic and around the world. The formula she used to achieve these sales was not unique but she was good at what she did.

Dr Flanders encouraged people to write to her with their sexual problems, experiences or fantasies. Thousands did so, and she used their letters as the basis for her books in which she discussed the psychoses of sex.

They were ostensibly classified as educational literature although the balance between confessions and psychology was heavily weighted in favour of the sex.

A life-size cardboard cut-out of Dr Flanders was in the entrance of the piano bar to welcome the guests. It showed a curvaceous woman in her late thirties in a figure-hugging business suit and with a lot of dark hair, although this evening she wore an elegant black shift dress and her hair was much more under control.

'You look better in the flesh,' he told her.

'I guess so,' she said, staring at her cardboard alter ego. 'I don't know about you, but it scares the hell out of me.'

'It's the suit. Makes you look formal and too old. We'll scrap it and do it again.'

'An executive decision?'

'An executive decision from an admirer.'

'You mean that as well as publishing my work you've read it?'

'Yes.'

'And approve?'

'On both counts.'

'Both counts?'

'Your books both make money and contribute to a deeper understanding of sexuality.'

'You think that's important?' she said.

'Of course. Sex is still a taboo subject. People are afraid of it, afraid of admitting what they really think about it. They bottle it up. You tell them it's good to talk about their experiences and fantasies. You are a very necessary release valve.'

'You make me sound like a bathroom fitting.'

He laughed and shook his head.

'You know what I mean. You're the expert with words, not me.'

She shrugged.

'There are those who wouldn't agree. They claim it's an easy way to write a book. Place an ad in the glossies asking for confessions, then sit back and sift the mail.'

'But it works wonderfully well,' he said.

She laughed and said, 'It does, doesn't it?'

'Maybe your critics are jealous.'

'Maybe they are. But it has given me something of a reputation as a vampire of sensation.'

'I like that,' he said. 'Vampire of sensation. Maybe we could use it on the cover . . .'

They both laughed, and she said, 'I know *your* reputation, too.'

He raised an eyebrow and said, 'Sounds like you think I might be a suitable case for treatment?'

'I don't treat people. I listen. I encourage them to talk. Or write.'

'You sound like the Samaritans.'

'Well, that's an improvement on a faucet.'

'I said release valve.'

'Same thing.'

They stared at each other and he realized that she really was a good-looking woman.

He said, 'I get the impression you don't approve of my reputation?'

'As long as what you do is not against the law or standards of basic humanity, I neither approve nor disapprove.'

'But you don't approve of Caroline?'

Tess smiled.

'Are you having an affair with her?'

'No. I am helping to liberate her.'

She laughed loudly.

'I've heard *that* before. Are you aware that one man's liberation can be a woman's domination?'

'Does it matter if both parties are over the age of consent and agree to the arrangement?'

'The semantics of sex,' she said. 'You are starting to

justify an arrangement you may have doubts about. Is the justification innocent . . . or culpable?'

They were both continuing to smile but Penn lowered his eyes as if he did not wish her to see what they might show.

'You are an interesting woman, Tess.' He raised his eyes again but now he was showing nothing. 'You think I take advantage of my power, don't you?'

'I don't know you well enough to form an opinion, but I think there is a self-evident danger in power. You obviously recognize it.'

'Yes, I do.'

'You also enjoy the power.'

'I worked hard enough to get it. I earned the right to enjoy it.'

'A man of driving ambition. I know all about the Penn success story. The ambition doesn't seem to have eased any. What continues to drive you, Charles?'

'That's a personal question.'

'It was meant to be.'

He waved his glass of wine to indicate the room.

'Wrong time, wrong place.'

'I guess so.'

'But perhaps we can talk again?'

'I'd like that.'

'No one has been as direct as you for a long time.'

'That's because I don't need you, Charles. My reputation is made. My books sell. If you didn't sell them, someone else would.'

'No ambitions, either?'

'Not for wealth or power. I have enough of both.'

'For what, then?'

'Now you're asking personal questions, and it's still the wrong time and place.'

They laughed and Penn saw Caroline moving towards them through the crowd.

'I think this might be a good time for me to circulate and stoke a few rumours.'

'With that young woman?'

He shrugged.

'I have my reputation to maintain.'

Penn gave her a half-bow to excuse himself and moved to the side of Caroline Lee. He put his arm around her waist and his hand strayed lower than was polite. The rumours, she could tell, were already starting.

Dr Tess Flanders smiled. He was very much a suitable case for treatment.

Penn had told Caroline to order the limousine for midnight. The party was still in full swing at the hotel when the witching hour arrived and everyone either saw or heard that he and the young public relations executive left together.

Roy, the same black driver, but now wearing a short-sleeved white shirt, held open the rear door and Caroline climbed in.

Penn did not immediately follow her into the limousine but closed the door and remained outside for a few moments, talking to Roy. Eventually, he got in and sat next to her on the wide white leather cushions.

'Where are we going?' she said.

'It's a surprise.'

He turned to catch her look and smiled into her eyes. Her smile in return was hesitant.

They drove along the front of the harbour on the Paseo Maritimo and through the suburbs of the city. Soon there were no more bars and no more suburbs and no more street lights. They took a road through the country towards Esporles.

'Is my wish still your command?' he said, softly.

'Yes,' she said, her voice a whisper.

He looked out of the window to his left at the darkness. he could sense her nervousness. He turned his head and gave her a reassuring smile.

'You look lovely,' he said.

'I'm glad you approve.'

He looked down at her legs.

'Show me,' he said.

The girl eased herself lower and towards the edge of the seat, put both her hands on her thighs and slid the dress upwards, exposing the tops of her tan stockings and the white suspender straps that held them taut.

'All the way,' he said.

She took hold of the hem of the dress and lifted it to her waist. Her thighs looked wider because she was sitting. She wore loose white silk panties. Penn nodded his approval.

'Beautiful,' he said.

The driver called from the front, 'Here, Mr Penn?'

'Yes.'

The car turned off the main road. There were no street lights, no other traffic. The limo left this minor road, bumped onto rough terrain and stopped. Roy switched off the engine and the only sounds in the car were of the three of them breathing. When Roy began to turn in the front seat, Caroline pushed down the skirt of her dress.

Caroline stared into the chauffeur's eyes but he intimated nothing and looked to Penn, who nodded. Roy took off the peaked cap and put it on the seat alongside him, got out of the car and closed the door. Caroline thought he would keep on walking, but he came round the car, opened the right-hand rear passenger door and looked in at them.

Penn said, 'Move a little closer, Caroline. Make room for our friend.'

The girl gulped. Her mouth was suddenly dry. But she moved further across the white leather closer to her employer. Roy got into the back and sat on her right. The limousine was wide and comfortable but the man took up a lot of room. She could smell his body odour and she stared at his huge black hands as they lay upon his knees.

'Now show me again,' said Penn.

Caroline turned her head quickly to look at him and saw that he was serious and totally calm, as if the request was perfectly reasonable.

She looked into her lap and saw her hands, small and pale, upon the material of her dress. It was almost as if she were watching someone else's hands, as they once more pulled the skirt upwards, revealing more and more of her legs. She glanced sideways one more time, in case he changed his mind, but Penn was watching her rising hemline.

'Higher,' he said.

The material went above the tops of her stockings and she felt her pulses racing.

'All the way,' breathed Penn.

She scooped the skirt in her hands and lifted it to her waist and laid her head back against the seat, her eyes closed.

'Beautiful,' said Penn. 'Do you not agree?'

'Uh-huh.'

'Stretch your legs, Caroline. There is plenty of room.'

She stretched her legs across the deep white pile of the carpet.

'Open your eyes, Caroline. You must watch.'

Caroline opened her eyes. Roy was staring at her legs. Penn was staring into her face. He smiled again: a renewal of trust? Of reassurance?

'Watch,' he whispered. He looked back at her legs. 'Touch her,' he said to the man. 'Feel her warmth.'

She watched as Roy shifted sideways on the seat and reached over to place his huge right hand upon her leg just above her knee.

'So delicate a limb,' said Penn.

The man's hand moved, stroking her in a gentle movement. His palm covered her leg, his fingers dipped around it.

'Higher,' said Penn. 'From silk to silken flesh.'

She watched the black hand move up her leg to cross the stocking top and slide inexorably onto her flesh. Her insides were quivering. Her own hands, still holding the skirt of her dress, had become rigid in their grip.

'Feel her warmth,' said Penn.

The hand stroked her naked thigh, his thick forefinger brushing between her legs.

'Find her heat,' said Penn.

That large forefinger dipped beneath the loose silk of the panties and stroked downwards through her pubic hair. It encountered the lips of her sex and manoeuvred between them. The hand was so black on her pale flesh, so black beneath the white silk of her underwear. The finger dipped over her clitoris and into her heat.

'Find the wetness,' said Penn.

The finger dug deeply inside her and she groaned. It moved and stirred and released her wetness. The man began to move the finger in and out of her vagina and she was amazed to hear the slurping noises that indicated she had become extremely wet so quickly.

Penn said, 'Does that feel good, Caroline?'

'Yes,' she murmured, her gaze fixed on the huge black hand between her legs.

'Your panties need removing, Caroline. Ask Roy to remove them.'

Her features did not feel as if they belonged to her any more. She could feel nerves quivering in her cheeks and neck. She could feel the finger like a boy's penis moving inside her. The black man stared into her face.

'Please,' she whispered, dropping her hands to her sides. 'Take them off. Take off my panties.'

Roy knelt on the white carpet in front of her and both hands went beneath the dress to her waist and tugged the panties down. She raised her buttocks from the seat to facilitate their removal.

The flimsy silk slid down her legs and Roy lifted her feet, still in their high-heeled shoes, one at a time, to remove the garment completely.

Penn held out his hand and Roy gave him the panties. He raised them to his face and inhaled their aroma.

He said, 'The finest perfume in the world.' He inhaled again. 'Smell her, Roy. Taste her.'

The man knelt up and unfastened his shirt. He took it off with slow deliberation and draped it over the front seat. His torso was magnificent. His muscles gleamed and rippled. His blackness was overpowering now the white shirt had gone. It was as if a barrier had been removed. He was the night.

He reached forward and opened Caroline's legs, his hands stroking her flesh above the stockings. He dipped his head and she yelped as his tongue slid over her skin.

It was warm and wet and pulsed as it licked up between her legs. His fingers preceded it and prepared her, opening

19

the lips of her labia, and she yelled loudly as the tongue found her opening and dug deeply inside.

The closest Caroline had ever been to a black man was on the Tube. And now she was staring down at the tight curls of his hair, at the huge hands that were pushing beneath her thighs and cupping her buttocks, lifting her legs over his shoulders. Now she was feeling his onslaught, his mouth a hot, wet and hungry beast at the portals of her sex, his tongue devouring her clitoris.

Her small white hands grasped his head, grasped the curls, and she felt Penn watching her. She glanced sideways at him, her blue eyes wide and staring, and thought what an amazing present he had given her. Then her eyes rolled upwards in her head, her lashes fluttered and she climaxed uncontrollably, thrusting her soft vagina into the mouth that was eating her, her legs twitching with the spasms of orgasm.

When her senses returned, she was sprawled on the seat, her legs still apart, her skirt around her waist. Roy knelt on the carpet near her feet and Penn sat silently in the corner, her panties held to his nostrils.

Penn lowered the panties so she could see that he was smiling.

He said, 'Now it is time for you to return the favour.'

For a moment she did not understand what he meant. Did Penn want her to fellate him? Then she understood. Penn wanted her to fellate Roy. She shuddered. She did not know if she could perform such an act. It had been different when the black man had been at her feet, but could she kneel at his?

Roy moved back onto the seat next to her. He seemed bigger than ever without the shirt.

'Caroline,' Penn said, as if reading her mind. 'Don't disappoint me. Kneel.'

She slid off the white leather and onto the thick carpet. Her dress dropped down her thighs so that she was almost respectable again. The thought caused her to smile. She thought that perhaps hysteria was not very far away. Could she really do this?

'Between his legs, Caroline.'

Roy opened his legs and she knelt between them and rested her hands upon his thighs. They were so big, so strong. She could sense his power. A different kind of power to that of Penn.

'Open his trousers,' said Penn.

Her hands moved across the trousers and she felt Roy's erection beneath the material. She gulped. Its size was intimidating. Roy lay back in the seat. He wore no belt and she unfastened the waistband and pulled down the zip. He wore white boxer shorts that bulged as if concealing a small animal. No, definitely not small. A large and dangerous weapon.

'Get it out,' whispered Penn.

There was no turning back, and besides, she was curious. Would it be any different to a white penis? Her hands pulled at the waistband of the shorts and, this time, he raised himself from the seat so that she could tug down the trousers and the underwear until they were around his thighs.

Oh my God.

Her eyes widened. Her mouth hung slackly open. His penis was huge and still not fully stiff.

'Touch it,' said Penn.

This was a negative replay of what had gone before. Then it had been black-on-white and now it was white-on-black as she watched her pale hands move across the trunk-like thighs and, finally, take hold of the slumbering monster at his groin.

Only the proportions were different. Her hands looked too small to cope.

She held it and stroked it. She caressed it and he grunted: it stiffened and throbbed beneath her touch.

'Suck it,' hissed Penn.

He still held the white silk panties to his face.

Caroline licked her lips and bent her head. She licked the length of the shaft and nibbled at it. Her hands began a rhythm upon the shiny taut black skin and she manoeuvred the penis upright, holding her face above it as she drew back the foreskin. The glans beneath was pink: she was captivated by the sight and her inhibitions began to fade.

'Suck,' came the command from the other corner.

She dipped her head, stretched open her mouth, and took the glans of the penis inside.

At first it was an effort but with lubrication it became easier. She felt small quivers of delight inside herself when Roy moaned and his hips bucked in appreciation of the skill with which she fellated him.

It was a strange sensation to be kneeling between such powerful thighs and using her mouth in such an intimate way with a total stranger. A stranger who also happened to be black and whose naked African hue dominated the white interior of the limousine.

Caroline felt she was taking part in a primeval act. In her fevered imagination she saw herself as the victim of a sacrifice, a captured white *memsahib* who had become the plaything of a tribal leader.

'Enough,' said Penn.

The word did not at first register, and it was only when she recognized the other sounds, the bestial slobbering of her lips, that she understood the repeated command. Breathless, her face wet with secretions, she knelt up, still holding the rampant penis in her hands. She stared at her employer.

Her senses whirled. She was intoxicated and it was not alcohol that was affecting her. It was sexuality. She became aware of how she must look, aware of the dampness of her face, and she remembered the noises she had been making. She flushed with shame at the depth of her abandonment.

Penn said, 'Come, Caroline. Sit here.'

He patted the seat alongside him and she moved to sit once more between the two men. Penn stroked damp hair from her forehead and turned her to face him.

'You wonderful girl,' he said.

He laid her face against his shoulder.

Behind her, she felt Roy lift her dress and expose the nakedness beneath.

Not this, too? Surely, not this?

The man manoeuvred her with those big strong hands so that her hip rested against the seat. His bulk was a cliff face that lay against her back as he moved her legs apart with his knees and his erection went between her legs.

Caroline raised her head and stared into the face of Penn, who held her shoulders.

'I don't think I can,' she whispered.

'Of course you can,' he said, and kissed her forehead.

Roy used a hand to guide his monster weapon and he parted the lips of her sex again with his fingers. But this time, instead of his hot and welcome tongue, he inserted the head of his penis.

'Aahh . . .'

The moan caught in her throat. Her eyes and mouth were wide in consternation. Her left arm was trapped by the seat but she gripped Penn's arm with her right hand, while he continued to hold her by the shoulders, as if to steady her, as if to hold her for inspection.

Roy took his time. The phallus went in slowly and he paused after each inch, while Caroline gasped and groaned. She had given herself up to the inevitable and no longer knew her reasons why. Her attention was concentrated upon the hot limb of steel that was being inserted into her.

'No . . . no . . .' she muttered, shaking her head: surely it would not fit. She felt tears upon her cheek.

'Yes,' said Penn.

Yes, thought Caroline.

This was inevitable and now she had to know if she was capable of what Penn expected of her, capable of accepting the whole amazing length of this black phallus.

The images in her head became jumbled, the hysteria crowded closer. Penn's face was inches from hers and his eyes devoured her, while behind she was being submerged beneath the black power of Africa, being overwhelmed by the distinctive racial body smell and the odour of sex.

God, she could take no more. Surely, there could be no more?

And then Roy held his breath, pushed one last time – and she felt as if she were an offering on a spit. Her insides boiled and his muscled hips were flat against the softness of her bottom.

Her eyes closed and she almost passed out at the totality of his insertion. None of them moved for a long time and her breathing became shallow, as if she were in a trance. She once more became aware of her surroundings as he flexed the weapon inside her, releasing tremors of pleasure that caused moans to dribble from her throat.

For a while, he was content to continue flexing the phallus while his hands moved over her, stroking her thighs, mauling her buttocks, delving beneath the crêpe de Chine of the dress to push up her brassiere and take her small breasts in his huge palms.

Her eyes closed and opened, her mind drifted on the waves of sensation. Each time her eyes opened she gazed into those of Penn, who held her gently and stroked her face but who showed no emotion.

There came a time when the flexing stopped and she sensed that Roy was waiting. Penn looked over her shoulder at the man who was embedded inside her.

'Fuck her,' he said.

Roy eased the phallus halfway out and eased it back in. It was a piston that was starting slowly and creating its own lubrication.

Caroline groaned but her vaginal passage adapted and his strokes got longer and her wetness increased. Her breath was no longer shallow: it was ragged, and Roy's was laboured.

He held her hips steady and the strokes were long and firm as his pace began to quicken.

'Oh God, oh God, oh God . . .' she murmured.

The pace continued to increase and the suction of her vagina upon the penis as it was withdrawn became a sigh which was followed by a slurp and a slap as his groin slammed against her buttocks. Her body was shaking and it no longer seemed to belong to her but to the two men who held her.

Her eyes were closed and her senses filled with the sounds and smells of their own creation, of sweat and sex and tortured breath and gasps and moans. Such was the strength of the onslaught to which Roy had built that she slumped in the arms of Penn.

Caroline had been so high for so long that she was limp

and lost in the maelstrom when a tidal wave of sensation overwhelmed her without warning. She put back her head and screamed into a shaking fit of orgasm.

Roy gripped her hips tighter still, plunged the giant phallus deeper still, and discharged a salvo of fierce power inside her.

She was still on the edge, still quaking with the intensity of the climax, when she felt Penn's mouth upon hers. His lips opened hers and he stole her breath as his tongue delicately made love to her tongue.

Caroline thought she might have passed out for a short while for she was unaware of Roy disengaging or leaving the back of the limousine.

When she opened her eyes she found she was lying upon the seat. Her clothes, apart from her panties, were in place. Her shoulder rested in Penn's lap and he held her head gently in his arms.

'Are you all right?' he said.

'I'm not sure.'

He smiled and stroked her face. His eyes still searched her face. She licked her lips.

'Did all that happen?' she said, in wonder.

'Yes. It happened.'

'Good grief.'

He kissed her forehead. The front door of the limo opened and she heard Roy climb into the driving seat. The car engine started, they bumped off the rough ground and onto a road and she fell asleep.

Chapter 3

Penn delivered the keynote speech the next day, at the morning and final session of the conference. As expected, it was received with undiluted enthusiasm.

Dr Tess Flanders, youthfully attractive in white slacks and blue silk blouson, watched and listened and, at the speech's conclusion, she smiled rather than contributed to the applause.

The conference was formally closed, although the company staff would not be returning to London until the next day, and the managing director released them from further business.

'The party starts here,' he said, to laughter and cheers.

Drinks were served in the piano bar, which was where Penn, casually elegant in a tan linen suit, was eventually able to talk to Tess.

He said, 'I watched you watching. Didn't you like the speech?'

'It was a fine speech.'

'But?'

'It could have been a bad speech and they would still have applauded.'

'True. But I don't make bad speeches.'

'Arrogance or assurance?'

'Probably both. Have lunch with me and perhaps you can tell me.'

'What about . . . Caroline?'

She articulated each syllable of the name.

'What about Caroline?'

'Won't you be lunching with her?'

'My relationship with Caroline is not based upon social engagements.'

'What is it based upon?'

'Maybe I'll tell you at lunch.'

'Where do you propose to lunch? Here?' she said, meaning the hotel. 'Are you sure your loyal followers would allow us the luxury?'

'Not here.'

Tess smiled. She knew Penn's interest in her was more than that of a publisher for one of his best-selling authors but she did not for one minute think it was sexual. Perhaps he wanted her help?

'All right,' she said.

He beamed, turned and motioned to Caroline who was in an adjacent group. She joined them.

'I'm taking Tess to lunch. Can you call Roy and have him outside in five minutes?'

'Right,' she said, flipping open her mobile.

'And I'll want you at two-thirty for the Miramar meeting. Okay?'

'Okay, Charles.'

'It's a formality. There's no work. So you enjoy yourself until then, and, when we get back, the party goes on.'

Her smile said she was ready for anything.

'Right,' she said.

She pressed buttons and called Roy.

Penn took Tess by the arm and said, 'Shall we go?'

They left the cocktail party and took the lift to the ground floor. By the time they left the hotel, the limousine was out front and Roy was holding open the rear door.

Tess was surprised at his choice of restaurant. It was simple and inexpensive and in a side street off the elongated plaza of Es Born that ran inland from the bay.

They sat in a cool and shaded patio and had fresh bread smeared with olive oil, crab and a dressed salad with a bottle of Rioja white. By the time they had finished, they were the only people there.

'How did you know about this place?' she asked.

'I used to come to the island a lot.'

'Before fame?'

'I'm not really famous.'

'Before power, then?'

He smiled and drank wine.

'This power thing interests you, doesn't it?'

'Combined with the sort of reputation you have, yes.'

'Do you think I abuse it?'

'I don't know. Do you?'

He gave her a long look, as if he were undecided.

'Sometimes it's difficult to judge. Sometimes the distinctions become smudged.'

'Are you bothered about the reputation you have? Or do you like it?'

'I suppose I like it. It is, after all, extremely helpful. Young women know what to expect. I do not have to try too hard to seduce them.'

'So why seduce them at all?'

'I enjoy it.'

'Have you enjoyed seducing Caroline?'

He sat back and chewed his lip. He seemed amused by his thoughts. Instead of answering her question, he asked one of his own.

'The letters you receive,' he said. 'What sort of percentage would you say are true?'

'That's difficult to evaluate. I ask people to tell me their fantasies as well as make their confessions.' She hesitated and thought about it. 'I suppose maybe half the stories the writers say are true are actually fantasy. But that doesn't invalidate them. It's just another piece of the sexual equation.' She laughed. 'When you hit the bottom line, mankind is obsessed with sex.'

Penn said, 'Is that a bad thing?'

'Any obsession is unhealthy. What I try to do is encourage people to embrace sex, rather than be obsessed by it. I want them to bring those secrets out of the closet and not be intimidated by them. The more we discuss them – confess them, if you like, in books like mine – the less reason to be obsessive.

'If a guy enjoys being tied up and whipped with celery, great. If a girl wants to make it with three hunks at the same time, go for it. But understand it first. And don't feel guilty about urges you think no one else has. Let me tell you, Charles, there is no such thing as a new perversion.'

He had become serious.

'I believe you.'

Tess paused, looked at him, and said, 'Are you happy with your sex life, Charles?'

'That's a very direct question.'

'I'm a very direct lady. Besides, you invited me to lunch because you wanted to talk.'

'Did I?'

'I have degrees in psychoanalysis, psychotherapy and clinical psychology. I am also a thirty-eight-year-old woman who has been around the block a couple of times. Men like to tell me things.' She smiled conspiratorially. 'Sometimes they get a kick out of it.'

Penn smiled and nodded.

'I can believe they do,' he said. He took a deep breath. 'All right. I'll tell you some of it. Caroline, for instance. She is a public relations executive. She is twenty-four years old and is good at her job and very ambitious. I attend, perhaps, two informal jaunts like this with Pennworld in a year. She knew my reputation and she made herself available to me, professionally and . . . sexually.'

Tess said, 'Did she say that?'

'She actually said that my wish was her command.'

'And that gave you carte blanche to use her for your sexual gratification?'

'In a way. But it is not that simple. I don't have your qualifications but I'm a fifty-one-year-old man who has been around the block many times. I know an innocent when I see one. I know when a girl gets herself into a situation she doesn't want to be in and wonders how the hell does she get out. Believe it or not, I've played Sir Galahad as well as Rasputin. And I can tell you that Caroline was no innocent and is no innocent.

'My reputation does two things. It make seduction easy but it also focuses the mind. A girl who makes herself available to me has already made a decision. I lead and she follows, but only because she wants to. Only because she needs a guide.'

Tess said, 'So you are a humanitarian. You put into practice what I preach?'

She said it with a smile – but not a mocking smile.

'Perhaps I do. I encourage women to embrace sex.'

'Has Caroline fulfilled your expectations?'

'Yes. But not in the way you might think.'

31

'In what way?' she asked.

He chuckled and shook his head.

'Oh, come on,' Tess said. 'I'm not easily shocked. You've read the books?'

'All right,' he said. 'I'll tell you. I have not had sex with Caroline. Nor have I had what I suppose you would term gratification. But I have introduced her to new sexual experiences and, I think, she has thoroughly enjoyed them.'

'Stop being mysterious, Charles. What did you do? Piss in her handbag?'

He laughed as he poured more wine for them both. But when he continued speaking, his voice became lower and his tone more urgent.

'Last night, I took Caroline for a drive into the country. Roy drove. The black gentleman? We parked and Roy got into the back with us.'

He toyed with his wine and now, as he talked, he stared into the glass.

'I told her to display herself. To lift her dress. I told Roy to touch her. I told her to ask him to remove her panties.' He sipped the wine. 'She did. She asked him. And he knelt between her legs and used his mouth to give her an orgasm. Then I told her to return the compliment. I told her to kneel down and fellate him.' He took another sip of wine. 'She did that, as well.'

Tess felt as if the patio had become even quieter as he talked. A bird that had been singing had temporarily flown away. Even the distant sounds from the kitchen had ended.

'Go on,' she said.

'Then I held her. Face to face. And Roy had sex with her. He entered her from behind and had sex with her.

All the time, I watched her face. I knew she wanted to be pushed further than she had ever gone before. I saw it in her face. If that desire had deviated, if I had had any doubts, I would have stopped the situation continuing. But she wanted it.'

He smiled tightly.

'I held her. Our faces were very close. Roy had raised her dress and she could feel him behind her. She knew what was to happen.' He shook his head. 'Her expression. So frightened, so eager.'

'You controlled it,' said Tess.

'Yes.' He stared across the table at Tess. 'I looked over her shoulder at Roy and I said "Fuck her". Those exact words. Brutal words. Sex words. "Fuck her." And I looked into her face and saw the effect the words had had. Just saying it almost made her orgasm.'

He sipped wine and the bird came back and continued singing.

'Afterwards?' she said.

'Afterwards, we went back to the hotel where I escorted her to her room and helped put her to bed.' His smile had regained a little lightness. 'He is a big chap, is Roy. And then I went to my own room and went to bed.'

Tess said, 'Your sexual gratification is cerebral?'

'So far.'

'No masturbation?'

'No.'

'No involuntary emissions?'

He chuckled at her questions.

'No.'

'You're saving it?'

He shrugged.

'Probably. I don't like to plan too far in advance. But, if the circumstances are right, I will probably indulge in physical gratification as well as cerebral.'

They exchanged looks. Penn was relieved that there was no judgement in her eyes. He had never made such a confession before. And the funny thing was, that was what it had felt like: a confession rather than an explanation of a philosophy or a description of events. It had certainly not been a boast.

Tess took a drink of wine.

'Are all the girls young?' she said.

'All the girls?'

'The ones you lead into temptation?'

'Yes.'

'Is that because you prefer them to be young?'

'Yes.' He shrugged. 'They are beautiful and there is no emotional involvement.' A spot of colour blushed his cheeks for a moment. 'I've found it is a mutually satisfying arrangement.'

'Is there never an emotional involvement?'

'There hasn't been, yet.'

'Yet?'

'Who knows what can happen? Maybe one of these days I'll fall in love.'

'How will love fit in with cerebral gratification? Voyeurism? A Lolita complex?'

He laughed loudly.

'That's a pretty swift diagnosis, isn't it? Especially for someone who doesn't treat people, just listens.'

'I'm sorry.' She smiled. 'I like you, Charles, but I think your power has made you smug. I think you maybe need to reassess a few assumptions. We all do, from time to time.'

'Perhaps I do. Lolita complex?'

'Maybe you're frightened of mature women.'

'Like you?'

'You're safe with me. You know that. We're both covered by the Hippocratic oath.'

'Perhaps I prefer younger women because they're more beautiful than older women?' He raised a hand and grimaced at his gaffe. 'That is in no way intended to be a reflection upon yourself. You know you are a beautiful woman.'

Tess smiled broadly.

'Stick to the truth, Charles. I'm not bad for thirty-eight and I know all about cellulite. But you're right. A good twenty-year-old body is better than a good forty-year-old body. But is the preference influenced by safety? You can tell an inexperienced girl what to do but a mature woman might ask questions. She might start playing mind games with you?'

Penn said, 'And that wouldn't do, would it? You do think I'm arrogant, don't you?'

'Sure. You're arrogant. You made a fortune and built an empire. Your middle name should be Midas, not Rasputin. You're entitled to arrogance. Without it, you wouldn't be you. But there should be room for humility, as well. And self-doubt. They're not failings. they're strengths. All part of the human condition, along with a healthy sexual appetite.'

He held her gaze and said, 'And there's the rub. Is that what you mean?'

'*Is* your sexual appetite healthy?' she said.

'I don't know. What do you think?'

'I think that by expressing doubt, you've made a start.'

'I've got used to my . . . what would you call them? Sex games? I've been playing them a long time.'

'Why?'

They stared at each other and, for a moment, she thought he was going to tell her something more, but he held back the words. Instead, he looked at his watch.

'I'm not used to such direct questioning,' he said.

'Sycophants wouldn't dare, huh?'

'I suppose that's true.'

'Yes-men will only say no when you fire them or go bankrupt. Do you want to talk to me again?'

'Yes.'

'I'll be in London for the next month. Maybe longer. Come and see me.' She smiled. 'No charge.'

'Will you use me in a book?'

'You might not be interesting enough.'

He laughed.

'No. Probably not.'

Penn finished the glass of wine and his body language said he was ready to go. Tess sipped her wine.

'Have you learned anything?' she said.

He shrugged. 'What if I reassess what I do and come to the conclusion I enjoy it? What if I decide I don't want to change? That I *can't* change?'

'You're expressing doubts again. That's good. You're acknowledging the possibility you might want to change. A sexual obsession is like drug addiction, Charles. You can change if you want to, but it won't happen overnight. Do you want to?'

'I don't know, Tess. Perhaps we've been playing another form of mind game. Whatever. It has been a stimulating lunch.'

Tess looked at her watch.

'You have a business appointment with Caroline, right?'
'Right.'

'Then we'd better go.' They got to their feet. 'I'm flying to London this afternoon, but don't forget. Come and see me if you want to play more mind games.'

Chapter 4

Penn had been stimulated by the lunchtime discussion. He had enjoyed having someone neutral with whom to talk. Tess Flanders had said they were both protected by the Hippocratic oath but could he really trust her confidentiality?

When he saw her again in London, as he intended, he would then have to make the decision whether or not to divulge anything deeper. She was easy company and it had been refreshing to talk to someone who did not treat him with total respect. But, so far, it had all just been words.

He still had business to take care of and he had not yet finished with Caroline Lee, a young woman whom he managed quite comfortably to compartmentalize into a different section of his conscience. Any self-assessment concerning his behaviour was for the future. It did not yet apply.

Caroline wore a tan business suit and matching high-heeled sandals and carried a briefcase instead of a handbag. She looked the essence of efficiency but he noticed, from her behaviour, that she had already entered into the spirit of the end-of conference party and had been drinking.

The meeting was to formalize Penn's investment in a Spanish leisure company and was with two of its directors. As the rest of the city enjoyed its siesta, they were driven in the limousine to a hotel complex at

Santa Ponsa, where they were shown up to a pent-house suite.

José Santos was of a similar age to Penn although at least two stone overweight. His face was full and pale like a moon and his hair wispy and red.

In contrast, Carlos Pinochet was a small and dark man of about forty whose thin dark hair was swept back from a high domed forehead.

They were dressed informally in slacks and polo shirts.

The hotel complex was part of the leisure group and was the first step in another direction in Penn's expanding business portfolio.

They were greeted with celebratory champagne and Penn could tell the two men had started their personal celebrations some time earlier.

It was just as well they had no inkling of his plans for the make-over of their company. Penn intended to turn it from a break-even venture that was in danger of collapse into a profitable asset that would become the basis for further expansion.

In the short term, they were welcome to enjoy the fruits of the day. In the longer term, their day had been and gone, and they were destined to be the first casualties of an executive sweep.

He reflected it was also just as well that Caroline had no inkling of his plans for her. He encouraged her to enjoy the wine as the men signed the documents.

If Caroline had been more sober, she might have become aware earlier of the way the two Spaniards looked at her, but she was concentrating on being the perfect personal assistant to her employer.

She returned the papers to her briefcase and was surprised

that the drapes were being drawn. The men spoke to Penn in Spanish, a language she did not understand, and she looked to him for guidance.

'José has invited us to watch a promotional film. It shows the many facets of the company.'

'Right,' she said.

Two long and low settees were set at right angles in the room and formed an open square that faced a large television set, video player and hi-fi equipment. Penn indicated the settee that faced the screen and she sat down. Jose sat to her left and Carlos to her right. Penn sat alone on the second settee.

It was at this point that Caroline began to feel butterflies in her stomach. José filled her glass again and she drank it quickly to calm her nerves.

The room was in shade and the men spoke softly in Spanish. Being excluded by language made her feel vulnerable. She glanced at Penn but he was looking at the screen.

Carlos used a remote control and the screen came to life. The film was in German and the opening sequence showed the front of a hotel. But she sensed this was no promotional film.

Young men and women were drinking in a bar in the hotel but again Caroline was excluded by language. But then, she guessed the language didn't matter. Three men and a woman left the bar and entered a lift. As the lift ascended, one of the men held the woman from behind and his hands went over her breasts.

Caroline's face coloured. She dared not look to either right or left at the two men who flanked her. But she could see that Penn continued to watch the screen, so she did the same.

José said, in English, 'I am sorry, Charles. This is the wrong film. We have made a confusion.'

Carlos froze the image on the screen.

Penn still watched the screen and said, 'What a pretty girl.'

'Yes. She is . . . pretty. But the film is strong. You know? Perhaps we should turn it off?'

Caroline, in her peripheral vision, watched Penn turn his head and look at her.

'What do you think, Caroline?' he said.

'I don't know,' she said.

'Have you ever seen a pornographic film?'

Now she turned her head and looked directly at him.

'No,' she said.

'They can be quite educational, as well as stimulating. Would you like to be educated?'

Caroline felt trapped by the presence of the men on either side of her and by the loaded questions Penn was directing at her. This was unexpected, again. But then, she had known his reputation and, after last night, should she be surprised at anything he led her into?

'What do you think, Caroline?' he persisted. 'Shall we watch it?'

'Why not?' she said.

He smiled.

'Why not, indeed.'

José said, 'Okay?'

Penn said, 'Yes, José. Okay.'

Carlos used the remote and the image on the screen unfroze.

The men escorted the woman to a hotel room. Once inside, two of the men continued drinking while one of them lay down upon a bed with the woman and they began to kiss.

Caroline knew what the outcome would be and her stomach churned. She had never watched anyone copulate, not even herself and her boyfriend in a mirror.

The couple who kissed upon the bed reminded her of a party she had attended as a teenager when she had watched a boy climb upon a girl in a darkened bedroom. They had thrust against each other, even though they had been fully clothed.

She remembered being in the same room, kissing another boy who had similarly been moving against her. It had been an exciting experience but one she had felt guilty about. Now what should she think?

On screen, the man had raised the woman's dress and exposed her limbs and underwear. The other two men in the film had stopped drinking and were beginning to undress. Caroline's mouth was dry and she tilted the glass in her hand and saw that it was empty.

As if waiting for the gesture, José poured more champagne into the flute. She drank it quickly and did not object when he filled it again.

She was aware that Penn was observing her and not the screen. But she could not stop watching the video images and besides, she did not trust herself to return his gaze for fear of what he might see in her eyes.

The film lasted twenty minutes and they watched it in silence. Towards the end, as the three men moved upon the bed and fitted themselves into the woman from varying angles, she was aware that the two Spaniards had also stopped watching the screen and were watching her.

Caroline's thighs moved together. She moved her bottom on the seat. She had an irritation between her legs that she had never experienced before. The girl bit her lip and felt a tear in the corner of an eye. She was wet between her legs and began to feel ashamed.

When the film ended, Carlos switched off the video and television with the remote. The silence was a prelude to a storm. She looked across the room at Penn who sat, legs crossed and face without expression. He stared quizzically back.

They did not speak. Caroline licked her lips and shuddered. Penn smiled.

The Spaniards turned to her, as if unsure of her reaction. José turned her head and his large moon face came closer and eclipsed the room. His fleshy lips were apart and for a moment Caroline was repulsed as the butterflies in her stomach fluttered more fiercely. Then, with a shock, she realized the repulsion was lust, and her lips parted and she welcomed his kiss.

Her eyes closed as his mouth fed hungrily at hers, his tongue deep inside, his hands pulling at the buttons of her jacket so that it fell open to reveal her small breasts in a white lace brassiere.

Other hands, the hands of Carlos, were on her legs, pushing up the tight skirt, delving beneath and moving over her stockings and onto her nakedness. The hands directed her and she obeyed. She raised her hips and the skirt slid higher until it lodged around her waist.

The cups of the bra were pushed up and her breasts freed and covered by hands. Her panties were tugged down and removed. Hands parted her legs and a mouth licked between her thighs and found her heat and wetness.

She lay back, half upon the settee, her legs stretched across the rugs. Carlos, the thin Spaniard, knelt between them and sucking at her vagina. José now had his mouth over a breast and hands grasped at her soft flesh.

Her eyes remained closed for there was no reason to see. Her body tingled all over with desire. She was hot enough to conflagrate.

Penn watched with satisfaction, his thoughts of self-assessment shelved. Another meeting with Dr Tess Flanders no longer seemed so certain.

Caroline had submitted totally to her own desires and those of the two men. He watched her slim body being moved by them, reacting to them.

Carlos unfastened his trousers and pushed them down his thighs. He knelt up between her legs and his firm buttocks quivered with eagerness. He held her hip with his left hand while he used his right to guide his penis.

Then he pushed with his hips and his buttocks quivered again and Caroline cried out as he sank his weapon inside her. The dark Spaniard pulled the girl's legs around him, lifting her feet from the floor and holding her with both hands upon her buttocks.

His thrusts were fierce and each one elicited a cry from her throat until José knelt upon the settee, trousers open, and fed his erect penis into her mouth.

Penn uncrossed his legs and rearranged his erection in his trousers. The men were using Caroline. She had ceased to be a person and was a vehicle for their sexual release. If he had judged Caroline correctly, she would be in a similar state, and a welcome recipient of their attention.

Awareness returned to Caroline for a moment as Carlos came inside her. Her vagina contracted around his penis and she felt triumphant at making him orgasm so soon, and then she came too, and became lost once more.

Carlos fell away and she slid from the settee and the phallus slipped from her mouth. She rolled onto the floor, thick rugs beneath her buttocks, and her legs were parted and another penis was presented at the portals of her sex and pushed deep inside.

José was heavy upon her but it was not an unpleasant sensation. She welcomed the obscenity of the fat man upon her and her hips thrust back, matching his lust. He tensed and climaxed and, as he shook his seed inside her, he triggered a second orgasm in Caroline.

For a while, after he had withdrawn, she lay where she was, alone on the rugs, aware that her breath was ragged, aware of the sudden smells that had been released and of the wetness between her legs. Her vagina was bruised and open and wanted more.

Someone was speaking quietly in Spanish. Liquid was being poured. Her eyes opened and she stared up into the face of Penn, who remained sitting in the same place, his legs casually and elegantly crossed, his eyes, as always, all-devouring as if he wanted to scour her mind.

Caroline rolled onto her hands and knees and, in that position, crawled to the settee where he sat. She rested her arms on the seat alongside him and stared hard into his face.

'Did you enjoy it?' she said.

'Yes. Did you?'

'You knew I would.'

'Yes.'

'How did you know?'

'I know women. I know sex. I know you would not have done this without my help. Perhaps you will never do this again. But you have done it once, and perhaps once is enough.'

Caroline licked her lips and gulped for saliva.

'You're a manipulating bastard,' she said.

He smiled, as if he took it as a compliment.

'And *you* like to fuck. Don't you, Caroline? You like to fuck and be fucked.'

'Yes,' she whispered.

'This is perfection. No complications,' he said. 'Safe sex with strangers. Abuse and lust without danger.'

She reached and touched his trousers and found his erection. Her hand squeezed it.

'What about you?' she said. 'When do *you* fuck me?'

His smiled widened at her use of the word.

'Perhaps in the car. Perhaps when we get back to the hotel. Perhaps only in my mind.'

'Are we going now?' she said.

'Not yet. It isn't over yet.'

Her eyes widened.

'It isn't over?'

'There's much more to come. Enjoy, Caroline. This may never happen again.'

The two Spaniards returned and lifted her to her feet. They were naked and now they unfastened her clothing and removed it, the immediacy of lust gone and replaced by brooding intensity. Caroline was left standing only in tan stockings and white lace suspender belt.

José was behind her, his belly pressing against her back, his hard erection against her buttocks, his hands pushing the flesh around it. Carlos was at her front and he wrapped her hands around his penis. As she masturbated him, he kissed her with a slobbering mouth and his hands mauled her breasts.

Penn watched, nursing the sexual desire he had been cultivating since he had first met the girl twenty-four hours earlier. Had it only been twenty-four hours? Without her heeled shoes, she looked small and frail between the two men, who touched her, thrust against her and mauled her.

Phillip Mason

Her mouth was open and her head tilted back upon the shoulder of José, her eyes half closed. Sensation had robbed her of identity. It was unlikely to surface again until she had been sated and the double assault had been concluded.

Carlos sat on the settee and she was pushed to her knees between his legs. She accepted his penis into her mouth and sucked. José knelt behind her and inserted his new erection into her vagina. As he thrust, the flab of his body shook like blancmange.

Penn touched his own erection. Although outwardly calm, he was inwardly existing at a high level of sexual tension. He had learned to maintain this tension for hours and days on end.

Others might shed their lust in an orgasm, but he nurtured his. Each adventure intensified it. The lulls between, for meals and speeches and business, were rest periods that did not affect the cumulative result.

At its height, his nerve ends jumped simply from looking at a girl and imagining what might come to pass. Now that it *had* come to pass, his nerve ends positively sang as he watched Caroline being figuratively deflowered by the two Spaniards.

Now they changed positions and laid her upon her back on the thick rugs on the floor. They knelt over her face and she held a penis in each hand and fed them alternately into her mouth. She tried to take both at the same time and failed, rubbing them across her face so that they left sperm trails upon her lightly tanned skin.

All the time, her hips writhed as her vagina pleaded for attention, and now they provided it. The fat one knelt between her legs, lifted her thighs and inserted himself into her, while the thin one continued to use her mouth for his solitary gratification.

48

Penn sat and soaked up the smells, the urgency, the sounds of slapping flesh and moans, the slither of sweating bodies and the sight of the delicate girl being so thoroughly used. And, as his pleasure stretched to its zenith, he saw, without warning, another girl superimposed where Caroline lay.

For a second, Caroline became Tamara. The flash went, as if drug-induced, but as his mind recognized the deceit the flash occurred again and remained longer. Now he watched Tamara lying there, beneath the thrusting bodies of strangers.

The image went and he was aware his breathing had changed. He was also aware, with that mixture of deep loathing and desire that he recognized from another age, that the vision had heightened the thrill of the experience. The zenith he thought he had attained was a false ceiling. The pleasure had intensified tenfold.

He felt sick and empty and his hands were shaking. He stared at the tableau of copulation before him and his mind was on the brink: it was his choice. His mind said so. New mind games, of his own devising.

But it was not his choice, it was his compulsion. His obsession. His mind imposed the vision again: Caroline became Tamara, his gut wrenched viciously and he almost came in his trousers.

He forced himself to look away and lifted his eyes to the ceiling. He heard José orgasm again. The man gasped and cursed in Spanish, and Penn, once more in control, looked again and saw him roll away and curl up with his back to the rest of them, a huge foetus of blubber.

Carlos changed his attack, now that he was in solitary control. He rolled Caroline onto her stomach and climbed upon her back. He pushed her knees apart and, using his right hand to guide himself, sank upon her buttocks with a satisfied sigh.

He took his pleasure upon her for a few minutes in this manner, pounding against her soft globes of flesh, his attack pushing her against the rug, making her cry out and moan, her hands clawing for purchase and sexual release.

Now he raised himself from her, his penis angry and glistening, and turned her onto her back. Once more he crouched between her thighs and slid it back inside, holding himself upright on his arms as he thrust into her and stared into her face.

Her head rolled from side to side and she raised her legs and wrapped them around his taut body as she ground herself against him, yelling as she came again.

In orgasm, her legs lost their grip and dropped alongside him but his movements were increasing in urgency and, with deep concentration, he withdrew, slithered up her body and straddled her breasts. His right hand maintained the rhythm upon his weapon. His back arched, he directed the phallus and ejaculated his sperm into her face.

At the very last moment, the vision returned and Penn watched the translucent liquid splash against the cheek and lips of Tamara. He shuddered, gripped his erection for a brief moment, and recalled reality and Caroline.

Carlos got up on shaking legs and staggered to the bar where he poured himself a drink. José rolled over, climbed to his feet and went to the bathroom.

Slowly, Caroline's identity filtered back. Penn knelt by her side and used his handkerchief to wipe the sperm from the hollows beneath her eyes. Her breathing became more controlled and her eyelids fluttered.

'Careful,' he said. 'It will sting if you get it in your eyes.'

He completed wiping her face and now, when she looked at him, her gaze was once more unsure. He helped her to her feet and to the settee.

'Are you all right?' he said, his tone solicitous.

'Yes.'

Was she all right?

Caroline remembered only vaguely what had happened. It was so far from any other experience that it was like a dream, like last night had been a dream. Her thighs ached pleasurably. She remembered that she had orgasmed but she could not remember how many times. She felt as if she had completed an examination, but did not know if she had passed.

Penn dressed her. He put her feet into the skirt and slid it up her legs, made her stand while he zipped and fastened it around her waist. He allowed her to sit again while he put her arms into her bra and fastened that, too, and slipped the jacket on.

He knelt at her feet to fit her high-heeled shoes as if she were Cinderella.

'Prince Charming,' she said, and he smiled.

He was still elegant in his tan linen suit, still in control. She realized she was still a little in awe of him as she watched him pick up her panties, hold them briefly to his nostrils, and then push them in his top pocket as if to replace the handkerchief he had used upon her face.

Penn picked up her briefcase and helped her to her feet.

'Time to go,' he said.

They left the suite. José was still in the bathroom and Carlos sat, naked and subdued, at the bar. No one spoke. In the lift, Caroline remembered the film. She remembered she had not washed or cleaned herself and could feel wetness between her thighs as her vagina leaked sperm.

She was still not sure if she were in command of all her faculties. Probably not. Anyway, it did not matter for she had Penn to take her arm and guide her through the quiet lobby of the hotel, into the brief heat of the sunshine, and help her into the air-conditioning of the limousine.

It was over and if it had been an examination she knew she had passed. It had been unbelievably bestial and she had embraced and enjoyed every moment. Her orgasms had stretched and been more intense than she could remember except, perhaps, for the night before.

Caroline stared at the back of Roy's head and remembered it being between her thighs: she moaned softly and moved upon the seat and closed her eyes. She needed to lie down for a while, now that it was over.

Penn took her hand, lifted it to his mouth and licked her fingers. He inserted the tip of one into his mouth and sucked it gently. She opened her eyes and looked at him.

'You were quite magnificent, my dear,' he said.

No. It was not yet over.

He escorted her to her room, his demeanour dissuading anyone from stopping them, attempting a conversation or even exchanging a greeting.

The drapes had been closed against the sun and, after he had pulled back the covers, she lay thankfully upon the bed, closed her eyes and, perhaps, even dozed for a short while until she became aware of her clothes being removed.

She opened her eyes and saw that Penn was naked. His body was lean and well muscled and, even without clothes, he exuded power.

He rolled her onto her stomach, pulled off the jacket

and unclipped the bra. He unfastened the waistband of the skirt and unzipped it and slid it over her hips and down her legs. She lay face down, her arms limp at her side, and he lay alongside her and stroked the curves of her bottom.

'Go back to sleep, Caroline. I have held this back a long time. It will not take long.'

Caroline closed her eyes and feigned sleep. His hands parted her thighs and his fingers stroked her vagina, which still gaped. They slid in the slickness of sexual juices.

He moved and lay upon her back, and guided his erection directly to the mouth of her sex. It slid inside, hot and hard and incredibly large, and he eased himself down upon her, so that his groin flattened her buttocks and his thighs lay against her thighs. For a time he did not move his hips but simply stroked her body.

His palms moved over her legs and hips, slid beneath her and beneath the loosened cups of the bra to caress her breasts. His fingers moved through her hair and stroked her face and he kissed her ear and her neck. She moaned and turned her head and his lips found hers and they kissed, gently, his tongue sliding along her teeth.

Now he groaned and moved his hips and pushed his erection deeper inside her. She could tell he would not take long, that the urgency he had been storing was too great.

He sank his face in her neck and hair and moved upon her with several hard strokes, buried the last one and held it there, gripped her hips, and came with fierce intensity.

The tension went: his body softened upon her and he kissed her neck and gently disengaged himself.

'Go to sleep,' he whispered, climbing off the bed and pulling the covers over her, and this time she did.

Penn stood by the bed. He felt renewed and yet a little

sad. He heard her breathing change and knew she was asleep. He dressed quietly.

This girl who had so recently been devoured by sex had reverted to childlike innocence in slumber. All the memories of what had happened to her had been shed and her features had relaxed and were at peace.

Was it their youth, their innocence that attracted him?

Was Tamara the girl who might rescue him from the games he played, the games with which he was obsessed? Or did his salvation lie with Dr Tess Flanders?

Chapter 5

The dossier Penn had had compiled about Tamara Fenwick contained more photographs than written documentation. Her father had been a vicar but had died when she was a child, and she was estranged from her mother, who had an antiques shop in Brighton and a third husband.

Her background was middle-class and she had attended a minor public school but had acquired few academic qualifications. She was one of those people who had become well known for being well known, for being an escort to show-business stars, and for being in the right place at the right time when photographers' flashbulbs popped.

What fame she had had been achieved, in part, by her reciprocal friendships with the paparazzi of the London scene, her ability to organize parties at which the right names would appear, and for being beautiful.

It had been reported that a television company was interested in engaging her as a presenter of a sophisticated late-night programme but, so far, this project had not got any further than the gossip columns.

Penn looked at the newspaper cuttings and the photographs. Tamara on the arm of a middle-aged Hollywood star, Tamara climbing out of a limousine with a rock legend, Tamara sharing a joke and a cocktail with a minor royal.

He read the personal details. He had asked for nothing

to be held back but he still wondered whether his staff had provided him with what they thought he wanted to read rather than the full facts.

Tamara was sexually active but not promiscuous. In a famous magazine interview she had declared she had lost her virginity to a chorister at the age of fourteen. The experience had been so enjoyable, she had said, that she had subsequently gone on to seduce a boy soprano, two altos and a tenor from the same choir.

Her one lengthy relationship seemed to have been with rock singer Jamie Philpott from the band Nadir. It had been a long-term but stormy commitment.

The longest they had lived together had been three weeks, but they had wandered in and out of each other's lives for three years. When she had tried to break the pattern and set up home with a video film-maker, Philpott had turned up after three months and ruined their domestic bliss.

Penn drew a circle around Philpott's name.

This was a young lady who was used to being in the presence of the rich, famous and powerful. She was used to dealing with and manipulating them, and had gained her own fame from their patronage.

How would she react to him?

Would she see his advances as a chance to further her career? Would she see him as a sad middle-aged suitor ripe for the taking?

Maybe she had heard of his reputation and maybe she would wonder about his motives, just as he was wondering about her reaction?

He telephoned the number on the dossier.

'Yes?'

A girl with a sleepy voice.

'Tamara?'

'Who wants her?'

'Charles Penn.'

'Charles Penn?' The girl repeated his name as if casting a fishing line to see what might arise from the depths of her memory. 'Oh.' Life began to emerge from the sleepiness. 'Charles Penn.'

'Yes. Is Tamara there?'

'This is Tamara.' She laughed. The voice had become gently vibrant. 'I'm still in bed.'

The thought fired Penn with a frisson of desire.

'I'm sorry if I woke you.'

'That's all right. I should have been up ages ago. Lots to do. How was Crete?'

'I haven't been to Crete.'

'Haven't you? I thought you were going to a seminar, or something.'

'It was in Majorca.'

'Oh, Majorca. Do people still go there?'

By people, Penn guessed she meant a certain class of people.

'I did.'

'Was it good?'

'It was very worthwhile.' Her voice was half tease, half disinterested, and he could not understand why he was so attracted by her. But he was. 'Look, Tamara, I wondered if I might see you again? Perhaps dinner?'

'Dinner?' She made it sound like an alien concept. 'I'm not really good at dinner. Why not come round here?'

'When?'

'This afternoon, if you like.'

'It is this afternoon.'

'Oh? Is it? Well, give me a couple of hours. Four o'clock?'

'Four o'clock.'

She blew him a kiss down the telephone and the line went dead.

He stared at the receiver before he placed it back in its cradle. He did not know if he was making a mistake but he would only find out by going to see her at four o'clock.

Tamara lived in a first-floor apartment in The Walk near the Chelsea Embankment. Penn pressed a button, stared into a security lens and pushed open the door when the buzzer indicated it had been unlocked.

He walked up the stairs and found the door to her apartment was open. He entered a small lobby, closed the door behind him, and called, 'Tamara?'

'In here.'

Penn followed the voice and went into a large untidy but luxurious room that was furnished with soft leather sofas and cushions that were scattered on a thick carpet. One wall was covered with a tapestry, the others with mirrors, original paintings and framed theatrical posters.

Tamara stood before a mirror fixing an earring. In this large room she seemed smaller than he remembered. A slight girl who wore what appeared to be a cream silk slip, which was fluid over the curves of her body, and a string of pearls.

She turned, smiled and came towards him. She wore no brassiere and beneath the slip her breasts moved and her nipples puckered the silk.

'Hello, Charles,' she said, and kissed him on the cheek.

He kissed her in return. For a moment they remained close together and he was aware of her body and her perfume. Then she smiled and moved away.

'Drink?'

A bottle of champagne was already open and sitting in an ice bucket on a sideboard.

'Thank you.'

She poured and he walked over and took the glass from her. They toasted each other.

'I'm glad you called,' she said.

Their eyes were locked again, as they had been the night they'd met and had monopolized each other's company.

'You knew I would.'

'Yes,' she said.

She turned away, crossed the room and sprawled on a sofa. The thought occurred to him that she wore nothing at all beneath the slip.

Penn looked out of the window. His throat was dry so he drank the champagne. He was annoyed with himself for his caution. He had to do things his way, the only way he knew, even if it meant making a fool of himself. He went back to the sideboard and poured more wine before facing her.

'This is an unusual situation for me,' he said. She did not reply, but kept staring at him with those wonderful green eyes. 'You are very beautiful.'

She smiled, but still did not speak. He moved from the sideboard and sat on another sofa that faced her.

Now she said, 'You have something on your mind.'

'Yes.'

'Tell me.'

'You may think me foolish.'

'I won't know what to think unless you tell me.'

'All right. Since we met last week, I haven't been able to get you out of my thoughts. I haven't wanted to get you out of my thoughts. I think I may have fallen in love with you. There. Is that foolish?'

She shook her head.

'It's not foolish. It's a beautiful thing to say and I am very flattered.'

'Perhaps the foolish part comes next. Do you think you might feel something similar for me?'

'I don't know. And that's an honest answer. I've thought about you, too, Charles. I felt it. What happened between us that night. But I'm not used to declarations as serious as this. I don't know what I feel.'

Penn felt a surge of hope. He had not been rejected. There was a chance.

'Perhaps we can see each other,' he said. 'See what happens.' He smiled. 'See if there really is magic there, or if it was just the smoky atmosphere.'

Tamara laughed. Her eyes had never left him and she had listened with concentration to everything he said. This was part of the attraction. She gave him her complete attention because she wanted to, not because she had to.

'I think there may be magic, Charles, but I'm not looking for commitment. I'm not ready to be tied.'

'I realize that.' He coughed. 'I also realize the difference in our ages.'

Tamara said, 'I don't. I felt no difference. I felt we had known each other for years.' She smiled. 'Perhaps we have, in a previous existence?'

'I don't know the reason but I do know that I felt something special. I still do.' He stared longingly at this elfin creature who sat opposite him. 'All I ask is that you allow me to see you. I will make no other demands. I would like to be your friend, your mentor if you like.'

She sipped the wine, her eyes still upon him. She had never once looked away.

'You are a very intense person, Charles. I can feel your power. And you say all the right things. I would be very happy to have you as my friend and mentor, for however long the magic lasts.'

'And if it develops into something else?'

'Let's wait and see. You know, this could simply be infatuation, on both our parts.'

He raised an eyebrow.

'Both our parts?'

'Oh, yes. I am physically attracted to you, Charles. Your mind, your body, you ... I can't split you into different pieces. But there is always a danger with infatuation. If this is infatuation.'

'What danger?'

'That it will fall apart once we've been to bed together.'

Penn was uncomfortable. He was not used to being led. He was not used to listening to the wisdom of a twenty-three-year-old, particularly when she was talking sense.

'There is that possibility,' he conceded.

They stared at each other across the lengthening silence. He had only imagined the physical side of a relationship with Tamara as occurring sometime in the future, not now.

Tamara said, 'I don't go to bed with everyone I find attractive. I am, in my own way, a very moral person.' A smile played at her lips. 'My father was a vicar. But we could put the magic to the test right now ... unless you want to live with the possibility for a while, and see what develops?'

It was Penn's turn to feel flattered. At his age, he had turned the head of this beautiful young woman. But he did not want to risk losing everything before their relationship had had a chance to develop. Besides, it was not part of his plan to indulge in direct sexual contact. That was never part of his plan.

'I can think of nothing more wonderful than putting the

magic to the test. But I think we should wait.' He laughed. 'To be honest, I'm in such a state I think I would be useless in bed. Besides, if you will permit it, I would prefer to pay court to you before that happens.'

'So would I,' she said. 'I knew you were a gentleman, Charles. But it's nice that you have confirmed it.'

He was relieved. The magic was intact and in no immediate danger. He wondered if she had been setting him a test? He wondered if she would have gone through with it if he had said, yes, let's go to bed.

Penn went back to the sideboard for more champagne, wrapped a cloth around the wet bottle and took it to fill Tamara's glass as well.

She said, 'You do know I am no virgin and no saint, Charles?'

'I know that,' he said, and returned the bottle to its bucket. 'Neither am I.'

'But I can tell you that I am not currently involved with anyone. And, as I said, I do not go to bed with every attractive male I meet. But even so, I am what you might call a free agent.'

Penn nodded.

He said, 'I don't intend to be a nuisance, Tamara. I just want us to share some time together and see if we are compatible. The future is unpredictable. You might meet someone tonight who knocks you off your feet. Someone with whom the magic is unmistakable.' He smiled self-deprecatingly. 'So might I, for that matter, although it's less likely.

'I have no wish to clutter your life. I just want to be close when you need me. If I can be of help in your career, for instance, let me be. But I realize your personal life is your own, even now. Even after what we have discussed.'

Tamara smiled warmly at him.

'You are a very understanding man. I suppose the word is "mature". Younger men can be so tedious at times, so demanding, so impatient. But you know all the right things to say. I'm glad you came, Charles. Glad you told me. I'm glad we have given ourselves a chance.'

'So am I,' said Penn, and no longer felt middle-aged and foolish.

She sipped the wine.

'I think you will be very easy to love,' she said. 'But that's not the same as being in love.'

'I know. But give the magic time to work. It may happen.'

'Yes. It may.'

Penn was delighted with the outcome but now that he had achieved this first step, he was aware of a persistent cloud at the back of his mind.

The cloud had gone with him to Majorca and had manifested itself during his sex games with Caroline Lee. It had frightened and aroused him.

He remembered how, in his mind, Tamara had taken the place of Caroline as she lay upon the rugs of the penthouse suite in Santa Ponsa in the lustful embrace of two Spaniards.

Penn also remembered his lunch with Dr Tess Flanders. She had said he was obsessive. She had talked of a Lolita complex and much more. And she had been closer to the truth than he had cared to admit.

If the magic between Tamara and himself was to have a chance, he must consult with the sex therapist as soon as possible.

Chapter 6

For her stay in London, Dr Tess Flanders had rented an apartment in the Barbican.

'Where do you want to meet?' she asked when Penn telephoned her. 'Here or at my office?'

'I didn't know you had an office in London?'

'I use the Dorchester. It's excellent for newspaper interviews and has the right ambience for photographs. And I let the reporter pick up the tab for lunch.'

'I would prefer to see you at your apartment.'

'Cheapskate.'

They both laughed.

Penn said, 'I'll buy you lunch as well, but the apartment first.'

'Okay. Privacy guaranteed.'

He was pleased the cordial relationship they had formed on Majorca had been instantly rekindled. When they met at the apartment, he was at once at ease. He knew he did not have to try to impress. He felt he could shed the mantle of power that he was always aware he carried.

Tess wore slacks and a blouse and a welcoming smile. They drank coffee and chatted, about her work and her home in Virginia, and about the several apartments and houses he owned around the world.

'Wherever I hang my hat is home,' he said.

'But where do you hang your heart?'

He smiled and became reflective and accepted the opening.

'That's what I want to talk about. I've met someone and I might be in love.'

'Might be?'

'I'm too old to talk in certainties. If I was younger, if circumstances were different, then maybe I wouldn't hedge my emotions quite so much. But I think I know the way these things work. If I allow it to happen, I could fall in love. But I don't know if I want it to happen.'

Tess said, 'Who is the girl?'

He took a photograph from his pocket and handed it to her.

'My Lolita complex again,' he said, with a half-smile. 'Her name is Tamara Fenwick. Her picture is often in the gossip columns and she's angling for a career in television.'

'Well, she has the looks. Does she have any talent?'

'I don't know.'

'Are you going to help her in television?'

'Yes.'

'She knows who you are? What you could do for her?'

'She knows.'

'Have you told her how you feel?'

'Yes.'

'And?'

'She said she was flattered and that she reciprocated . . . in a way.' He shrugged. 'She said I would be easy to love, but she didn't know, at least not yet, if she could fall in love with me.'

'How old is she?'

'Twenty-three.'

'What are you worried about? The influence of power?

That she might say she is falling in love with you for all the wrong reasons?'

'That's part of it. She also said I might be suffering from infatuation.'

'You could be.'

'She suggested we could find out whether it was infatuation or not.'

'How?'

'By going to bed. She offered to go to bed with me to see if I still felt the same the morning after.'

'Clever girl.'

'You suspect her motives?'

'Whatever her motives, she's a clever girl.' Tess looked again at the photograph. 'She is certainly lovely. I don't see any man working off an infatuation with just one night of passion.'

Penn had intended to use the meeting to test his own theories in discussion with Tess, but now that he was in her presence, he felt he could trust her. He needed someone in whom to confide and explain in detail his worries about the development of a relationship with Tamara.

'I've known many young women, Tess. But Tamara is someone I actually enjoy being with and talking to. And that's where the major problem comes in.'

'Sounds serious.'

'You touched on it in Majorca. Voyeurism and the Lolita complex. It's true. I like to watch.' He took a deep breath. 'Over the years I have made all kinds of excuses to myself but, if I'm honest, I actually *need* to watch. Without the excitement of watching, I don't think I could become aroused enough to perform.'

He looked at her helplessly and spread his hands.

'You see the problem,' he said. 'When I finally meet a girl I'm ready to love?'

Tess took her time before replying. She cogitated upon what he had said.

She eventually said, 'You mean that love might not make a difference? That before you can make love to Tamara, you might have to watch her in a sexual situation with someone else?'

Penn nodded enthusiastically.

'That's it exactly.' He sighed. 'It's not the best basis for a close and loving relationship, is it? No basis at all for a marriage.'

'You are considering marriage?'

'I don't know. I've avoided marriage for years for this same reason.' He bit his bottom lip, aware that he was uncharacteristically showing his nervousness. 'I was married before. A long time ago. It didn't work out.'

Tess said, 'For the same reason?'

'Yes.'

She changed her position in her chair and made herself more comfortable.

'Voyeurism is natural,' she said. 'Everybody likes to watch.'

'That may be so,' said Penn. 'But not everybody NEEDS to watch.'

Tess nodded placatingly and said, 'Okay, so it may be habit-forming and you've been hooked on this habit for a long time. You told me in Majorca that you wanted to avoid serious relationships. That's why you picked young women and why you took the role of sexual guide. Right?'

'Right.'

'By doing that, you placed yourself out of the emotional equation. You were the ringmaster, if you like, the master of ceremonies. You enjoyed the cerebral gratification of being in control.' She paused and thought some more. 'Were you also sexually excited, watching a girl being seduced?'

'Yes.'

'And did you usually gain your own sexual gratification as well?'

'Yes.'

'So basically there's nothing wrong with you. You're capable of sexual arousal, you're capable of orgasm. And now you think you may be falling in love. You've just been playing mind games too long, Charles. They've become habit-forming but it's not an incurable habit. Your sex life needs a change of emphasis.'

Penn said, 'Easy to suggest. Difficult to achieve. I've tried.'

'But not impossible. You see, Charles, you already know what's wrong and you are an intelligent man. You also know the emphasis can be changed.'

'That's the problem, Tess. I am not convinced it can be. I have never had a normal sexual relationship with anyone. My problem goes back to the first time I was in love. Perhaps if I told you, it might explain the problem more fully.'

'Go ahead, Charles. We've got all day.'

He smiled with relief that he had broached the subject and was now, at last, about to share it for the first time in his life.

'It started when I was eighteen. I was in love with a girl called Julia, who was about the same age, maybe a year younger. I suppose that started as infatuation as well, because I knew I didn't have a chance with her. Her boyfriend was in his twenties. Black leather jacket and a motorbike and from the wrong side of the tracks.'

He laughed at the image his words conjured, but it was basically true.

'Rick had everything going for him, including Julia. Funnily enough, he took a liking to me. He called me "Brains" and treated me sometimes as a confidant and sometimes as his pet intellectual. His description, not mine. Although we never spoke about it, he knew how I felt about Julia.'

Penn sat back and remembered. His fear and grudging admiration for Rick, and his devotion and unfulfilled desire for Julia.

'He taught me all about mind games,' Penn said. 'There was a big crowd of us that went around together, but I was the one that Rick insisted was always with him and Julia. I was Robin to his Batman. Perhaps at first he wanted me there so he could watch me watch Julia with adoring eyes. But then he developed it. He developed the whole situation.'

The memories were strong enough to make him feel the first twitches of arousal.

'Rick began touching her while I was there. Insisting I stay. Telling me to stand guard in case other people came. Each time he touched her more intimately. I suppose he did it at first to show his power. Maybe to inflame me. He made her fellate him while I watched. He had sex with her while I watched. Eventually, he gave her to other people and they had sex with her . . . while I watched.'

He paused because he was uncomfortable and he laughed with embarrassment.

'I'm sorry,' he said, changing his position discreetly. 'Just talking about it, even now, has given me an erection.'

'That's okay. Do you want a drink? Water? Alcohol? Anything?'

'No, thank you. I just want to tell you. Now I've started I dare not stop.'

'How long did this go on?'

'About two years. It was odd. All I felt for Julia was a deepening love. I thought it appalling that she was being made to suffer such indignities. But at the same time, it became a compulsion. It was tremendously arousing.'

Tess said, 'You were a young man. You were full of sexual desire. How did you gain satisfaction?'

'Alone, mainly. I masturbated. This odd relationship filled my life at that time. There was no room for other girlfriends. In a way, I counted Julia as my girlfriend. And every week when I went out with her, I would watch her have sex with someone else and then I would go home and masturbate with the image still in my mind.'

'How did it end?' asked Tess.

'Rick and Julia got married and moved away and I got a job abroad in one of the less civilized parts of Africa. I put my efforts into my work and stayed celibate for two years. That was no real problem as there was a shortage of single white females and the only women available were black prostitutes.

'I drank a lot, and when I needed sexual relief, I made the occasion last longer than a two-minute hand-shake. I wrote about Rick and Julia and what they had done. I described the situations and the sex scenes I had witnessed in detail and with obscenities and then, when my lust was at its peak, I allowed myself to orgasm.'

Tess said, 'So you took your obsession, your compulsion, with you to Africa?'

'Yes.' He smiled, sadly. 'And I enjoyed it.'

'What happened when you came back?'

'I was twenty-two and still a virgin. That can be a handicap. Opportunities arose, but being a twenty-two-year-old male virgin made me nervous of a sexual situation where it was one-on-one. Where the only audience was a girl who might start laughing because I didn't do it properly or came too quickly.'

Penn laughed at himself and shook his head.

He said, 'You'll never guess what I did?'

'What did you do?'

'I went and found Rick and Julia. Looked them up, to see how they were going on. They were pleased to see me. Genuinely pleased. I think maybe I had provided a spark to their sex lives. A spark that had been missing since they had been married and I had been in Africa.

'Inevitably, Rick started the games again. I stayed with them for a long weekend but by the end of it I had had enough. I left. Walked out on the games.

'Some time later, Julia phoned. Rick had left her and I had always said I would be there if she needed me. I still loved her. The old-fashioned type of love, you know? The pedestal type of love. Despite everything that had happened, I still treated her as if she were a virgin who had to be wooed.

'Well, we eventually got married but there was no happy ending. At first we were okay. But then I found that the relationship seemed a bit empty. Julia was not enough. To arouse myself before we made love, I had to think about the times I had been the silent witness. The watcher. The voyeur.

'Julia discovered my problem at a party when I saw her with another man. She knew I was watching and later we had the best sex of our marriage. From then on, we were back to playing games. It was no basis for love and no basis for a marriage. We split up and I've avoided real relationships ever since.'

Tess nodded.

'And now you are worried in case the only way you will be able to have sex with a woman you love is with the aid of a third party?'

'Yes.'

Tess nodded and considered a response. Penn, now that he had made his confession, felt emotionally naked. He needed a diversion while he regained his composure.

'Do you think I could get a cold drink? A Coke or something?'

'Sure.' She pointed. 'In the kitchen.'

Penn got up and went into the kitchen and got a Coke from the refrigerator. He popped the tag and drank from the can. He walked back into the living room and found Tess was still sitting in the chair.

'I'm sorry,' he said, holding up the can. 'Did you want anything?'

'No.' She shook her head. 'It took a lot of guts to tell me what you did.'

'Thank you. But praise doesn't help.'

'How about writing it out of your system? That might help.'

'Writing it?'

'Like you did in Africa. Whatever episode sticks in your mind. Write it down in as much detail as you like and use whatever language you like. Release it. Put it on paper as erotic stories.'

'If I write it down, what do I do with these stories?'

'Give them to me.'

He grinned, still self-conscious, and said, 'Another book?'

Phillip Mason

'No. A second opinion. You've already got your own opinion.'

Penn drank the Coke and thought about becoming a writer. Years ago it had been an ambition, before other ambitions involving money had taken over his life.

'You think it might help?'

'It might and it will give me a greater insight. Talking about it is one thing, but writing it down involves a much greater depth of concentration and commitment. You'll bring those incidents back to life.

'At the moment, they're memories in a cupboard at the back of your mind. Memories that might be faulty, affected by dust and cobwebs. Dig them out, write about them and your mind will go back thirty years: you'll remember more than who did what to whom, you'll remember how you felt, how Julia looked, what was said.

'Write them, Charles. See if they still turn you on.' She smiled. 'See if they turn *me* on.'

He laughed. He was glad he had confided in her. She had made it easy and was still making it easy. This was no session on a couch where he was expected to bare his soul, this was an adult conversation between two mature people.

'Okay, I'll write them. I enjoyed being a storyteller once. I might enjoy it again.' He shrugged. 'But how do I it?'

'As directly as possible. Put in whatever details you think are important or relevant. Starting will be the difficult part but, once you *have* started, you will find it comes easy. What are you doing tonight?'

'I'm seeing Tamara at Stringfellows about midnight.'

'Then sit down at eight and write the first episode. Let me have it tomorrow. Send it by messenger.' He looked doubtful, and she added, 'And that's doctor's orders.'

*   *   *

Because they were doctor's orders, at eight o'clock that evening Penn sat at the desk in his apartment at Wapping that overlooked the Thames and Tower Bridge.

He wore jogging shorts and a T-shirt and had tried to get himself into the right frame of mind by working out in his gym and having a long shower. He had hoped the physical effort might work as a form of meditation or mind-relaxant.

Now he sat before the screen of his computer and stared at the keyboard. He had once wanted to be a writer and produce the great novel and had faced this same dilemma before. Only back then it had been a blank sheet of paper in a typewriter and not a blank screen.

The emptiness of the paper had defeated him then. It had taunted him because he knew it would take a great deal of effort to fill even one sheet, never mind the three or four hundred necessary for a book.

Now the screen taunted him, except this time he did not have a book to write, just episodes from his life of more than thirty years ago. Surely he could manage that?

The great novel. He remembered his hopes. At the time, he had given himself all sorts of reasons why it did not happen. Ultimately, he had blamed it on time. He simply had not had the time, not while he was making money and building a business empire.

But when he thought about it now, he realized it had not been time or the hours of solitary hard work that had killed his ambitions to be a writer. It had been much simpler than that. It had been the fear of failure.

What if he had written the great novel and it had been rubbish?

This time, there would be no literary critic reading what he produced. This time it was for him and Tess Flanders only to read. Would it turn him on, like it had in Africa? Would it turn Tess on?

The thought made him smile. He had never asked her the obvious question. This was a woman who dealt professionally and lucratively with other people's sexual experiences and fantasies and who appeared to be fazed by nothing, however bizarre.

He had read her books. He had read of the young woman who had a crush on her dog and the elderly man who enjoyed wearing his wife's frocks. All human life was there in her books and, while some of it was definitely not to Penn's taste, there were sections that were. There were sections that definitely turned him on.

But what turned Dr Tess Flanders on? Would his stories do the trick?

Penn took a deep breath and let his mind roam over those strange and intense years of his youth. Where should he start?

The first time Rick made him a voyeur, he supposed, but it had happened in stages. There was no real beginning, just a series of hesitant steps that had developed until Rick suddenly realized the power he wielded . . . and that he enjoyed wielding it.

The party was probably the first time. Penn would start with the party. He took his time focusing his mind on a particular night, remembering the ancillary details that might bring the memory to life. He began to hit the keyboard and the words began to appear on the blank screen.

Chapter 7

Charles Penn's story

I suppose I started watching them in the car. I would borrow my father's car and act as their chauffeur. Rick came to expect it at weekends.

On those occasions, after we had been out somewhere – to a pub or a party or somebody's house – he and Julia would sit in the back of the car while I drove them home. They would kiss and he would touch her and make her touch him.

Because I was driving I never got a proper view of what they were doing. But I could hear and, sometimes, I would alter the rear-view mirror so that I could see.

He would open her blouse or push up her skirt. She would try to stop him going too far but there were times when he made her masturbate him. I didn't see it all but I heard it, and I did see her crouched over his groin, saw her arms moving as her hands worked on him just outside my field of view. Of course it aroused me. It made me stiff.

But the most arousing sight I actually saw were her stocking tops when her skirt was pushed up. If it was a tight skirt, she would have difficulty getting it down again quickly. I would only get a glimpse for a moment but it always turned me on.

It changed the night we went to a party. It was a big

house, someone's parents were away and everybody got invited round.

It's funny but I remember the music. The Beatles had just made it big. Started another rock-and-roll revolution. Gerry and The Pacemakers, The Searchers, Billy J. Kramer and Freddie and the Dreamers were all in the charts. Their records were being played at the party.

We took beer and wine and cider and someone raided the houseowner's drinks cupboard. Rick had a bottle of vodka. It wasn't full and he'd mixed it with orange cordial. We ended up in a bedroom together. Him, me and Julia.

I'd already had beer and when he insisted I had a drink of the vodka I put it my lips but only pretended. Besides, I didn't much like the taste. There's nothing worse than warm vodka.

There was only a single bed in the room. I think it was a spare room. There was nothing intimate about it. We sat side by side on the edge of the bed, Julia in the middle, and shared the bottle: I could tell Julia was getting drunk.

They were playing a game. He poured vodka in her mouth and she had to hold it until he put his mouth over hers and they could share it. He did it this time and then gave me the bottle to hold and when he put his mouth over hers and they swallowed it, he kept his mouth there and kissed her. A wet, open-mouthed kiss.

We had been laughing but the atmosphere changed. I sat there grinning like an idiot, holding the bottle, while he kissed her, slobbering at her mouth. He had one arm around her neck and his other hand went over her breasts. He mauled them and she put a hand up to push his hand away. But he took hold of her wrist and put it down by her side and then continued mauling her breasts.

I had seen him kiss her before, seen him touch her before,

but not this close, not this blatant. My face went red and I had an instant erection. At eighteen it did not take much to give me an instant erection.

He pushed her back across the bed and continued to kiss her and pull at her breasts through her dress. She was wearing a dress that zipped up the back otherwise he might have pulled it open. I continued to sit there, not knowing what to do. Being pushed back had caused her skirt to ride up and I stared at her legs. I was hot and shaky at being so close, at seeing her legs like that, slightly apart and the skirt moving higher.

Rick stopped kissing her but held her down on the bed with his left hand. He lifted his body from her and grinned at me. He had a very infectious grin that was also dangerous. He grinned with his teeth and I had seen him grin like that just before starting a fight. If there was a fight, he always started it. And he always finished it.

Anyway, he grinned at me and put his right hand on Julia's leg. He pushed his hand up the skirt and pushed the material higher. I didn't know where to look. Whether to look at him or at Julia's legs.

Julia tried to stop him and reached with one hand to push at his arm. He turned his head to stare down at her and, while he did, I looked at her legs and saw the skirt was above the tops of her stockings. Tan stockings and white suspender straps and his hand upon her thigh.

He said to her, 'I want to look,' and she took away her hand but closed her eyes and turned her head away.

Rick stroked her legs and said to me, 'Beautiful, aren't they?'

'Yes,' I said.

He was inviting me to watch so I did. I watched his hand go between her legs beneath the skirt where I could not see and she gasped and raised her hips from the bed.

'She likes it all the time,' he said to me, quite conversationally. 'She likes being touched. Don't you?'

When she did not reply straightaway his hand went beneath the skirt once more and I saw the bulge of the dress as he gripped her between the legs. She writhed again.

He said, 'Don't you?' and she said, 'Yes.'

Then he said, 'You like being fucked, don't you?'

'Rick!' she said, and opened her eyes to stare at him, and I dared not look at her face.

His hand moved beneath the skirt: her eyes closed, she bit her bottom lip and her head rolled to the side.

'You do, don't you? You like being fucked?'

'Yes,' she said.

'Say it,' he said. His hand moved again and she moaned. 'Say it.'

In a small voice, she said, 'I like being fucked.'

Rick looked back at me, our faces close, and his smile was dangerous and lecherous.

'Watch the door,' he said.

'What?'

'Stand against the door and make sure no one comes in.'

I nodded, got off the bed and went and leaned against the door. There was a small catch to lock it and I flicked that into place.

I was literally shaking with fear and excitement. Rick pushed at Julia and spoke to her in a low voice and she moved so that she lay properly in the middle of the bed. He lay alongside her and kissed her and his hand pushed up her skirt again and she pushed against his shoulders and whispered something to him.

He turned his head and said, 'Turn off the light.'

I switched off the light and, even though I couldn't see as well as before, I was grateful for the darkness. The curtains were open and there was a moon. I could see enough.

Rick knelt up on the bed and took hold of the skirt in both hands and pushed it upwards. Julia raised herself and it slid up around her waist. Now he lay on her and they continued to kiss. Her arms were wrapped around him and she pulled at him with her hands.

He had one leg between hers and was moving himself against her. She was rubbing her groin backwards and forwards against him.

From the neck to the waist she was fully dressed but from the waist down she was deliciously on view. Rick ran his hand along her thigh, from nylon to flesh, and pushed it beneath her to grope her bottom.

My erection was so fierce I thought it might explode but at least they were not looking at me. It seemed as if they had forgotten about me.

I held the vodka bottle in my left hand and my prick in my right. I held it through my trousers and rocked against my hand. My throat was so dry I took a drink of the vodka and orange. It made me want to cough but I choked it back. I didn't want to make any noise that might make them remember I was there.

Rick's hand left Julia's bottom and came over her hip as he lifted himself and put it between her legs. She started groaning. He did this for a while and then raised himself again and used both hands to unfasten his jeans. Then he took Julia's hands and pushed them down between them and I could see her arms moving as she masturbated him.

It was at this point that I came in my trousers. I could no longer keep myself under control. I remained by the door, gripping myself tightly in my right hand, and came silently but with tremendous intensity.

I hadn't been able to delay it or stop it: while it was happening it had been an amazing experience, staring at the girl I loved who was lying half-naked upon a bed and masturbating another man.

Not being able to see everything that was going on didn't matter. I was there and I knew what was happening, knew that his prick was in her hands, those lovely, delicate, feminine hands.

Rick began to pull at her panties. But she struggled again and whispered to him and he laughed.

'Okay,' he said.

He got off the left side of the bed and looked at me. I felt guilty at watching and ashamed in case they guessed I had come in my trousers, but he just grinned at me.

'Keep guard, Brains,' he said.

I nodded to him while I tried to watch Julia in the periphery of my vision as she got off the bed on the opposite side.

Rick pulled back the covers of the bed and began to take off his shirt. He was no longer looking at me. Julia had avoided glancing in my direction, choosing to pretend I was not there. She had her back to me and, for a moment, my heart sank in disappointment as she pushed down the skirt of the dress. But it was only so she could reach behind her to unzip it.

I lay against the door in the shadows while the moonlight cast a pale glow across the bed and I watched Julia drop the dress from her shoulders so that it pooled on the floor. She stepped out of it. All she now wore was white bra, panties and suspender belt, and the tan stockings.

My erection came back almost as instantly as it had left

as I stared at her lovely body, pale and, as far as I was
concerned, mysterious, crossed by the white straps of her
underwear, her legs sheathed in nylon stockings.

She continued to ignore my presence, got into the bed
and pulled the covers up to her neck.

I had been aware that Rick was also undressing and now
I saw that he had no inhibitions and had removed all his
clothing. His prick was stiff, thrusting out from his groin,
and he stroked it as he smiled down at Julia.

He got beneath the covers with her, and rolled against
her. They kissed, rubbed themselves against each other and
then paused and his arm came out and threw her bra onto
the floor. They continued embracing and he disappeared
beneath the covers and emerged minutes later to drop her
panties over the side of the bed.

My senses were swimming again. They were making
noises, grunting and moaning. Sometimes I thought Julia
was complaining or trying to restrain him and I felt guilty
again. If I loved her, should I not step in and ask her if this
was what she wanted? Should I not try to protect her?

But how could I? She was Rick's girlfriend, not mine.
She might not welcome my interference, she might prefer
to pretend I was not there. Besides, Rick would give me a
good hiding.

What made me feel more guilty was that I didn't want
this to stop. I didn't want Julia, the girl of my dreams, to
call a halt. I wanted it to continue.

He lay on top of her and again she stopped him and
they whispered and Rick turned his head to stare in my
direction.

'In my jeans,' he said. 'Back pocket.'

For a moment I didn't know what he meant. But I knew
better than to keep him waiting, so I went to the side of

the bed, picked up his jeans, felt in the back pockets and found a Durex.

His hand stretched out from the bed and I gave it to him, at the same time catching a glimpse beneath the covers. Julia had turned her head away but I could see her breast beneath his chest, the curve of a delicious breast, and its nipple, large and brown.

He winked at me and I returned to the door and the darkness and breathed through my mouth as I watched and listened while he tore open the packet and threw it onto the floor. Then he raised himself beneath the sheets as he fitted the condom. He chuckled and changed his position and Julia murmured something and then groaned and his hips pushed forward.

All I could see were their outlines beneath the covers, Julia's legs spread and Rick lying between them. But it was the most exciting experience I had ever had.

He waited for a moment, then raised himself and thrust again. Julia groaned again and then he began to do it quicker and harder and she breathed in time to the thrusts, groaned in time to the thrusts.

I didn't touch myself. I leaned back against the door, my prick stiff again and still sticky in my trousers, and I watched him fuck the girl of my dreams.

Julia began to say, 'No, no, no,' but I don't know why, and he was grunting and the bed was creaking and she moaned and her knees came higher beneath the covers. He gasped and his back arched upwards and I watched him shake as he came inside her, and I came again, no hands, just watching, and I had never felt so alive.

Afterwards, Rick lost interest in the situation, for which I was grateful because now I felt the embarrassment was about to set in. He got out of bed, pulled off the Durex and got dressed while Julia still lay there.

'Pass my things,' she said to him, and her voice was a little slurred.

'Brains can pass them,' he said, and indicated that I should do just that.

My face was red again. But I picked up her panties and trembled at their touch, and her bra, and went to the side of the bed and offered them.

Julia looked at me for the first time. Her face was different, maybe a little puffed, maybe a little drunk, and she took the underclothes and pulled them beneath the covers.

She said, 'Don't ever tell anyone.'

'No,' I said, wanting to fall on my knees by the side of the bed and pledge my loyalty. 'Of course not.'

Rick opened the door and light from the hall came in. Julia closed her eyes and pulled the covers over her head.

'I'm going to get a beer,' said Rick. 'Guard the door, Brains.'

He left and closed the door behind him. I went to it and clicked the lock again and waited, once more not knowing quite what to do.

'Shall I wait outside?' I said.

'No,' she said, nothing more.

So I stayed and she eventually got out of the bed. I pretended not to look and she kept her back to me so that I could look: I watched her put the dress on and reach behind her for the zip.

'Can you do it for me?' she said.

I went to her and took hold of the zip and was within inches of her naked back and the white strap of her bra. I felt intoxicated with love for her and wanted to tell her so but instead I pulled up the zip.

It seems strange now, looking back, to have been so intoxicated with what I thought was love when it was really lust. But, whatever it was, it had made my prick go stiff again.

I thought then we would leave the bedroom. But she made the bed and straightened the covers so no one would know. Then I noticed the used Durex on the floor. I picked it up and put it in my pocket, not caring that it might leak and make a mess, because I looked upon it as a love token.

After all, that Durex had been where I could only dream of going.

When we got to the bedroom door, she smiled at me and said, 'You're sweet, Charlie. I know I can trust you.'

'You can,' I said, and meant it with all my heart.

Then we went back to the party and I joined Rick. Julia went to the bathroom and, when she joined us she looked as normal as ever. Perhaps still a little drunk, but normal, as if nothing had happened.

That was the first time. Maybe it was even the best.

Chapter 8

Charles Penn waited two days before he telephoned Dr Tess Flanders and left a message on her answering machine. For a man who was supposed to be self-possessed and arrogant, he had been experiencing a great deal of angst lately.

Tess called him back that evening at his apartment.

He said, 'I wondered if you had had time to read it.'

'I read it as soon as it arrived. You have a natural aptitude, Charles. Maybe you should write an erotic novel.'

Penn laughed.

'Maybe I'll save it for my autobiography. What did you think?'

'More to the point, what did *you* think? Did you enjoy writing it?'

'Yes. I did.' he laughed nervously. 'It had the same effect as when I was in Africa.'

'You indulged single-handed?'

'No, of course not.'

'You didn't?'

Her voice was weighted with scepticism.

'Okay. So I did.'

Why did he feel like a guilty schoolboy? Why had he even told her?

'One thing I noticed,' she said. 'You didn't describe them. You described Rick's smile, but that was all, but nothing about Julia. Maybe that was because you had their images fixed in your mind and wanted to cut straight to the action.'

'I suppose so,' he said.

'So what was she like?'

'She was dark. She had dark hair. A pretty face. Nice legs. A slim body.'

'And Rick?'

'I remember his smile. He must have been twenty-four or twenty-five. He'd signed on on a ship in his teens and been to America. To us, the crowd we went around with, he was Marlon Brando. You know? *The Wild One*.'

'I know.'

'People did what he said. Julia certainly did. She was totally under his power. I was amazed her parents put up with Rick but they did. Her father was a bank manager. Maybe they were intimidated by him as well.'

'Did they know he was sleeping with their daughter?'

'I don't think so. At least, they didn't want to know. Daughters didn't do that thirty years ago. Or they were not supposed to do that.'

Tess said, 'Have you seen Tamara?'

'I saw her the night I wrote it.'

'Have there been any developments with Tamara?'

'No. We talked in the club, but there were a lot of people there. She was making contacts. Trying to put together this TV thing.'

'Have you made an offer yet?'

'No.'

'Why not?'

'The abuse of power, I suppose. If I do suggest it, she might feel obliged to reciprocate in some way.'

'And you still don't want to go to bed with her?'

'I'm still not sure that I could.'

'When are you next seeing her?'

'Tomorrow evening. I'm taking her to dinner and then dropping her off at a club.'

'She goes to a lot of clubs.'

Penn laughed.

'It's what she does.'

'Okay,' said Tess. 'Then write another piece tomorrow, before you see her.'

'Do I send it to you by messenger again?'

'Unless you want to deliver it yourself?'

'I'd prefer to do that. I have this fear of having my secret confessions lost on the streets of London.' Tess laughed and he added, 'And besides, I find it easier to talk to you in person, rather than on the telephone.'

'Okay. How about the day after? When are you free?'

'Any time I want to be.'

'Bravo. The arrogance is back.'

'Do my nerves show that much?'

'A little, but I am a trained observer. Come round at one. I'll give you lunch.'

'I appreciate it.'

'You haven't tasted my cooking.'

When Penn replaced the receiver, he picked up the new dossier that had been delivered to his office that afternoon. This went deeper than the original: a discreet and very expensive firm of private investigators had followed lines of specific enquiry.

There were more photographs, but these were from private sources and had not appeared in the gossip columns. Pictures of Tamara at home and at parties and on holiday.

One series of prints showed her taking her clothes off in an amateur striptease sequence and had been obtained from an early boyfriend. They were innocuous, except in what they suggested: that after she had disrobed, the boyfriend had obviously had sexual relations with her.

Penn had obtained the negatives as well as what prints the boyfriend admitted to possessing. The cost had been high but he had achieved two aims: the protection of Tamara's future reputation and an insight into her teenage years.

He stared at the enlargements he had had printed. Tamara had been eighteen years old when they were taken and had not yet acquired the air of sophistication that she now carried so comfortably, and her hair was long and untidy.

There were ten shots. She was dressed as a schoolgirl in white knee socks and posed with her skirt raised while sprawled upon bed. The shots progressed so that she was shown without a skirt, then without the blouse although she retained the tie. Then without her white cotton brassiere.

The photograph Penn kept staring at more than the other was one where she knelt upon the bed on her hands and knees and faced the camera. Her eyes were wide and a little lost, her lips slightly parted, the tie dangled from around her neck, and her small breasts hung delightfully beneath her, the nipples neat and budlike.

Penn stared at the background of the picture, at the bottle of wine on the bedside table, the poor quality of the furnishings and the bed covers, the sad wallpaper.

The pictures had been taken in the boyfriend's bedsitter in Putney. It was a time when Tamara had obviously been short of money but not short of admirers.

He imagined the boyfriend touching her in between the poses, kissing her, fondling her breasts, and, ultimately, having sex with her. The thought aroused him satisfyingly.

There was also information about Jamie Philpott, the

rock singer who had drifted in and out of her life. The stories surrounding him were legend and, Penn had to admit, fairly routine as far as rock stars were concerned.

The band he fronted, Nadir, had indulged in the usual on-tour parties with groupies. Their music was quite wild and their behaviour matched it.

Photographs had been obtained from hotel rooms and dressing rooms that showed female fans, several of whom had stripped to black stockings and underwear for the privilege of sharing a bottle of Bud with the boys in the band.

Whatever else the girls had offered as party favours was not shown in these particular photographs. But Penn had issued instructions for all efforts to be made to acquire more explicit evidence.

Background briefing notes told him that the band were famous for their gang-bangs.

They also said Jamie Philpott was an honours graduate in art from Sheffield University and was estimated to have a personal bank balance of £1.3 million. Of course, if the music ever stopped his bar bill alone would eat into the interest at an alarming rate. His fondness for cocaine would eat into the capital.

Penn stared at the photographs of Jamie Philpott. There were several and on every one he was sneering at the camera. It was part of his image to be rude. What on earth did Tamara see in him?

He snorted and laughed.

Apart from his dark good looks, long hair, lean physique and an undoubted talent as a singer-songwriter.

Could love be blind? He hoped so.

Tamara had also lived for three months with Alex Brown, who made promotional video films for rock bands and award-winning television commercials. Brown was forty and had a successful freelance career, as well as a taste for young women.

Touché, credited Penn.

In these days of video and instant cameras, Penn had no doubt that there would be film of Tamara in poses more compromising than that almost innocent schoolgirl striptease. If there were such films or photographs, he wanted them.

Alex Brown was not a man to be persuaded to part with such merchandise, if he had any, for straight cash. He might be a gentleman who would never release such damaging footage, or he might be waiting for the right time to make a killing. So Penn had decided to remove this matter of conscience from Brown's domain.

He had instructed the firm of discreet private investigators that he employed to discover whether Brown was likely to have such material and the probable places where it might be kept. Then they were to burgle Brown's home and business premises and take the material into safe keeping.

The same instructions applied to Jamie Philpott.

Penn finally turned to the last report. This was accompanied by two photographs, one that showed Tamara in her actual school uniform and the other portraying her as a member of the choir that had figured in her famous magazine interview where she had claimed to have seduced four boy choristers.

The report suggested this was an untruth. The rumour that had circulated at the time was that the choirmaster, a gentleman of forty-six, had seduced Tamara when she was sixteen.

No one's past warranted close inspection. Penn knew that better than anyone. And nothing he had so far discovered altered his feelings for the beautiful young woman.

Everybody's life was full of indiscretions, and he had a burning desire to discover hers. Not to destroy her or to judge her, but to know her, to protect her. Perhaps because he was still playing games.

Still a voyeur.

Tamara was not ready when he went to her apartment the next night to take her to dinner.

After she had buzzed him in from the street, she once again left her front door open for his arrival. He went into the main room and called her name. She shouted back:

'Pour yourself a drink, darling. I'm sorry I'm running late, but I've had rather good news.'

A bottle of pink Pol Roger champagne was in the ice bucket and he poured himself a glass.

'What's that?' he called.

'A television producer called. He wants to do a pilot. You know, a show.' She entered the room wearing high-heeled shoes and a pink peignoir over her underwear. 'It looks as if it's actually going to happen.'

'That's wonderful,' he said. But he was distracted as she came to him, kissed him on the cheek and held out her glass for more wine.

The peignoir hung open and flowed behind her when she walked. Her silk underwear was also pink. A delicate shade of oyster. A flimsy excuse for a brassiere, French knickers with high-cut slits up each side, and a suspender belt with gossamer straps that held taut pink stockings that had a wicked sheen.

'Isn't it, though? It's not the same chap I've been talking to, but somebody new. A different company.'

She turned and went to the fireplace. Penn sipped the champagne to moisten his mouth that had suddenly become dry.

'What's his name? I may know him.'

Tamara put her glass down and picked a box from the mantelpiece.

'Monty Radcliffe. The company is Badger UK.' She laughed, as she rummaged in the box. 'I thought it sounded rather silly but apparently they do a lot of things for Channel Four.'

Penn said, 'I don't know Radcliffe, but I've heard of Badger. They're pretty good.'

She found a pair of earrings, replaced the box, turned and gave him a wide smile.

'Then this could be the start of a whole new experience,' she said.

'It certainly looks that way.'

Now she turned to a mirror and fixed the earrings while Penn admired her slim body through the peignoir.

'So you can see why I'm late. Nearly ready now, though.' Tamara walked back across the room towards the bedroom from which she had emerged. 'Would you mind, Charles?'

He put down the champagne and followed. The bedroom was in varying shades of pink that blushed as deep as rose. The cover on the king-sized bed was pink silk, the drapes at the window were pink satin, the carpet and rugs also pink.

The dress that hung on a wardrobe door was black and a stark contrast. Tamara shed the peignoir as she walked and let it float to the ground behind her, affording Penn an unrestricted view of her delectable body.

She took the dress from its hanger, stepped into it and

lifted it over her shoulders. It was crêpe silk with a bodice that was fitted to the waist and a full skirt that hung caressingly from her hips.

'Would you?' she said, turning her back to him.

The dress was open to her buttocks. He remained calm, took hold of the zip and gripped the material to add tension. Her skin glowed with youth and he could smell her perfume. Ralph Lauren's Safari.

He could feel her warmth through the knuckle of the hand that held the zip. He admired the curve of her hips and her long elegant spine, and the further curves of her neck and shoulders as his hand slowly moved upwards and closed the black gash of material.

'Thank you,' she said, and turned and leaned against him briefly while she kissed him again on the cheek. 'And now, believe it or not, I am ready.'

Her eyes were wide and her smile girlish and he grinned in response because, after that almost casual moment of intimacy that had aroused him so much, she suddenly made him feel young.

'And well worth waiting for,' he said.

Tess Flanders was wearing a dress and high-heeled shoes when she opened the apartment door for Penn the next day.

'You have legs,' he said, in mock surprise.

She laughed and led the way into the main room.

'I don't show them too much for fear of exciting the local populace,' she said.

'They are very nice legs,' he said. 'I didn't mean to be rude.'

'I know, I know. I usually wear slacks for comfort, but this morning I had an interview at the office . . .'

'The Dorchester?' he said.

'. . . The Dorchester, with a very nice young man from *The Independent*.'

'And he was worth the dress?'

'I have discovered that a hint of stocking can still win the hearts and minds, even of young men.'

'I believe you.'

'Anyway,' she picked up a glass of white wine. 'I started without you.' She held up the glass. 'Chablis? Or would you prefer something else?'

'Chablis is fine.'

Tess pointed to the sideboard.

'Help yourself.'

He put his briefcase on a chair and did so.

Tess sat in an armchair and said, 'How was your date?'

'Very enjoyable.'

'Where'd you go?'

'Le Caprice.'

'And after?'

'Tamara went to work and I went home.'

Penn sat opposite Tess. She really did have very nice legs.

'Work?' Tess asked.

'She's making a pilot for a TV series. She had people to see.'

'The TV has worked out?'

'It depends on the pilot.'

'And the pilot depends on you?'

'Yes. But Tamara doesn't know that. She thinks she got the chance herself. I told you. I don't want her to see me as a means to an end.'

'Are you still in love?'

'I'm still considering the possibility.'

She smiled and shook her head.

'Mr Impetuous,' she said. 'Did you do your home-work?'

'Yes.' He opened the briefcase and took from it the pages he had completed on the word processor before he had gone to meet Tamara. He handed them to Tess. 'I'm still not sure if it's doing any good.'

Tess put down the glass of wine.

'Do you mind if I read them now?'

'Of course not.'

'If you want something to read, try an erotic novel. You might get the urge to write one yourself, like I said. Or maybe publish some?'

She pointed to the table next to his chair where a dozen paperback books were scattered.

'I thought you only dealt in fact?'

'It's a thin line, sometimes,' she said. 'Besides, I enjoy erotic fiction and you Brits do it so much better than in the States.'

'I'm glad we're good at something.'

He browsed the titles and the authors: Maria Caprio, James Allen, Phillip Mason.

'They're the best,' Tess said. 'Read and, in the immortal words of Tim Leary, tune in and turn on.'

'Didn't he also say something about dropping out?'

'That's optional.'

Penn smiled and shook his head. This attractive American woman continued to surprise him and he remembered a question he had failed to ask her when they had spoken on the telephone. He looked up from the book he held but she had already started reading the second instalment of his confessions.

The memoirs of a voyeur?

Would it make a book, he wondered?

Tess was reading intently. When she had finished, he would ask her the question he had pondered since he delivered the first instalment. But in the meantime, he would read.

He opened a book by Phillip Mason called *The Innocence of Miss Jones*. What an appealing title. He thought he might like it.

Chapter 9

Charles Penn's story

It was a Sunday afternoon in the summer and I had borrowed the car. A Ford Zephyr. It was a big car. Lots of room. A bench seat at the front.

I drove, Julia sat in the middle and Rick next to her. We went into the country. I suppose Rick had something in mind but he didn't tell me or Julia. He was playing games, as usual.

He told me when to turn off the road and when to stop. We parked on a track near a wood and it started to rain. It was an isolated place and there were no other cars around or people.

'Well, we can't go for a walk,' he said. 'We'll just have to make our own entertainment.'

Rick climbed over the front seat into the back. He sprawled there, laughing, and said to Julia, 'Come on. Climb over.'

Julia was giggling. Games again. She slid over from the front into the back. I remained in the driver's seat. I turned sideways and looked over at them. I suppose I guessed what Rick might have in mind. At least, I was hoping he had something in mind. I wasn't disappointed.

Rick said, 'All this way and it's raining. It's a shame. Brains can't get to see Mother Nature.'

Julia was still giggling and she said, 'Shame,' too, and kept laughing.

'Maybe we should give him a nature show right here,' Rick said. Julia stopped giggling, the breath seeming to catch in her throat, and suddenly she also knew he was going to do something that perhaps she would not want him to do.

Rick said, 'Did you enjoy it at the party, Brains? Huh? Remember? That little show?'

I bit my lip and I knew my face was red. Julia was blushing but she was also looking at me and I thought her eyes were accusing.

'Did you enjoy it?' asked Rick.

'It wasn't a question of enjoying it, Rick, I was watching the door.'

Usually I could talk myself out of tight spots. I preferred negotiation to fist fighting, but there was no option here. I wasn't faced with a fist fight but with the dominance of Rick's personality.

'I don't want lies, Brains. You enjoyed it, didn't you?'

His voice had dropped an octave and carried an implied threat.

'I suppose so,' I said.

'Of course you did. You a virgin, Brains?'

'Well . . .'

The question took me by surprise. He knew I was, he knew I hadn't had a girlfriend of my own for months. He had eyes that could stare into your soul and he just knew. But Julia was still looking at me and, although she still blushed, her interest was obvious.

'You're a virgin,' Rick confirmed. I said nothing but my face went a deeper shade of red. 'I'll bet you creamed yourself that night.'

He was humiliating me and yet he was the person I considered my closest friend. I know now that he was nothing of the kind, that he was using me as he was using Julia. But I was so influenced by him at that time that I really did think of him as a friend.

So I was humiliated but that didn't matter as long he went on to the next stage. I didn't mind being humiliated if he let me watch while he and Julia did things together.

Pathetic?

I suppose so, but I was eighteen and full of sex and didn't have the confidence to find it anywhere else. Besides, just sitting there in the car with the rain beating on the roof and listening to Rick talking about that night, with Julia sitting there in trepidation, was highly arousing.

Rick said, 'How about biology? We could give him a lesson on biology, couldn't we?' He looked at Julia but she did not reply, and he looked back at me. 'Hand in hand, and hand in gland, and gland in gland.' He laughed. 'That sort of thing?' His smile was predatory. 'Interested?' he said.

He knew damn' well I was interested but I dared not say anything. I looked at Julia. Her face was still flushed and she was nibbling her bottom lip. She still stared at me but from lowered eyes.

'Interested?' he repeated.

I shrugged.

'Whatever,' I said.

My mouth was dry and I wanted to say 'Yes, please' but Julia was staring at me. I couldn't tell what she was thinking but I didn't want to offend her.

'Let's start with the female form,' said Rick. 'Ah!' He turned in the seat towards Julia. 'And purely by chance, we have one here.'

Julia was wearing a blue shift dress. She was sitting sideways on the seat with her knees together and her arms wrapped around herself.

'First,' said Rick, his smile firmly in place, 'we have the kiss.'

He put his arms around her and kissed her. Although at first she sat there coldly beneath his embrace, after a while she began to respond. Her head moved, her mouth became mobile, her arms unfolded and she kissed him back.

Rick built her fervour and then broke away. Her flush had changed. I didn't understand it at that time. I thought maybe she was even more embarrassed but I suppose she was also aroused.

Thinking back to the tension in that car I suppose we were all very aroused. Me at what I might see, Julia because whatever happened would be perpetrated upon her body, and Rick because he had the power to inflict his will upon us both.

'That's better,' he said softly to her and eased her shoulders back into the corner of the seat. He placed her arms by her side and straightened her legs out in front of her. 'The beautiful female form,' said Rick.

He put his hands upon her knees and began to slide them up her nyloned legs beneath the dress. The material moved upwards on his wrists.

Julia gulped in nervousness and, as he went higher, reached forward and placed her hands over his.

'No,' she said.

Her eyes glanced in my direction.

'Yes,' said Rick. 'Brains is okay. He's keeping watch. Besides, he needs the education.'

He laughed. A snigger, really, but I didn't care. I just

wanted his hands to keep on pushing higher up her dress, to show me what was beneath.

Rick said, 'Don't you think he deserves a little reward? You've seen the way he looks at you, Julia. You know he's devoted to you. You're devoted, aren't you, Brains?'

'Yes.'

That much at least was true.

'See?' said Rick. 'He won't tell anybody. It will be our secret. Okay?'

His hands started again on their journey beneath the dress. Julia capitulated with a nervous sigh, moved her hands and put them back by her sides, and lay there subservient beneath his touch.

The dress slid across the darker bands at the top of her stockings. I imagined what his fingers were touching and my prick throbbed. His hands went higher still as Julia closed her eyes and the dress went above the stocking tops. I could see her flesh and the tabs of her suspenders, the taut white straps heading to my personal heaven.

I was so close to them and this was in daylight and her legs and thighs were there before me, more than naked in tan stockings and white suspender straps.

Out of sight of Rick and Julia, I held my stiff prick in my trousers and gulped for breath. It seemed as if someone had sucked all the air out of the car and replaced it with tension.

He stroked her thighs. He pushed a hand beneath her and groped a buttock and, because he moved her legs, I could see the mysterious white V of her panties.

Rick parted her thighs and his fingers stroked that tight stretch of nylon between her legs and all the time Julia sat with her eyes closed and head back and nibbled into her bottom lip.

'There is so much pleasure to be gained from a girl,' said Rick, his voice gentle. 'All this lovely, soft flesh to touch. Hand in gland?'

He pushed a finger beneath her panties and she tensed but did not try to stop him. I watched the bulge his finger made beneath the nylon and then the bulge disappeared as his finger sank inside her as she gave a small, involuntary moan.

I kept gulping for saliva and breath and my eyes were fixed on the hand that was between her legs and the movement of his finger.

Rick turned and smiled at me, that smile he did with his teeth, and I shuddered and wanted to stop him, wanted to apologize to Julia for her humiliation, wanted to take his place. And wanted to come.

'You know something?' he said to me, confidentially, as if Julia could not hear. 'My dick has gone hard. Has yours gone hard?'

He laughed, removed his hand from Julia, sat back on the seat and stroked the bulge in his trousers. Julia opened her eyes and watched him, but he watched me.

Rick reached sideways and took hold of her hand. He pulled it towards his lap and she had to move closer to him on the seat. She did not push down her skirt. He placed her hand on the bulge in his trousers and rubbed himself against it.

'Ooh, that feels good,' he said.

He turned sideways and put his arms around her and kissed her. As they kissed, he placed both her hands upon him. When he took his own hands away to stroke her face and neck, she continued rubbing him through his trousers.

They kissed for a long time, as if they had forgotten I

was there. He dropped his right hand and put it back up her skirt. She turned sideways and his hand went beneath her and cupped a buttock as her hands still worked on his erection.

Julia no longer seemed so shy or embarrassed and appeared to be using her palms and fingers in a way she had practised often. Their mouths broke apart, he whispered in her ear and she began to unfasten his jeans.

I watched her delicate fingers opening the waistband and pulling down the zip. I watched them delve inside to move his shirt away and then they were tugging at his underpants. One hand went inside and then the other. They grasped and moved rhythmically. Then Rick groaned and he stopped kissing her and lay back on the seat.

He stared at me, mouth slightly open, a knowing expression in his eyes. Julia leaned against him, her hands working upon him, her head against his chest, and when she looked at me I thought, for the first time, that I saw a slyness in her face. But I told myself it could not be so.

Her mouth was open and her features had become heavier. Her hands and wrists moved with a practised rhythm and her dress still lay rumpled high upon her thighs.

'She's good,' said Rick, softly.

He reached down, took hold of the waistband of his underpants and pushed them down. He raised himself from the seat and pushed the pants and his jeans down his hips so that I could see exactly what she was doing.

Julia looked away. She no longer wanted to watch me watching her.

His prick was big and engorged. Her hands moved over it lightly. From time to time she would touch the glans of his prick with her fingers or run her palm across the top and he would groan and his hips would rise. And all the time that she did this he watched me.

'Do you like watching?' he said.

I licked my lips. I knew he wanted an answer.

'Yes,' I said.

'Lovely hands,' he said. 'Julia has such lovely hands.'

He held my gaze until I dropped it to watch her lovely hands masturbating him with consummate skill.

'You want to watch something else?' he said.

What else? I couldn't imagine. Was he going to have sex with her here, in the back of the car, in broad daylight?

I nodded. Yes, I wanted to watch something else. I just didn't trust my voice any more.

'Julia has a great mouth,' he said, and, for a moment, the rhythm of her hands faltered. 'You know what I mean?'

I shook my head.

'She has a great mouth for sucking,' he said, and the realization slowly dawned. He ran his tongue around his lips. 'A great mouth for sucking my dick.'

I was in such a high state of excitement and anticipation and horror that I could easily have had a heart attack. I remember my first reaction to what he was saying was that he would surely not make her do that. Not that. Not here on a Sunday afternoon. But I saw his smile and knew that that was exactly what he intended.

'Would you like to see Julia suck my dick?' he said.

Of course I would. He knew I would, but he waited for my answer.

I nodded.

'Julia,' he said, 'Charlie wants to see you suck my dick.'

No, I thought. Don't say it like that. Don't blame me. I'm just here to watch.

He put an arm around her and he ran the fingers of his other hand through her hair.

'Come on, now. Be a good girl and show Charlie how it's done.'

Rick pushed her head down towards his lap. I expected her to resist but she didn't. She knew it was useless to resist, I told myself. She knew she could expect no help from me.

Her head went into his lap and she held his prick upright by its base. He held her hair away from her face so that I could see her profile, could see her mouth open and take the head of his prick inside.

I watched her suck, saw her cheeks working as she sucked, heard the noises she made, and then she began to move her head up and down upon his swollen prick. The noises got louder and his smile got tighter.

Her fingers also worked on his prick, at its base. He began to shake his head slowly, raised his hands and stretched them sideways along the back of the seat, while his girlfriend, his plaything, my love, conditioned to suck while he took his ease, continued to do just that.

His face changed with the pleasure and soon he announced, 'I'm going to come.'

Again, I was shocked. Surely not? He would not come in her mouth? She would not allow that? But she would and he reached down with one hand to hold back her hair so that my vision would not be impaired.

Rick tensed, his hips lifted and the muscles in his stomach became taut. Julia stopped sucking. She gulped and her lips clamped around his prick, her hands holding it steady, and as Rick came in her mouth, I came in my trousers.

Julia kept on gulping and swallowing. When Rick relaxed and his prick began to soften visibly, she lifted her mouth and licked her lips, her tongue peeping out, checking the corners of her mouth for any part of his discharge that she might have missed.

'Good, wasn't it?' he said to me, knowing that I, too, had come. All I could do was nod in reply.

That was all that happened that day. Rick lost interest after his orgasm. But there were other occasions. In the car, when they were in the back seat and while I drove, she would masturbate or suck him and he would describe what she was doing as I listened to the sounds.

There were times at parties when I would be in the same room while they went to bed in the dark and fucked. Twice he instructed me to sit next to him on a bed while she knelt at his feet and sucked him until he came.

Then, near the end of the summer, we went out for a drive again to those same woods, only this time it was not raining. The day was warm and the woods were empty.

We walked for a while. He kept touching her and rubbing himself against her and stopping to pull her to him while they kissed. I watched and wondered what else they might do.

He tried to push her against a tree but she refused and said the tree would dirty her blouse, which was white. She wore it with a thin blue pleated skirt.

'All right,' he said. 'Then lean against Brains.'

'What?' she said, thinking he was making a joke. But he wasn't.

'Lean against the tree,' he told me. I did what he said and stood with my back against the tree. 'Now you won't get your blouse dirty,' he said to Julia and placed her in front of me and pushed her until her back was pressing against my chest.

Julia giggled, but seemed to have doubts about the arrangement. But Rick, as always, could not be denied.

Her shoulders were against me but she arched herself away so that no sensitive areas were touching. That situation, of course, did not last long.

Rick stood in front of her and she put her arms around his neck and they kissed. As he pushed against her, he pressed her body back against me and her bottom rubbed against my prick.

I was mortified that she would feel my erection and recognize it for what it was and know, once and for all, of my arousal. But there was nothing I could do except endure the embarrassment and humiliation – and the deep and searing pleasure.

My prick was standing upright in my trousers and was deliciously accommodated in the cleft between Julia's buttocks.

Now I stood revealed for what I was, a lecherous youth rather than a devoted admirer. Rick, of course, had known the state I would be in and had known exactly how our bodies would fit together.

He pushed her legs slightly apart and rubbed himself against her. Incredibly, she moved in response to his thrusts, causing her buttocks to move against my erection.

I was in heaven and hell. The sensations were unbelievable. This was more than I had ever dreamed of achieving. My stiff prick rubbing against her softness, feeling her body shaking with desire, if not for me, then at least the next best thing, against me.

But I was in such a state that I feared I might come and she would feel my orgasm against her and be repulsed. For I had been placed there for her to lean on, not for me to ejaculate against her.

My reasoning was not sound. It never was where Julia and Rick were concerned. I still believed Julia to be an innocent girl who was being led into corruption by Rick. I still dreamed of rescuing her and making her life a bed of roses. But at that point, all I wanted to do was to wallow in the moment and try to stop from coming.

Rick opened her blouse. His hands were on her breasts, his groin still thrust against her and her bottom still moved magically against my erection. There was a moment when she almost overbalanced and I put my hands upon her waist to steady her. She did not object so I left them there.

He crouched to suck her breasts. Her head fell back against my shoulder and I breathed in the smell of her hair. As he sucked, he lifted the skirt and his hands moved over her thighs above her stockings. He gripped her hips in both hands and deliberately moved her against me: I almost came but held myself in check.

His hand went between her legs and she squirmed at his touch. Again I was close but refused to throw away the moment by falling over the precipice for the one glorious instant of ecstasy.

This was also ecstasy. Painful ecstasy, but ecstasy none the less. Holding myself on the brink, in such a high state of arousal, was like a stretched climax that might foreseeably last for ever, or at least for the duration of the game.

Rick used Julia and me in this manner for several minutes, inflicting upon me tremendous pleasure and uncertainty, and drawing from Julia moans and groans and little whimpers of 'Please, please . . .'

A voice broke into our private world. A voice from the other side of the wood behind me. I caught my breath and Julia stopped moving to listen but Rick simply smiled. Teeth in a piranha grin.

Julia said, 'Someone's coming,' and tried to push down her skirt.

Rick said, 'So what?'

'They might see,' she said, urgently.

'Then I'd better finish.'

He stepped away from her and turned her so that she faced me. My expression must have been as startled as hers.

'Hold her,' he said, and pushed her forwards.

Julia put her hands on my shoulders and I held her waist. Our eyes locked. Her face was flushed, her mouth open, her eyes wide. Her blouse was open and her bra had been pushed up to free her breasts, the tips of which were visible below the white cotton cups. Rick lifted her skirt and pulled at her knickers and her eyes widened further as she guessed his intention.

'No,' she murmured, looking at him over her shoulder.

'Yes,' he said.

'We'll be seen.'

He laughed and pulled her knickers down. She glanced back at me and then dipped her head against my chest and hung on to my shoulders.

I stared over her at Rick who continued to grin as he unfastened his jeans. He took a Durex from a pocket, held it up for me to see and winked.

Then he tore open the wrapping which he threw on the ground and fitted the rubber sheath. He lifted her skirt higher and moved closer to her and I felt her adjust her stance. He moved again, using his hand between her legs, and then pushed and Julia moaned as he sank his prick inside her.

The voices were coming closer. Youthful voices, shouting and swearing. Youths who thought they were the sole occupants of the wood. I wondered what would happen if they found us before Rick had finished: visions of mass rape flashed through my mind. I gripped Julia's waist tighter and she leaned closer against me, her breasts pushing against my chest while Rick grimaced behind her as he pounded in and out of her.

He was grunting with effort and concentration. I could here the noises of their union and the slap of his groin against her buttocks and thighs.

'Please, please,' murmured Julia.

Her fingers seemed to grip me tighter as she shuddered. Rick gasped, held himself inside her and came quickly.

The voices were closer. If we moved, the youths would be able to see us through the trees. I realized I hadn't come, that my erection still throbbed and that my level of excitement was still high.

Rick stepped away from Julia. She straightened with relief, reached beneath the skirt to pull up her knickers and then turned away to rearrange her bra and fasten the blouse. Rick pulled the Durex from his now flaccid prick and dropped it on the floor, a trophy of conquest, and fastened his jeans.

As he finished, the youths came out of the trees. Eight of them, aged from early to late teens. A gang of ruffians looking for mischief and trouble. Their talk tailed away as they saw us and they ambled to a stop, their eyes darting from one to the other of us.

Rick was standing with his feet apart, his thumbs in the belt loops of his jeans, the used Durex between his feet. He was being Marlon Brando again.

The youths saw the Durex and looked at Julia. She took a step backwards and I moved to stand in front of her. If Rick was Marlon Brando, I was Ivanhoe with a guilty conscience and a stiff prick.

One of them, who carried a broken tree branch in his hand, said, 'What's been going on here, then?'

Rick just smiled.

Another said, 'Have you two been fucking her?

And a third added, 'They've been fucking her.'

The first tapped the broken branch in his palm, smiled and said, 'Is she a good fuck, then?'

'Yes,' said Rick, quietly. 'She's a very good fuck.'

The youths were beginning to smile. Sensing sport, sensing sex.

The first one, their leader, said, 'How do we know you're telling the truth?'

And the second added, 'Maybe we should try her ourselves. Maybe we should fuck her.'

Rick grinned. For a moment, I thought he might actually give Julia to them, and I knew that this time I really would put my life on the line in her defence. I stepped closer to her.

But Rick reached into his back pocket and produced a closed knife. He held it in front of him as if it were an exhibit, then thumbed the switch. The blade shot out.

He said, 'I don't think that would be a good idea.'

The youths bristled but it was obvious they had no stomach for a fight against a madman with a naked blade. If their intimidation had worked, they would have happily raped Julia, but Rick had faced them down.

Instead they resorted to making obscene suggestions that became bolder as we left them and walked back towards the car. Julia was in front and I stayed close behind her, while Rick swaggered at the rear.

There was a moment when she paused. I caught up with her and was able to be of assistance again while I held her arm as she negotiated a fallen tree.

'Thanks,' she said.

'Are you all right?' I said.

She paused and gave me a smile that was open and honest and innocent again. She nodded and said, 'Thanks for being there, Charlie.'

When we got to the car, I drove. Julia and Rick sat in the front alongside me on the bench seat. Julia was in the middle, her thigh against mine. My erection still throbbed as I wondered how long I could maintain this sexual euphoria that had been boosted into the stratosphere when she had said, 'Thanks for being there, Charlie.'

The confrontation with the gang and my obvious readiness to do battle on her behalf had reinstated me as her devoted admirer in her eyes. At least, that was what I told myself. Even Rick kept making references to my bravery on the drive home.

'You were ready for them, eh, Brains? You'd have gone down fighting.'

The sex was not mentioned. It had been superseded by the danger.

I dropped them off at Julia's house and went home. I said I had a headache, locked myself in my bedroom, undressed, pulled back the covers and lay naked on the bed.

With my eyes closed I relived the afternoon. I started from the time I had picked them up and remembered everything that had happened, went through it in detail to ensure the memory was firmly in place and that I would never forget. That's why I have remembered it in such detail now.

Then I masturbated slowly. I thought of the first time I had watched Julia masturbate Rick in the back of the car, how her hands and fingers had flowed over his prick, and I made my hands and fingers do the same.

I remembered how she had sucked him and swallowed his spunk when he came in her mouth, how the pink tip of her tongue had touched the corners of her mouth in case she had missed a drop.

Finally, I replayed in my mind the afternoon in full again. Taking my time, rewinding and replaying the parts I liked best, remembering her softness.

I caressed my prick and kept just the right side of orgasm. Then I laid my pillows in the middle of the bed, covering them with a handkerchief, and lay upon them and pressed my groin against their softness and imagined it was Julia.

When the pleasure was at its height I finally allowed the orgasm to happen. I gave it permission. And it rushed in and overwhelmed me as I came upon the pillows, gave up the ghost and passed out.

I don't think I have ever experienced a stronger orgasm from masturbation in my life. It was so amazing I was still stiff after I had come, still aroused, so I tried to repeat it.

That afternoon I lay in my bedroom for two hours, masturbating, and came five or six times but never with the same intensity as that first time. Eventually I stopped and slept for a while because I was exhausted and my head now really did hurt and my prick was extremely sore.

Writing this has had the same effect as when I remembered the details that afternoon. It has always had the same effect, every time I have recalled it. It has given me an erection. Writing it down has made the memory more vivid and made the erection stronger.

Writing it down has evoked the past in a way I did not think possible. I can almost taste the desire and the fear of that afternoon. And the softness of Julia as Rick pressed her against me . . .!

The memories are still in my head and I shall masturbate

because of them but not yet. I shall take my erection with me when I go to see Tamara and I shall not deal with it until later when I return.

Do I now add masochism to my list of perversions?

Chapter 10

Tess put down the pages and stood up. Penn put down the book and looked at her enquiringly.

'Well?' he said.

'I need a drink.'

He watched her go and pour some Chablis. She raised the glass in his direction and took a sip.

'Well?' he repeated.

'You write very well.'

She walked back and resumed her seat.

'Has it told you anything?'

'Were you really in love with Julia?'

'At that time. Yes.'

'Not puppy love? Infatuation?'

'I no longer know. It was a long time ago. At the time I thought I was in love. It felt like love. All-consuming. Many-splendoured thing. All the clichés.'

'And yet, until I asked, you didn't even describe what Julia looked like. Your descriptions are still sketchy. It's the action you describe so well, not the girl. It's as if Julia was a cipher.'

Penn shook his head.

'She was more than that.'

'Maybe so, at the beginning. Every teenager falls in and out of love countless times. Week by week. Maybe you had a pure and innocent crush on her at the beginning.

But you didn't give yourself the chance to get over it and meet someone else.

'By being the third person in this relationship, that innocent love got stuck in a time warp. You fixed Julia in your mind as she was when you first met her and fell for her. But she didn't stay that person. Not under the influence of Rick. She changed. She was no longer the person you had fallen in love with.

'Your infatuation just added to the compulsion. In your mind she was that young, innocent girl of your dreams every single time Rick made her perform sexually. Obviously she was no longer young and innocent. But it gave you a bigger kick to think she was. That's where the Lolita complex started. Maybe that's one of the reasons why you have a preference for young girls.'

Penn said, 'I'm not sure I know what you are getting at.'

She laughed and said, 'Neither am I, half the time. This is not an exact science.'

'You think I wasn't really in love with Julia?'

'I think you had an infatuation. I think that infatuation became so tied in with the pleasure you got from watching that you eventually became unable to separate the two. I also think you're a pretty good writer.'

Penn smiled and said, 'So there's no instant cure?'

'There never is. Besides, I want to read more. I want you to write more. Put it all down, work it out and confront it, and we can keep on kicking it around and see where it takes us. You obviously enjoy writing about it.'

'Yes. It excites me.' He paused. 'Tell me honestly, Tess. Did reading it excite *you*?'

'Did it turn me on? Of course it turned me on. It's a hell of a story.'

He wondered what Tamara would think if she read it. Would it turn her on?

Tess said, 'How did you feel when you went to meet Tamara? I mean, after writing this. The state you were in.'

'Very alive,' he said.

'You do this a lot? Delay orgasm?'

'It started as I described it in the story, and it developed over the years. There's a similar concept in Zen. I learned to enjoy the journey more than the arrival.'

'Sounds painful. Particularly if the journey takes too long.'

'I once delayed it a year, just to prove that I could.'

Tess gazed at him in amazement.

'A year?'

'Yes.'

'Without an orgasm?'

'Yes.'

'Without fulfilling sex?'

'There was lots of fulfilling sex. I just never came.'

'How can you have fulfilling sex without an orgasm?'

He smiled and said, 'I watched. I participated. I copulated. I was fellated. I just didn't come.'

'Ouch,' she said.

Penn laughed and said, 'There were times when it was a little uncomfortable but it was a most amazing year. My senses became supertuned to sex.'

'What happened when the year ended?'

'It's funny, but the first orgasm was a disappointment. About average on the Richter scale. It took three or four orgasms before they returned to a reasonable strength. I guess my body had adapted to the journey and had forgotten the destination.'

'And you still practise this self-denial?'

'Not for such extreme periods. The length of a seduction, maybe. With Caroline in Majorca, for instance, it was forty-eight hours. During that time, I watched her involved in three sexual liaisons before I . . .'

He didn't quite know how to put it.

'Before you fucked her?' supplied Tess.

Hearing the attractive woman use the word gave him a pleasurable shock.

'Yes. Before I fucked her.'

'What about Tamara?' she said. 'Will you practise the same philosophy?'

'Tamara is different. I don't know what will happen.' He shrugged. 'That's my problem. I don't know if I can do anything at all without the stimulation I have got used to. Except . . .'

'Yes?'

'Last night, when I went to pick her up, she wasn't ready. She was in her underwear.' He shrugged. 'It seemed quite natural for her to walk around her apartment in her underwear. Perhaps, because I have been honest with her about my intentions, she sees no need for false modesty. But there she was in stockings and high heels and not a lot else.'

'And?' Tess prompted.

'And I was very aroused. I felt I could maybe have taken her to bed then and there and made love all night. Without stimulation.'

'But that *was* stimulation, Charles.'

'I beg your pardon?'

'You watched her in her underwear. She paraded for you, innocently, as if you weren't there, in the intimacy of her apartment. You watched and you knew you were not supposed to touch. That's what being a voyeur is, Charles. Gaining pleasure from watching.

'It doesn't have to be a choreographed orgy. It can be a husband watching his wife get dressed or undressed. And what happens after the pleasure of watching? The pleasure of making love.'

Penn said, 'You're clever with words. But I'm not sure your philosophy applies in my case.'

Tess said, 'Sex is not that complicated, Charles. My philosophy does not include waiting a year to get your rocks off. My philosophy is do whatever turns you on and gives you pleasure, just as long as you don't hurt anyone else in the process.'

He said, 'But my problem is that I have a compulsion that is debilitating when it comes to making love.'

'Only because you think it is,' she said.

He shook his head, and said, 'Words.'

'You know, I get a lot of letters from husbands and wives who become involved with other people. Believe it or not, there are a lot of husbands whose greatest fantasy is to watch their wives having sex with another man. They then like to join in so that the husband and the other man are both fucking the wife at the same time.

'The husbands more or less fall into two camps. There is the husband who would get the same sexual enjoyment if the woman involved wasn't his wife. He just likes the idea of two men fucking the same woman.

'Then there is the husband who gets a large part of his enjoyment because of the jealousy that is created. He loves his wife and what they do together is private and special. Watching someone else do the same things to her is going to make him jealous and jealousy is one of the strongest aphrodisiacs known to man.

'Maybe, all those years ago, part of you was jealous of what Rick did to Julia. You were also pretty naive and a virgin. You would have enjoyed watching any pretty young girl in a sexual situation. You were also learning all the time and began to develop your own way of enjoyment. Your self-denial technique, for instance.

'Your enjoyment was intense but it became confined. You enjoyed watching and saving your orgasms. You told me this went on for two years. Then for another two years, you did nothing to break the habit. All you did was write about it, think about it and masturbate about it. You reinforced it. You even went back to find them to try to resume the relationship.

'This was at a time when you were sexually at your most potent. This was at a time when whatever you experienced in life would make a lasting impression – and it did. You built a high wall to protect your sexual creed and preferences, Charles. Now you have to knock a hole in the wall and let them free. Let them mix.

'Look at it this way: each story you write is a brick and you're giving those bricks to me. We're breaking down the wall, Charles, and you'll maybe discover a bit more about yourself as we do so. Before long you'll feel the benefit. Trust me.'

Penn smiled and said, 'Funnily enough, I do trust you.'

'Good, because there's something else I want to say and I don't want you to take it the wrong way. These situations I was talking about, where husbands want to watch their wives with other men? They can go awfully wrong. You know why? Because the women quite often get to like it.

'A husband may get cold feet once the fantasy is fulfilled. He sees the dangers and is maybe not so eager to do it again,

122

or maybe only just occasionally. But quite often the wife finds it liberating. She may feel suddenly more confident in her looks and sexuality. She may discover she enjoys fucking.

'There is a fallacy that man is the sexual beast. That his urges are more dominant than a woman's. Baloney. A woman unleashed is a fearsome sexual animal, Charles. They can be devious, demanding, manipulative, unscrupulous and insatiable.

'I have a feeling that Julia was not the shrinking violet of your memory. But you wanted her to be for the games you played in your own mind. And I'm not for one minute casting aspersions or attempting to influence you in any way, but maybe you should not take Tamara totally at face value.

'You have your own doubts. You have what you perceive as your problems, your compulsions, your desires. Maybe she does, too.'

Penn remained silent for a moment. He might not necessarily agree with everything Tess had said but it was a relief to be able to discuss these matters after all these years with someone who did not think his preferences were dangerous aberrations. He was also quite willing to talk about Tamara.

He said, 'Would it shock you to know that I have been having discreet enquiries made about Tamara?'

'It had never occurred to me, but now that you have told me, no, it's not a shock. I guess it's part of what you are. The international businessman. The guy who gets what he wants no matter the cost.'

'You don't approve.'

'I told you. I don't make judgements.'

'When I instigated the search, I gave myself reasons. I

told myself I didn't want there to be any indiscretions in her past that might crop up and spoil the future. If there was evidence of anything indiscreet, I wanted to stop it being a threat. Photographs, letters, videos.

'If any exist, I've given instructions to buy or steal them if they could be an embarrassment to her. And I told myself I wanted assurances that she was not a gold digger.

'But I suppose the real reason I instigated the search was that I wanted to peep into her privacy. You know? Be a voyeur, as always.'

'Have you just realized that?'

'Yes, I think I have.'

'Then you're making progress.'

'I'm not sure that I am. I'm enjoying it too much. There is a set of photographs a boyfriend took of her when she was eighteen. A striptease. They turned me on.'

'They would probably turn on any heterosexual male. Don't make it a big issue.'

'For a time, she lived with a video film-maker. I am actually hoping that he made films of her. I am looking forward to watching her in a sexual situation.'

'Point one, if there is a film it's something from the past. It's not a question of her being unfaithful. Point two, jealousy is the greatest aphrodisiac.'

Penn said, 'I keep trying to shock you and you won't let me.'

Tess laughed and made him smile. She was even more attractive when she laughed. A bright, intelligent woman who was also damnably attractive. It was a dangerous combination. He knew she was divorced. Maybe she was too formidable to be married.

She said, 'It's a professional pose. You are a very shocking man, Charles Penn.' She got up. 'And now I'm going to shock you.' For a moment he could not imagine what she meant. 'I'm going to serve you lunch.'

Chapter 11

Penn was not disappointed. Alex Brown, the video-film maker with whom Tamara had once lived, *had* shot footage of her. The three videocassettes lay on his desk together with a report from the private investigator who had obtained them after breaking into and entering Brown's home.

The report that lay in a pool of light from the desk lamp said Tamara was not the only home-movie star. Forty-four cassettes featuring several young women had been removed. The report described the contents of the videos as explicit but did not go into detail.

He stared out at the night and the panorama of the river and felt the familiar tensions rising. Did he really want to watch a film of the girl he thought he loved having sex with another man? He smiled at the night. Of course he did.

A box containing the other forty-one cassettes offered alternative entertainment and, in time, he would view them all. But the ones he wanted to watch right now were those of Tamara. He wanted to watch them before he went to meet her at the nightclub where she was holding court.

With the report was a photograph of Alex Brown that showed him to be slim and dark with sharp features and a closely trimmed beard. It said he had the reputation of a Svengali with young women.

He promised them at least a brush with fame, if not personal success, by featuring them in the promotional

127

videos he made for rock and pop recording artists. In return, the young ladies were happy enough to trade sexual favours.

Penn wore only a silk dressing gown. He had worked up a sweat in the gym to tire his body and had showered in a leisurely fashion while he anticipated the film show ahead. Now he delayed it a while longer to allow the excitement to grow. He opened a bottle of Bollinger and sipped a glass of the wine.

Tess was right. Whatever Tamara had done was in the past. It was not as if she were being unfaithful to him or breaking a trust. Tess was also right about jealousy. It was a marvellous aphrodisiac.

The videos were numbered one, two and three, to indicate the order in which they had been made. At last he got up and switched off the desk lamp, leaving the apartment in darkness and lit only by the moon.

He walked across to a wall that was filled with electronic entertainment equipment and slotted the first cassette into the player. He sat in a deep reclining armchair, untied the belt of his dressing gown and opened the silk to expose his tumescent phallus. With the remote, he switched on a television that had a forty-eight-inch screen and set the video film in motion.

This was no ordinary home movie shot with a fixed camera. Brown had combined footage from at least three cameras and incorporated many close-ups.

Tamara and Brown were in a bedroom. They kissed and embraced. She was girlish in a floaty dress and he wore jeans and a white T-shirt. Penn noticed the jeans and T-shirt were Armani. Brown looked old enough to be her father. With a pang, Penn realized he was even older.

Whatever else, Brown knew how to make movies.

Cameras lingered on caresses. His hand moved over her buttocks, her hand was pushed between their bodies to cup the bulge in his jeans. Close-ups of mouths open, saliva wet, tongues probing and slithering. Faces changing, becoming heavier with lust.

They lay on the bed and a camera watched his hand go beneath the skirt, raising it to reveal the tops of her tan stockings and white suspender straps.

Penn's erection lay against his stomach. He tensed the muscle that ran from it between his legs to his anus and his penis twitched and pulsed.

On screen, the usual happened, although this could never be usual as it starred Tamara. Her dress was removed. Her bra and panties were removed and Brown stripped to reveal a tanned and lean physique. He licked her breasts, slid down her slim and beautifully pale body, put his mouth over her vagina and sucked.

More close-ups of her face, eyes closed, lips parted, pleasure apparent. Close-ups of his face buried between her thighs, back to her face, head tilting backwards, mouth opening wider, and the shake and groan of an orgasm.

The images were tastefully erotic until Brown put his penis into her mouth. Then, for a moment, she glanced at the camera with those large green eyes and hesitated, but soon did his bidding and sucked.

Penn's erection continued to pulse as he watched the activities on screen. Brown lay between her legs and entered her and his rump thrust rhythmically upon her. He turned her over and climbed upon her back and they copulated again, with more close-ups of her face, of her fingers gripping the sheet, of his hips pounding her buttocks.

They changed their position and now she straddled him and sat upon him with his penis buried inside her. She moved upon it, her mouth open, making mewling noises in her throat, her breasts bouncing, and she came again.

Brown laid her upon her back once more and lay between her spread legs to make his missionary insertion, thrusting again with rising vigour until he came inside her.

The video finished and Penn pressed the rewind button until he found her first orgasm. He watched her face closely and gently stroked his penis. She really was so beautiful, so innocent.

Finally, he rewound the video, got out of the chair, removed the cassette and slotted in number two. He poured more champagne, made himself comfortable and pressed 'play'.

Tamara was dressed as a schoolgirl in pleated grey skirt, white blouse and tie, white ankle socks and flat shoes. She wore no make-up and looked incredibly young. She sat at a table upon which were books. She was writing in an exercise book.

A close-up lingered on her face, her teeth nipping her bottom lip as she concentrated on her work. Then a different shot of a different face as another camera picked up the outline of someone staring through the window from outside.

The figure wore black. As storylines went, Penn did not think this was original, but the anticipation made his penis harder still.

Brown silently entered the house through an unlocked kitchen door while schoolgirl Tamara continued to do her homework unaware of the danger. He picked up a handy knife with a long blade and made his way to the room where she sat.

The dialogue was brief but to the point.

'Don't scream,' he said.

Tamara gasped in shock and stood up, knocking over the chair behind her.

'Oh my God,' she said. 'Don't hurt me.'

'Who else is in the house?'

'No one. I'm all alone.'

He stepped closer and moved the knife in front of her face and she cringed back against the table and theatrically put her hand to her mouth. She was not a good actress but she did not need to be. The pretend situation was potent.

'All alone?' he said.

'Please. Don't hurt me.'

'I'm not going to hurt you. I'm going to fuck you.'

'Oh, no. Please don't. I'm a virgin. I've never done anything like that before.'

'Then it's time you learned.' He moved the knife closer and she tried to lean further away. 'You don't want me to use this, do you?'

'No.'

'So you'll do what I say?'

'Yes.'

'Everything I say?'

'Yes.'

'Good girl.'

He stepped away and dropped the knife behind a chair. She lowered her hands and held onto the edge of the table as she faced him. He went back to her and touched her face. She tried to turn her head away but he pulled it back.

'Everything,' he said.

Holding her head between both his hands, he pressed his body against hers and kissed her, forcing her lips apart and thrusting with his tongue as if he were copulating with her mouth.

When the kiss ended, he stepped back, gripped the blouse

and ripped it open as Tamara gasped. He pushed the blouse off her shoulders, at the same time roughly pushing the straps of the white bra down her arms. He pulled the cups of the bra down to reveal her breasts. He mauled them and bent down and sucked them into his mouth, first one and then the other.

All the time Tamara stood stiffly, head back and eyes closed.

Penn stroked his phallus and shivered with the exquisite torture of holding himself in check. He continued to watch, continued to make his penis pulse by the contraction of the muscle that ran between his legs.

On the screen, Brown picked up the chair that she had knocked over and made her sit in it. He unfastened his trousers and took out his penis.

'Suck it,' he said.

'I don't know how,' she said. 'I've never sucked one before.'

'Put it in your mouth.'

He gripped her head and she struggled as he wiped the glans of his penis across her face before pushing it into her mouth. He held her head in position with both hands.

'Suck,' he ordered, and Tamara sucked.

More close-ups of that young, exquisite face, and of Brown's hands as he reached down to grope her breasts.

Penn found the film compulsive viewing. What shocked him more than the scenes on the screen was the thought that Tamara had readily agreed to take part in such a home video and play the victim.

Brown removed his penis from her mouth without coming and made her stand. He bent her over the table and raised her skirt. He pulled down her white panties and pushed fingers inside her. She moaned and pleaded.

'Please don't,' she said. 'Please don't.'

'You'll enjoy it,' Brown said, his voice hoarse.

More close camera work as he manoeuvred his erection, still wet with her saliva, and pushed it into the pink flesh of her vagina.

Penn gulped and regulated his breathing. This had been the most blatant sexual shot yet. He now watched as Brown thrust against her, his hands gripping her hips. Tamara lay across the table among the scattered books, her arms spread as if in sacrifice.

Perhaps Brown meant it to be a short film. Perhaps he just lost control. But it ended when he began to gasp and shudder and he pulled out his penis, gripped it around the base and shot his sperm onto her buttocks.

The cum-shot, it was called. Penn had seen it many times on many films. He wondered, fleetingly, if Brown had ever marketed any of these films? Surely not, not if he starred in them himself. They had presumably been made for his own enjoyment and entertainment.

Penn rewound the cassette and slotted in the third video. He sat in his chair, pressed 'play' and, for a moment, thought there had been a mistake.

It appeared this had been shot in a cellar. Chains hung from hooks on the walls. There were wooden devices and frames designed for bondage and torture, a low metal-framed bed whose mattress was covered in a black rubber sheet, and a rack of whips and wooden paddles. The camera panned the room and lingered over the equipment and whips.

Brown entered the shot, naked except for black combat boots and a black rubber face mask. Penn might have been tempted to laugh – except that Brown led Tamara on a chain that was attached to a padded leather collar around her neck.

The pale beauty wore a rubber corset that ended below her breasts. Six wide suspender straps held taut shiny black stockings and she tottered on spike-heeled black shoes. Her wrists were held in front of her in a pair of leather handcuffs.

Penn was shocked. His erection stiffened and rose from where it lay against his stomach. He had not been so aroused for many years. He was once more in that highly charged situation of choice: part of him wanted to switch off the video and destroy it, and the other part wanted to watch and wallow in Tamara's subjugation. He watched.

Once again, the content of the film was not unusual. He had seen much harder pornography involving whips and chains and containment. But Tamara was the element that made it special. Her innocence once more shone through. Her eyes held a bewilderment that churned his stomach with helplessness and desire.

Brown lifted her arms and hooked the handcuffs onto a chain that hung through a metal loop on the ceiling. He pulled the other end of the chain until her arms were at full stretch and secured it to hold her in place.

He walked around her, surveying her body, before touching her, feeling her breasts and buttocks, running his hands between her legs, causing her hips to move, either in an attempt to escape or to encourage the attentions of his fingers. The man's penis had become stiff and he rubbed it against her buttocks and between her legs.

Had she been duped into this scenario, Penn wondered? Was she as bewildered and innocent as her large green eyes suggested? Did she now wish it to stop but knew she was trapped?

Brown picked up a cat-o'-nine-tails with soft leather thongs. At first he stroked her breasts with it, he trailed the thongs across her buttocks, he ran its gnarled leather grip between her legs.

Tamara began to moan.

Now he flicked it upon her body. He dealt with her breasts first and she twisted on the chain that held her arms so taut. Marks began to appear across her soft flesh. Brown altered his angle of attack and now concentrated upon her buttocks, flicking the thongs over those curvaceous globes, lightly at first, but increasing in strength so that the flesh quivered and bloomed pink and she moaned loudly and began to cry.

Was she crying in pain and distress or because she was enjoying it?

Brown released the chain. As Tamara's arms dropped, her body sagged. He led her to a complicated device that involved chains and a harness. He placed the whip next to it. Tamara sat upon a broad soft leather seat that was suspended from a wooden frame on chains, rather like a child's harness swing. Her feet rested on two high wooden blocks.

He unfastened the handcuffs and put her wrists into separate restraints that were also attached to chains that hung from a cross-beam. Now he moved her into the leather harness upon which she had been sitting until she lay in it, the leather providing a support beneath her waist.

Tamara hung from chains at her wrists, supported at her waist, her body horizontal to the floor, her thighs spread because her spike-heeled shoes rested on wooden blocks.

Brown, grotesque in the featureless mask and heavy boots, positioned himself between her legs. His erection was level with her vagina. He pushed her and her body swung slowly on the chains. It was the ultimate machine for copulation that presented the open sex of a woman at groin height to a man, while accentuating the fullness of her buttocks as her body arched over the harness.

As she swung, he touched her between the legs with his fingers and she moaned. He inserted fingers and she moved against them. Again, it was open to the viewer's interpretation as to whether she wished to avoid or engage them.

He finally inserted the tip of his penis, took hold of her hips, and drew her onto him. He groaned in pleasure and his hands went beneath her to hold and caress her bottom.

Penn also groaned as he watched. He stroked his engorged phallus with the silk belt of his dressing gown.

On screen, Brown increased the tempo of his engagement as he swung Tamara backwards and forwards upon his penis. He picked up the whip and flicked it across her breasts and she writhed and moaned. He now alternated, and flicked the whip beneath her onto her buttocks and she yelled and twisted in the chains.

They continued in this fashion for a long time, with close-ups and lingering shots of her face, and Penn began to admire Brown's stamina. Then the camera closed in on Tamara's face as she gasped for breath and orgasmed wildly.

Penn was beginning to feel drained. He pressed the pause button and froze Tamara's face upon the screen, got up and walked across the darkened apartment to the Bollinger. He refilled the glass, drank, and refilled it again.

He stared across the room at the frozen picture of Tamara in the throes of ecstasy. He was close to that state himself. He walked back to his chair and pressed the play button.

Brown helped her upright and released her from the harness and the chains. She staggered as he led her to a trestle and seemed grateful for its support when he leaned her over it. He attached her wrists to restraints on the far side of the frame. He also put a blindfold around her eyes.

As he was submitting her to the straps and the blindfold, his erection touched her and rubbed against her, and once she was in place he entered her immediately from behind, holding her hips while he pounded against her buttocks.

Still he did not come, but eased himself away, breathing heavily, and picked up the whip again. He flicked it over her bottom and she cried out and flinched. He struck her harder and she yelled.

'More?' he said.

'Yes. Please give me more.'

He struck her again and she wailed.

'Beg,' he said.

'Please beat me. Whip me. Please give me more. I'll do anything. Just give me more.'

He beat her again, with genuine fervour, and weals appeared on her buttocks. She was crying continually. Brown dropped the whip and entered her again and this time, Penn thought, the man would not be able to resist a climax. But resist he did, and pounded into her against her bruised flesh until her crying changed into the wail of orgasm.

Brown lay over her back and rested. He unfastened the wrist restraints and had to help her stagger to the bed. He laid her upon the black rubber sheet on her back and once more shackled her wrists, this time to the metal bedhead.

The camera closed in on her face and Penn could see she was exhausted. He felt compassion and love for her, but he also wanted the film to continue, he wanted to see more sexual activity and degradation inflicted upon her.

He felt guilty, jealous, lustful and humiliated at sitting here in the darkness of his apartment watching the girl he might one day marry.

But as he began to question the ethics of his viewing, he calmed himself by rationalization. What was happening on screen was not real, it was pretend bondage and beatings. No one was getting hurt and Tamara had enjoyed it: he had watched her orgasms and they had not been faked.

There was no reason for him not to watch. He needed to watch. He needed to take his tension to the edge without falling over.

Brown knelt on the bed and straddled her body. His penis glistened with her vaginal juices. He knelt up and wiped the glans across her blindfolded face. Her mouth opened and her tongue flicked. He put it inside her mouth and she sucked greedily.

The man's stomach was taut and his breathing was ragged. Penn was sure that this time his orgasm would not be far away.

As she fellated him, the camera panned her body, slim, pale and abused in the black nylon stockings and rubber corset, her legs apart and her vagina pink and open and wet.

He was thrusting in and out of her mouth, holding her head in his hands. He began to gasp and knelt up and pulled his penis from between her lips.

'Now,' he said.

Brown held his erection at its base between the finger and thumb of his right hand to heighten the sensation, and spurted his sperm into her face.

Tamara lay beneath him, blindfolded, her mouth open

to receive his communion. The globules were thick and splattered her features. The camera caught their trajectory and the close-up lingered on her face.

The video finished and Penn rewound to the final shots and froze the picture so that Tamara's stained face filled the screen.

He got up and crossed the silent apartment. The darkness had deepened. He stood by the window and stared down at the river and the lights of the traffic that crossed Tower Bridge.

Was there blame in the video? Blame that should be apportioned? Tamara had enjoyed what had been done to her, that much was obvious. But she was an innocent, Penn told himself. Brown was a man of the world. He had seduced her, led her deeper into the mysteries of sex until he had hooked her. Had he fed her drugs as well to make her more pliable?

Penn was suddenly angry at himself for blaming Brown. Was what the film-maker had done so very different to what he himself frequently engineered with beautiful young women? He had never needed to use drugs to make them pliable. The very thought was abhorrent.

Bondage was fine as a game but not in reality. And, similarly, Penn did not believe in persuading a woman to do anything against her will. They knew what to expect when they sought his company: he might surprise them but he did not disappoint them.

He used no persuasion, no threat, no blackmail, no inducement. Or did he? Power was the only real inducement and he had power.

The champagne bottle was empty and he went to the refrigerated bar and got another. Tess was making him question pleasures he had taken for granted. She was making him question his life.

Penn glanced across the room at the frozen image of Tamara on the screen and he was filled with love and desire. He knew he could at this moment take her to bed and make love to her. But so he should after watching three video films she thought would remain private for ever.

He popped the cork, poured wine into a fresh flute, then stopped and looked back at the screen. He put the bottle alongside his glass, left them and crossed the room to pick up the remote and rewind the video further. He pressed 'play' again and his suspicion was confirmed.

The first two films he had watched had been made using several static cameras that were moved and refocused during the action. But this last film had had something extra: a third person.

Some of the shots could only have been achieved by a mobile cameraman as well as the fixed cameras. He remembered other shots from earlier in the film, shots taken before the blindfold had been applied.

Tamara had agreed to a third person witnessing, as well as filming, the bondage, flagellation and sexual couplings. The presence of the third person had not inhibited her for she had orgasmed without restraint.

His pulse raced. She was still so innocent. She retained that same quality that Julia had retained, no matter what Rick did. And she performed before the ultimate voyeur – the lens of a camera.

Was that why he was so smitten? Was he trying to recapture a lost love of the past and this time make it work?

Penn suspected a different motive and his discovery of the third person fuelled it. Perhaps he would not have to change. Perhaps he would find contentment and love as a voyeur with the right woman.

A woman who would allow him to dictate the nature of her sexual activities, who would welcome the sophistication of the games he devised, who would accept his desire to watch, and who would be dutiful and submissive.

Tamara seemed to have all those qualities.

When he saw her in the VIP room of the nightclub, surrounded by the rich, the famous and the wannabes, he tingled with the knowledge of his insight, as well as from watching the three video films.

Her innocence was an aura that would never die and yet he sensed she was a submissive who would enjoy being told what to do.

She wore a plain silk violet dress with a scooped neckline and no brassiere. Her breasts were supple beneath it. Around her throat were pearls and she wore matching earrings.

He leaned down to kiss her and as she moved he could see into the dress. Other men had similarly enjoyed the same view this evening, he knew. What's more, she knew they had, and the thought thrilled him.

'You're beautiful,' he said.

She laughed and said, 'So are you.'

They made small talk. He watched her mouth and remembered how it had sucked the penis of Alex Brown and how his sperm had fallen onto these delicate features.

Later, they sat together behind a corner table while she rested her hand on his thigh and he flexed his penis into erection. He listened as she talked about her plans for the television pilot and he made plans of his own. Since watching the films he had become more at ease in her presence, as if the secret he held gave him a power over her.

The plan unfolded in his mind as he maintained his attentive pose. The first thing he would do would be to arrange for someone to warn her about him. To tell her of his reputation with young women.

Monty Radcliffe, the television producer, was the man. Radcliffe worked for Penn. It was true he was screen testing Tamara and putting together footage for a possible television show, but he was doing it because Penn had told him to. Penn had also told him not to let Tamara know that he was the financial backer.

Now he would give Radcliffe extra instructions. He would tell him to give her a fatherly warning about Penn's unsavoury reputation.

The producer could say he had once been part of a team researching a programme about Penn. The programme had not, in the end, been made because Penn had blocked it, but Radcliffe still had part of the research.

This, he would confide, described how the business tycoon had seduced many young women. How he was dominant and demanded to be obeyed. Radcliffe would say that any young woman involved in a relationship with Penn had to be prepared to do anything he asked.

Penn liked the idea immensely. From Tamara's reaction, he would be able to gauge whether he had been correct or not in assuming she was a submissive who would be a willing partner in his games.

If she reacted unfavourably to the report, he could calm her fears and remain the perfect gentleman. He could assure her that his love for her had reformed his character – and trust that Dr Tess Flanders could actually help make that happen.

'You know,' he said to her, 'I have known many women.'

'I would expect that,' she said. 'You are a mature, sophisticated and handsome man. I expect you have known very many women.'

'You might be shocked at how sophisticated I have been.'

'It takes a lot to shock me.'

He looked sceptical.

'You are still so young, Tamara. Your innocence is a perfume. I think you would be very easily shocked.'

'You know I am no virgin, Charles.' She smiled sweetly and pursed her lips. 'I have had affairs with sophisticated men before.' She stroked his thigh. 'Although none as handsome as you.'

He raised an eyebrow.

'So you are a sexually liberated young woman?'

Her laughter was infectious and he smiled.

'Is this a very clever inquisition?' she said. 'Are you trying to delve into my past? Hoping I might make a dark confession of erotic secrets?'

Penn kept his smile as he said, 'Are there any dark secrets to tell?'

'Everybody has secrets, Charles.' She leaned forward and kissed his cheek and he looked down her dress at her breasts. 'You like them?' she said.

'They're delightful.'

'My offer still stands.'

'It's very tempting. But I would still prefer to wait.' He smiled. 'Unless you have fallen in love with me?'

Tamara widened her eyes in seriousness.

'I think perhaps I am beginning to. One day soon, Charles, we shall have to put it to the test.'

He ran his fingers down her face, tracing her jawline. Then down her neck and lightly over her breasts, touching her softness with his fingertips. He was strongly tempted to accept her offer that very night.

But that was not the way the game was to be played. He would wait and anticipate. And he still had his memoirs to write.

Chapter 12

Charles Penn's story

Rick had an older friend. A barber called Eddie. We went to his shop to have our hair cut and that was where Rick would buy his condoms.

Eddie was about thirty-seven or thirty-eight which, to me, was ancient. He was average height, average looks, brown hair. The few times I saw him away from the shop, he wore a camel-hair overcoat and carried the week's takings as a wad so that people would think he was a success.

He was married with a couple of kids, had a nice house out of town, but he and his wife didn't get on. There were rooms above his shop that he was converting into a flat. From the way he and Rick talked, he'd been converting it for years. He was a bit of a wheeler-dealer and in those days, when censorship was strict, he always had a supply of Continental magazines.

This particular night was late summer. It was dark and I had the car. I picked up Rick and Julia.

Rick said, 'Go to Eddie's.'

I said, 'He won't be open at this time. It's half-past eight.'

'Just go there,' said Rick. 'He's finally finished the flat. I said we'd go and have a look.'

Julia said, 'Do we have to go?'

'We don't have to go,' said Rick. 'I want to go.'

'But I don't know this Eddie.'

'You'll like him. Won't she, Brains?'

'He's all right,' I said.

Eddie's shop was in a row of businesses that were all locked up and most had their lights out. But Eddie was there, as Rick said he would be, and he let us in.

He showed us upstairs. The flat had a living room, bedroom, kitchen and bathroom, and carpets had been laid. But there was no furniture, apart from a double bed whose mattress was still sheathed in a thick protective plastic covering. Fitted wardrobes had been built the length of one wall in the bedroom.

Eddie had plugged in electric heaters in the two main rooms and the place was hot.

'Just right for a love nest,' Rick said.

'Trouble is, the wife expects rent,' said Eddie.

'Then get a couple of nurses in. Next best thing. You know what they say about nurses?'

'It's a nice thought,' said Eddie.

Rick sat on the edge of the bed.

He said to Julia, 'We should get a place like this.'

'What do you mean?' she said.

Eddie said, 'Are you talking marriage, Rick?'

'I'm too young to get married. I mean for assignations. Isn't that what they call it in the movies?'

'Borrow it any time you like,' Eddie said, and smirked at Julia. 'I would if I had a young lady like this.'

'You approve, then?' Rick said.

Julia was standing next to him and he reached out and put his palm behind her knee. He pushed it up her skirt.

Eddie smiled at Julia and said, 'She's gorgeous, you bastard. Everything you said she was.'

Julia had frozen. She wore a knee-length tight skirt, V-neck sweater and high heels.

Rick looked around the room.

'Where's your supply?' he said.

'In the wardrobe,' said Eddie.

'Anything new?'

'One or two.'

Rick got up and went to the wardrobe. He took out a cardboard box, closed the door, and brought it back. He put the box on the floor and sat on the edge of the bed again. The box contained pornographic magazines.

'Sit down,' he said to Julia, patting the bed next to him.

Julia looked at me and glanced at Eddie. I couldn't tell if she was looking for help but I didn't offer any. As usual, I didn't know what to do. She sat next to him.

'They're a bit strong,' said Eddie.

'She's seen them before,' Rick said, which gave me a shock.

Julia didn't look up.

Eddie said, 'There's something I want to show Charlie downstairs. Come on, son.'

We left the bedroom and I followed him downstairs into the small back room of the shop.

'Have a seat,' he said, so I sat down. He dropped three magazines on the coffee table next to me. 'Second supply,' he said.

I picked up one of the magazines and started looking through it. It told a story in photographs with captions in three languages. The English translation was stilted and often unintentionally funny but the photographs were hard-core. They showed two couples having drinks, taking off their clothes and fucking each other in different ways.

Eddie said, 'She's a nice girl.'

'What?'

'Rick's girlfriend. A good-looking girl.'

'Yes, she is.'

He looked up at the ceiling.

'Lucky sod,' he said. 'I wonder how far he's got?'

The conversation embarrassed me. I guessed Rick and Julia would be having sex and I was frustrated. If Eddie hadn't been here, maybe I would have been up in the room with them, watching. But that was our secret and I didn't want to discuss their sexual activities with anyone else, least of all a middle-aged hairdresser.

Eddie left me alone for a short time when he went into the shop and I continued looking at the magazine.

When he came back, he said, 'Right. Let's go back up.'

I thought, if they are having sex, they won't have finished yet. But he was twice my age and I was used to doing as I was told, and maybe they weren't having sex at all. We went back upstairs.

Eddie pushed open the door to the bedroom and walked in and I followed. The main light had been switched off and a bedside lamp that was on the floor was on, casting a beam of light and lots of shadows.

On the bed, Rick was on top of Julia. Her thighs were spread and the tight skirt had become lodged around her waist. His trousers had been pushed down around his buttocks. Her legs were encased in tan stockings held taut by the straps of a black suspender belt.

Julia had turned her face away from the door, her hands on Rick's arms. He looked over his shoulder and smiled his piranha smile. Her black panties lay crumpled on the floor at the bottom of the bed.

The box of magazines was still on the floor and Eddie walked past them, his face suddenly heavy, his eyes fixed on Julia's flesh.

'This is better than looking at pictures,' he muttered.

Rick's smile broadened and he moved his hips, thrusting in and out slowly.

'And she likes it,' he said. 'Oooh. Lovely. You know what, Eddie? She likes being watched.'

'Does she, now?' said Eddie, stroking the bulge at the front of his trousers.

Rick continued to fuck her, slowly at first, and then he began to bang into her, so that she groaned and her fingers gripped his arms tighter.

'You like it, don't you, Julia? I know you do.' He kept up the pace as he spoke: his voice was low, as if there was nobody else in the room but them. 'You like men watching you. Wanting you. It makes you hot.'

Her head rolled so that her face was towards me. Her eyes were closed but she was biting her bottom lip and her face was flushed. Her features shuddered and she bit harder. I wasn't sure, but it seemed as if she had orgasmed but didn't want Eddie or me to know.

Rick stopped and kissed her neck. She opened her eyes briefly and saw me by the door, watching, as always. She shuddered again and closed her eyes.

He moved off her body and she put her hands over her vagina and he laughed.

'Modest, too,' he said. 'And you know what, Eddie? She has a great mouth.'

He slid up the bed and sat with his back against the headboard. He held his erection in his hand.

'Come and suck it,' he said. 'Show Eddie how good you are.'

Julia licked her lips. She opened her eyes but avoided looking at anyone except Rick, rolled onto her stomach and slid on the plastic until she was between his legs. She rested on her elbows, took his prick into her mouth, and began to suck.

Her legs lay straight out behind her, clad in nylons, the pale flesh above them crossed by the black straps of the suspender belt, her buttocks naked and round.

I remained standing by the door, my heart in my mouth once more, and my prick as hard as iron. Eddie crouched by the bed so he could watch her sucking Rick from close range. He shuddered, knelt on the carpet and unfastened his trousers.

'Do you mind?' he said, and began to masturbate as he watched.

'Not at all,' said Rick, turning to smile at me.

Julia used her mouth on him expertly. It was as if Eddie and me were not there. She held his prick and her head bobbed up and down as she sucked and licked.

When he had had enough, Rick lifted her head from his lap, swung his leg over her and climbed off the bed.

'I'm getting hot,' he said. 'Those heaters really work.'

He stood by the bed and undressed. He removed all his clothes, including his shoes and socks, while Julia lay face down, unmoving.

Rick got back on the bed and pulled down the tight skirt so that she was covered again, but only so he could unzip it. He opened the skirt at the waist and eased it down over her hips and pulled it down her legs. He removed her shoes at the same time. She did not resist.

He straddled her, so that his prick lay against her bottom, and pushed up the sweater.

'This, too,' he said.

She moved so he could pull it over her head and arms. He dropped it over the side of the bed and then unclipped the black bra. He slipped the straps over her shoulders and guided first one arm free, pulled the bra from beneath her, and slid the other arm out.

Julia lay flat, her arms spread where Rick had left them, her face turned towards me. Her cheeks were burning, I could see that, and her eyes were tight closed.

Rick held himself over her and rubbed his prick between the cheeks of her buttocks. He smiled at Eddie, who was sitting on the floor on the far side of the bed, and who continued to masturbate slowly.

'She loves it,' Rick said. 'Can't get enough.'

He opened her legs with his knees, adjusted his position, reached between her thighs with his right hand and guided himself inside her. He sank down on top of her with a big sigh and grinned again.

'What a fuck,' he said to Eddie. 'What a fuck.'

And that's just what he did, while Eddie masturbated at one side of the bed and I watched from the doorway. He fucked her again and she began to groan again. I told myself she was groaning in protest, but I suppose she was groaning because she was enjoying it, even though she did not want to admit it. Even though *I* did not want to admit it.

He kept it up for a while before once more sliding from her body. He sat alongside her, resting on one arm.

Eddie's eyes were devouring her, running down her body and up again, over her curves and limbs.

He licked his lips and said, 'Can I touch?'

Rick took his time before replying and then he smiled and said, 'You can touch.'

Eddie knelt up by the side of the bed and reached out with the hand with which he had been masturbating. He placed a shaking palm on the back of Julia's leg behind the knee. Her body twitched as she felt his touch.

He slowly moved his hand upwards, over the nylon stocking and onto the flesh above. I could see his hand shaking and he hesitated a moment, and then moved it higher, onto her bottom. His palm remained there, fingers spread, and I watched his hand tense as he gripped and felt the softness.

Rick said to Eddie, 'You know what she likes?'

'What?'

Eddie's hand still flexed upon her softness. A crab, waiting to invade dark places.

Rick opened his mouth and flicked his tongue as if he were a lizard.

Eddie shuddered and his hand gripped the cheek of her bottom, his fingers digging into the flesh. He looked at Julia's face but it was turned away, so he looked back at Rick, a question, a hope in his eyes. Rick nodded, lay down next to her and kissed her neck and her ear.

'Roll over,' he said, encouraging her with a hand on her shoulder.

Julia rolled onto her back and for the first time her breasts were exposed, her nipples pink and pointed. She opened her eyes briefly. Rick lay against her side and smiled down into her face. He kissed her, mouth open, tongue digging, his hand moved over a breast and her eyes closed again.

When the kiss ended, he looked at Eddie and nodded. Eddie moved to the bottom of the bed and slithered up the plastic surface of the mattress, another lizard. He pushed her legs apart and slid between them, and Rick bent to kiss her again and stifle any protest.

Eddie put his mouth over her vagina and began to suck greedily, his hands holding and groping her thighs and slipping beneath her to feel her bottom. Rick lifted his mouth from hers and she began to moan and her shoulders began to shake and he held them down.

Rick sucked her breasts and Eddie sucked her vagina and her body moved beneath them as if she was being prodded with an electric rod. Her moans got louder: this time she could not hide the orgasm and she shook into a climax.

My erection was stiff and upright in my trousers. I hadn't touched it. I didn't need to. It was as if my brain was a recording machine and I was absorbing every sight and sound and smell and expression, every twitch and moan. I remained the intimate observer.

I hadn't thought Rick could go any further than he already had. But again he had shocked me by allowing Eddie to touch Julia and become involved in the games.

For a moment I panicked in case he invited me to do the same. That was something I couldn't do, not directly and blatantly like that. It would destroy the relationship we had. Besides, if I touched her I might no longer be able to control myself.

Eddie got up from the bed. He stood by its side, his trousers open, and resumed masturbating. Rick kissed Julia again and spoke to her quietly.

'Poor Eddie,' he said. 'You've got him in a terrible state. You've made his dick go stiff.'

The barber shuddered as he watched and listened. I think I had forgotten to breathe. I existed by osmosis: these sights and sounds and awful suggestions that Rick was making, these awful things he was allowing, that he was making Julia do, had become my life force.

Rick continued to speak to Julia in a low and reasonable voice.

Phillip Mason

He said, 'I think you should touch it for him. It's the least you can do.'

Julia opened her eyes and stared into Rick's face but she did not reply. Rick looked round at Eddie and smiled.

He said, 'Come and sit on the bed, Eddie.'

The man moved round the bed and sat to the left of Julia. He leaned against the bedhead. His trousers were open and his prick was large and swollen.

Rick turned Julia on her side so that she faced him.

'Go on,' he said. 'Touch it for him.'

She reached out and took hold of it with her right hand. Eddie shuddered and groaned loudly as she masturbated him.

Rick lay behind her and kissed her neck and watched.

'He sucked you,' he said. 'You should suck him.'

He pushed Julia's head down into Eddie's lap. She opened her mouth, accepted his prick and began to suck. I thought my control might leave me and that I might come in my trousers.

'That's a good girl,' Rick said, and he manoeuvred himself so that he lay against her back and bottom, nudged apart her thighs and pushed his prick inside her again from behind. 'Oh, yes,' he said.

Eddie's expression was strained, his mouth open and his breathing laboured. Rick began to move behind her, causing her body to rock as he fucked her. His hand went over her breasts and he tweaked her nipples. Then his hand went to her vagina and his fingers flicked there, although, at that time, I didn't know what they were doing.

Julia's mouth suddenly opened wider, her body tensed and she came for a third time, much to my amazement. I thought that maybe she suffered from a sexual condition which was why Rick was able to take advantage of her.

The vision of her between the two men, one of them more than twice her age, the other the man she was supposed to love, became etched in my mind, certainly as the most erotic I had seen until then. It is still one of the most erotic scenes I have ever witnessed.

Both men were now in the grip of sex. There were no smiles or banter.

Rick said, 'Did you bring some?'

The barber reached into his shirt pocket and passed over a Durex. Rick took it, then pulled his prick out of Julia.

He said, 'You first.'

Eddie removed his erection from Julia's mouth and Rick pushed her face down on the bed. The older man took another Durex from his pocket, tore open the packet and rolled the condom onto his prick.

He glanced enquiringly at Rick, who lay on his side next to Julia, one arm around her shoulder, her face turned to him. Rick nodded and Eddie got on the bed, pushed his trousers and underpants down, and climbed on top of the girl I loved.

Rick kissed Julia as Eddie pushed between her legs and, with a gasp, put his prick inside her. He sank onto her buttocks, gave four or five thrusts, and came with a loud grunt. He shuddered on top of her for what seemed like an age and, all the time he was coming, Rick kissed her.

When he had finished, he rolled off, his prick now limp and the Durex hanging off the end like a sad deflated pink balloon. He got up, pulling at his trousers, and went straight to the bathroom.

Eddie might have gone but I was still there, my erection still stiff in my trousers, still untouched. Rick rolled Julia onto her back and he glanced up at me. His face was tense but he managed a half-smile.

'Okay, Brains?' he said.

I nodded as if it was my duty to be there as a witness. He lay on Julia, she spread her legs and he pushed inside her, this time wearing a contraceptive. He fucked her one last time as she lay limp beneath him and as he came, his face buried in her neck, she turned her head and her eyes locked with mine. I thought that she smiled.

Gold knows what I thought, I suppose I was looking for signs that she might one day see Rick for what he was and love me instead. That if she could allow a middle-aged barber whom she had never met before to fuck her then she might welcome my tender true love as an alternative.

Of course, she didn't. Not then. Not ever, really, although I fooled myself she did.

Rick went to the bathroom and I stayed in the bedroom and watched as Julia got dressed on the far side of the bed, turning her back to me out of modesty. I could hear Rick and Eddie laughing together, although Rick's laugh was a little edgy and I sensed danger.

When Julia was ready I said, 'Shall we wait in the car?'

She smiled at me, innocent and sweet once more, in the V-neck sweater and tight skirt, and she kissed me on the cheek, as if I had been a good boy.

Feeling protective, I led the way to the stairs and Rick came onto the landing.

'We'll wait in the car,' I said.

Rick nodded and said, 'I won't be long.'

I unlocked the front door. We went out into the night, got into the car and I started the engine so that the heater would work. Julia sat alongside me on the front bench seat, her thigh next to mine, and she put her hand on my leg.

'You're a good friend, Charlie,' she said.

For the life of me, I couldn't work out what she meant then, and I still can't work out what she meant now.

There was a light on above the shop, where the living room of the flat was, and I could see the shadows of two figures beyond the thin curtains. One of the shadows suddenly took a swing and hit the other, causing him to fall down. It looked as if the upright shadow then kicked the one on the ground before leaving.

A moment later, Rick came out of the front door and got in the car next to Julia. He was flexing his fist.

'Why did you hit him?' I asked.

Rick pulled a face that maybe said he didn't know.

'He gets on my nerves, sometimes,' he said.

I didn't understand it then, but that is one aspect I subsequently did come to understand. I realized that while the game was being played, jealousy fuelled Rick's sexual tension. He had wanted more and more excitement. But once he had come, the jealousy had turned to anger and the excitement had been replaced by self-doubt.

What about this, Tess? Analysis. Is this progress?

Chapter 13

Penn persuaded Dr Tess Flanders to visit him at his apartment. She was prompt at eleven o'clock on a morning when the sun was bright in a blue sky and the river looked at its best. She admired the view.

'Do you have soul, Charles Penn, or did you buy it as an investment?'

'The apartment?'

'Don't tell me. You rent?'

'No. I own the whole floor. And yes, I did choose it for the view. Does that mean I qualify for salvation?'

'Maybe. Or maybe the choice was another aspect of power.'

'Will I never satisfy you?'

Tess laughed and turned from the window. It was his turn to admire the view. She wore a svelte blue silk dress and high-heeled shoes.

She said. 'You should be careful how you phrase your questions.'

He laughed as well, and poured coffee from the percolator that had filled the apartment with a fine aroma. She joined him and added her own cream but declined sugar, and they sat in comfortable chairs. He had sent her the latest instalment by messenger two days before.

'You write a gripping narrative,' she said.

'You liked it?'

'Wrong word. It was interesting. Okay, fascinating. And yes, before you ask, it was also arousing.'

She crossed her legs and he admired her knees and the sheen of her stockings.

'Is it making sense?'

'Well, as you say, you've started analysing some of the reasons that make men do the things that men do. Over the years, you've formulated certain sexual practices and you've kept repeating them out of habit. I think you've already started wondering why.'

'But what if I decide I like these practices?'

'We've talked about this. There's nothing wrong in being a voyeur, but it shouldn't restrict other aspects of the sexual experience. For chrissake, it's boring, Charles. And sexual boredom is a main reason for divorce.'

Penn said, 'The thing is, I think Tamara might fit perfectly into my life without my having to change it.'

Tess raised her eyebrows.

'You've changed your tune. I thought this was true love?'

'It may be. But if it is, why can't we love each other and still play games?'

'Well, your games are pretty specific, and a young bride may not appreciate having the best man invited along on the honeymoon.'

Penn smiled at the scenario.

'Maybe not quite like that,' he said. 'Maybe what I mean is a combination of true love and selective games.'

'Sounds like you're chasing your ultimate fantasy. To recreate what you think you had with Julia.'

'What I think I had?'

'Perceptions change from a distance. Particularly from

thirty years. You're getting there. It shows in what you write.'

'Such as?'

'Well, you intimate a special bond between you and Julia. As Rick orgasmed, her eyes met yours, sort of thing. You keep saying you loved her but obviously the love went sour after you married. As we said before, maybe it wasn't even love *before* you were married.

'In the last piece you wrote, you describe that incident when Rick and Eddie were both having sex with Julia as one of the most erotic experiences of your life. Maybe you see the opportunity with Tamara of recreating that scene, that feeling. Of reliving the dream. Because that's what it is, Charles: a dream.

'Memory is selective. You keep the horny bits but maybe your memory banks have ditched the downside. You wallowed in humiliation, Charles, during this entire two years, then spent another two years wiping out the bad parts and keeping the scenes that turned you on. You really think you would like humiliation again?'

Penn said, 'It wouldn't be humiliation this time. I would be in control.'

'I don't think it's that simple,' Tess said. 'Back then all you did was watch. You were the intimate observer. What you have done since is different. As you say, you've been in control. It's impossible for you to recreate the past with Tamara playing Julia. You can't have a love affair that way.'

He shrugged, and said, 'Maybe I can.'

'Maybe she won't.'

Penn sat silently for a moment and considered the options.

'Let me show you a video,' he said. 'Two videos.' He got

up and went to the TV and video equipment. 'I told you that, for a short time, Tamara lived with a video film-maker. He's very good at what he does. Well, I suspected that if he was in the business, he might well have made films of Tamara. I was right. He did.'

He slotted the second film into the machine and went back to his chair.

Tess said, 'How did you get them?'

'Most things are for sale. If not directly, then through indirect means.'

He pressed 'play' and the film of the schoolgirl and the burglar appeared on the giant TV screen. They sat through it in silence, Penn casting almost furtive looks at Tess to try to gauge her reaction. The video gave him an erection but he was distracted by the presence of his guest.

When it finished, he went back to the machine and put in the bondage film.

'I think you need to see this one, too,' he said.

They again sat in silence while Tamara was abused in the dungeon. Penn's erection was this time quite fierce. The film ended and he switched off the video and TV.

'Well?' he said.

Tess ignored the question and said, 'You have a point to make.'

'She's a submissive. She enjoys games. Yet she retains her innocence. Don't you think that we could be perfectly matched?'

'For what? A weekend in Majorca? Last time you were saying this could be the girl you married. I don't think you can have a marriage based on your precepts. Not one that would last.'

Penn was depressed. He had wanted approval.

'Do you think I'm serious about Tamara?' he said. 'Or do you think I'm still playing games?'

'You'll always play games, Charles.' She smiled. 'When you showed the films? You were watching me watching them. Did you get a turn-on?'

He flushed and said, 'Yes.'

'Good God, you blushed.'

He laughed to cover his embarrassment.

'First time in years. But you haven't answered my question.'

'I think you don't know if you're serious about Tamara. I think you're scared about being serious about anyone, and that's not because you think being a voyeur might have affected your lovemaking capabilities. If you loved someone, believe me, you'd be able to make love to them without the need of any outside stimulation.'

Penn was uncomfortable with her diagnosis.

'Then I suppose I should tell you what I've done.'

'You intrigue me. What have you done?'

'Planned more games, I suppose. I've arranged a house party. I have a place in the country. Tamara will be there, along with the television producer she thinks is going to make her a star.' He shrugged. 'People of influence, a few show business names. Her old flame will be there. Jamie Philpott. The singer?'

Tess said, 'What is this? A test?'

'In a way.'

'Are you hoping she'll make a choice? You or the singer?'

'Maybe.'

'You wrote about a choice with Julia. You were offering her love that was tender and true, even after she had let a middle-aged barber fuck her. Remember? Something of a

163

dichotomy. Especially as you knew she would have chosen the fucking. And later? When you married? Not even then. You said so yourself. Not then, not ever. Although you pretended she did.'

Penn smiled, and said. 'I was younger then. These days, I have more to offer.'

'Now we're back to power and influence.'

'It seems like I can't win.'

'Not until you're honest with yourself.'

He laughed and shook his head but didn't say anything.

'What?' she said.

'I don't know if I dare tell you the rest.'

'There's more?'

'The TV producer? At the house party he'll have a confidential chat with Tamara. Tell her about my reputation with women. How I direct them in sex games. How I like to dominate.'

Tess said, 'You may scare her off.'

'It's a possibility. If it becomes obvious she doesn't like what she hears, I'll swear fidelity and claim it's a pack of lies. But if she does like what she hears . . .?'

'You have a playmate.'

'A match made in . . .'

'Hardly heaven.'

'But we could be so compatible.'

'For a long-term relationship?

He shrugged.

'Maybe.' He got to his feet. 'Anyway, I wondered if *you* would like to come to the house party? Cast your professional eye over my fantasies?'

'When is it?'

'This weekend. The house is in Sussex. I would be happy to arrange transport.'

'Okay. Sounds fun.'

'And now I promised you lunch. I have a car waiting downstairs.'

Tess got up and smoothed down her skirt.

'Nothing like a couple of blue movies to give a girl an appetite,' she said.

'I didn't ask. What did you think of the films?'

'On an erotic scale from one to ten?'

He laughed, and said, 'Yes.'

'No higher than four for the pair. I like something with a little more subtlety,' She smiled at him sweetly. 'But then, I am a woman.'

'I've noticed,' he said.

His plans for the weekend were meticulous. No one who was asked to the gathering refused an invitation. Not even Jamie Philpott.

Of course, the house party was presented to prospective guests as a chance to meet special people, maybe do a little business and enjoy the legendary hospitality for which Charles Penn was renowned.

The other aspect that ensured everyone would attend was that no one dared snub him. Philpott might have, but pressure had been put on him by his manager who had promised to make sure he was there. Besides, the singer was apparently looking forward to seeing Tamara again.

Penn, meanwhile, had his memoirs to occupy him.

He was enjoying writing about the past. It might have started as an experiment in therapy but part of his enjoyment was the knowledge that his epistles were for the eyes of Tess alone and that she would read these intimate disclosures.

The knowledge that his descriptions of lust would be read by her was an added stimulus. He wanted to excite her, turn her on, maybe shock her, although so far she had proved to be unshockable.

It was, in a curious way, as if he were making her a voyeur. As if she were watching from the shadows, peering into his past and his secret desires. He had never been so open with a woman before. Correction: he had never been so open with *anyone* before.

Perhaps the therapy would work, perhaps not. Perhaps his own games would produce swifter results.

Tess was right. Tamara did remind him of Julia. The innocence was the same. Maybe the games could be the same, only this time he would be in control.

The relationship need not be short-lived, as Tess had warned. He knew the pitfalls of sharing a wife. He had done it before. This time, he knew he could do it differently and provide both Tamara and himself with excitement, sexual satisfaction and maybe even happiness.

A lot depended on the weekend ahead. He looked forward to the challenges and opportunities. But before then, he had another epistle to write for Dr Tess Flanders.

This time, he felt, he should move on. This time he should face the dichotomy Tess had talked about. He should write about when it came down to choices.

Chapter 14

Charles Penn's story

Rick and Julia got married and I went to Africa. It sounds more dramatic than it was, like I had run away to sea, but jobs abroad were easier to get back in the Sixties. A lot of things seemed easier then, but maybe that's my memory playing up. (You said it was selective, Tess.)

While I was away, I kept mainly male company. I drank a good deal, as everybody seemed to out there, worked hard, saw a fair bit of the country, and, when I felt the urge, I wrote about being with Rick and Julia. Personal stories for my own consumption that I kept for maybe a week afterwards and then destroyed because they made me feel dirty.

When I came home, I was still a virgin. I was also a fish out of water with the people I had known before. Everything seemed to have changed. My attitudes, their attitudes. I seemed to have matured and gained ambitions while their horizons were fixed in their own backyard.

The thought of seeing Rick and Julia again had been at the back of my mind but maybe I wouldn't have done anything about it except that I bumped into one of Julia's girlfriends. She gave me their address and telephone number.

Once I had that information it was just a question of

time before I got in touch. It was inevitable. It was as if I had nowhere else to go.

They were living in the Midlands. I eventually plucked up courage one night after a few beers and telephoned and spoke to Julia. Two years and an instant erection. The memories flooded back.

The difference was that we were now both grown-ups. She was a married woman and I had just got back from Africa with the option of another two-year contract. We talked about what had happened to people in the old gang, about her parents, about what I'd been doing, what she and Rick were doing. But of course we never talked about what was uppermost in both our minds.

I arranged to call again when Rick was there. I did so and he gave me the invitation we all knew would be forthcoming.

Come and see us, he said.

Two days later, I was there.

They lived in a semi-detached house in an ordinary suburban area. She was a clerk in a bank and he worked in a garage. He still had his motorbike but they also had a family car. The house was furnished just like every other respectable semi-detached house, as if Julia's parents had given her the blueprint and she had followed it to the letter, even to the ornaments on the mantelpiece.

I got there late on a Saturday afternoon in May, not quite knowing what to expect but not wanting to have to spend long blank periods sitting in the front room wondering what to talk about.

Rick hadn't changed. He looked just the same in jeans and a T-shirt. Julia was as lovely as ever, although she had the veneer of a married woman. Maybe it was another blueprint given her by her mother. She was very much the lady of the house and proud of the fitted carpet and the ornaments on the mantelpiece.

We had a meal and she went to get bathed and changed before we went to a pub for a drink. Rick and I watched television and still we never talked of sex, although I could tell he was quietly brooding and I noticed a hint of his piranha smile on his face.

Julia came in and said she was ready, and I complimented her on her dress. It was white with a full skirt and with it she wore white high-heeled shoes. She sat in a chair opposite me while Rick went upstairs. I kept glancing at her legs: I think she noticed and I blushed.

She said nothing but kept crossing her legs and I kept glancing in hope. I got no erotic glimpses but the possibility that I might, and the sound of the nylon swishing as one leg crossed the other, gave me an erection. In those days, it never did take much.

Rick returned, still in his jeans but in a clean T-shirt. I went to the bathroom and washed and shaved and put on a suit.

When I went back in the front room, Rick looked at the suit and laughed but Julia said, 'At least someone's made an effort.' I didn't think too much of it at the time, but maybe it was an indication of the way their relationship had gone.

We went by car to a country pub. Rick drove and did not stint on his drinking. As we consumed alcohol, the barriers of two years dropped. We became less formal, Julia shed something of her married veneer and Rick became his old domineering self.

Back at the house, we watched television for a while. We watched it in the dark. It seems silly now, but back in the 1950s and 1960s, families would turn the room lights out so they could see the black-and-white pictures better.

Rick got bored with the TV and put an Elvis Presley LP on the record player. Songs of our youth. He switched off the TV but did not put on the lights. I was in an armchair and they were on the sofa. My stomach churned because I knew what was going to happen.

Nothing was said. That was the strange thing. No preliminaries, no excuses or explanations. No pretence. The only illumination came from the orange glow of a gas fire. Rick sat next to Julia on the sofa, turned her face to his and kissed her.

At first she didn't react. Her arms were by her side. As he kissed her, he felt her breasts. The dress fastened down the front and he undid the buttons and opened it. I could tell from the movement of his hand that he had slid the bra strap from her shoulder and the cup from her breast.

He dipped his head and sucked. His hand now went to her knee and began to push up her skirt. Still she didn't react. Still she sat there, unmoving, unprotesting, letting it happen. Even though the light was dim, I could see that her eyes were closed.

Rick pushed his hand between her legs and arched his arm so that his fingers could rub her crotch, but there was little I could actually see. I thought she moaned or grunted but her eyes remained closed. He dropped to his knees before her and reached beneath her skirt. She murmured and raised her hips a little. He pulled down her panties and slid them off over her feet.

He was about to discard them but hesitated, glanced over his shoulder at me, the silent witness, and tossed them towards me. They landed in my lap. White nylon.

I was in a high state of arousal and because Rick's and

Julia's attention was elsewhere had been able to touch myself and make my erection comfortable in my trousers. Rick moved between Julia's legs, pushed up her dress, and put his head down into her groin. I heard him licking and sucking. Now she reacted.

Her head rolled to one side, she moaned and her hips moved as she slid further down in the seat to give him greater access. Now I could also see her legs. Tan stockings, white suspender straps crossing luminescent flesh, and Rick's dark head between her thighs.

I picked up the panties. They were warm. Her eyes remained closed and I lifted the panties to my face and, for the very first time, inhaled her intimate aroma.

Julia moaned a few feet away. Her dress was open, but the darkness hid her breasts. Rick's hands were beneath her and her legs were over his shoulders. The sounds he made became louder and her head rolled and she gasped and grunted and came and I pressed her panties against my face.

Rick got up and unfastened his jeans but did not remove them. He knelt on the sofa astride her and I heard the sounds of Julia sucking him. She was sitting low on the sofa and her legs stretched across the carpet, the skirt of the dress still around her waist. Her foot was close to mine.

Rick was moving his hips against her face and she spluttered. He was obviously holding her head and she raised her hands between them, I suppose to try to control his thrusts.

Then he climbed off her and pushed her lengthways on her back on the sofa, pushed his jeans and underwear down from around his hips and climbed on her again, between her legs. Much of what they did was in shadow but I saw him

171

raise her thighs and push his prick into her. She moaned when it went in.

He lay on her and fucked her for two or three minutes, quite fiercely so that he banged moans out of her with each thrust. The sounds were intoxicating and my eyes were fixed on the curve of her thigh where it became a buttock, and on the length of stockinged leg.

Rick got off her again and pushed gently at her but she didn't know what he wanted.

'Kneel on the floor,' he said.

Julia knelt on the carpet facing the sofa. She lay forward with her head and arms on the cushions and he knelt behind her and pushed his prick into her again and fucked her. I couldn't actually see a great deal but I was so close that I could hear them and now I could smell them, smell the sex.

Unlike before, Rick was not putting on a show for me. He was virtually ignoring me and so was Julia. He stopped thrusting, withdrew his prick and held it in his hand, still close behind her, and she moved her hips.

'No,' she said.

'Yes.'

'Not there.'

He didn't reply but held her in place and kept pushing. She cried out and he sighed as his hips sank forward and I knew he had put it in her anus.

Maybe he was doing it because I was there, I thought. Maybe he was showing he could do anything with her and it didn't matter if I was there or not. It suddenly occurred to me that maybe he saw me, for the first time, as a threat.

The thought frightened me and thrilled me. It could result in a beating but it could also mean he thought Julia might, just might, now pick me if it came to a choice.

He held her hips and, at first, eased it in and out of her and she moaned quietly, her arms spread over the sofa. As it moved more easily, he pushed harder. He grunted with each push and began to gasp and I inhaled Julia's aroma from her panties again and he came.

Rick lay slumped over her back for a few moments, then moved away and got to his feet. I pushed the panties down the side of the chair. He pulled up his jeans and glanced in my direction and then back to Julia.

'Who wants another drink?' he said.

Julia pushed her skirt down as she got off her knees, turned and sat on the edge of the sofa.

'No,' she said, in a dull voice.

He looked at me.

'Sure,' I said. 'Why not?'

'Beer or whisky?'

'Beer.'

He left the room, fastening his jeans, and when he opened the door electric light from the hall shone in. Julia stared across the room at me. Her dress was open but she had replaced her breasts in her bra. She didn't seem to care that the dress gaped.

I couldn't work out what her expression meant. It might have been dull, accusing, frustrated or bored. Then she got up, smoothed the skirt and glanced around. I felt embarrassed that I had her knickers.

'I'm going to bed,' she said.

'Goodnight,' I said, trying to fit a lot into that one innocuous word, but she left the room without saying anything else and went upstairs.

Rick came back and still didn't put the light on. He gave me a bottle of beer and a glass. He had a bottle of whisky and a glass. He had been quite intoxicated before and I sensed he wanted to make a full job of it. I just hoped he didn't want violence as well.

We drank and talked. At first we talked about the old days and he told me about his time as a merchant seaman and visiting America. Maybe he wanted to put me in my place. I might have been to Africa but he had sailed the world and been to the Mecca of teenage dreams, that sort of thing.

He drank the whisky at a fast rate and soon became very drunk. That was when he started talking about sex.

'She likes you watching, you know. Always did. Big turn-on.'

I didn't say anything. I felt I was on very dangerous ground.

Rick didn't mind. He had enough to say for both of us.

'Julia was a virgin when I met her. But she was ready for it. Ready for anything. She loved sex.'

He refilled the glass and took a mouthful. I waited and at last he continued.

'She knew how you felt. I called you her lapdog. When I fucked her I said "Imagine Brains watching this. Send him crazy".' He laughed. 'It sent *her* crazy. So we did. Let you watch. And it did, didn't it?' The piranha was drunk but could still be harmful. 'Didn't it?'

'Yes. It sent me crazy.'

Rick drank more whisky and stared into the fire.

'There's nothing she wouldn't do. Butter wouldn't melt, that's what you thought. But there's nothing she wouldn't do. You were crazy and so was she, for sex. She did it with a cucumber, with a bottle. A carrot. She'd do it with anything.'

He lapsed into silence and kept staring into the fire. His face had a devil glow.

'You know what, Brains? This last year has been boring. You've provided a spark again.' He glanced directly at me. His grin was back and for a moment he seemed fully in control. 'You know what? There's nothing we can't do.'

He had another glass of whisky and a few minutes later he was asleep.

I sat for a while, wondering whether I should stay in the chair so he couldn't accuse me of anything when he woke up. But what the hell could he accuse me of?

He knew me, knew I was the witness, not the lover. Knew I wouldn't dare attempt anything with Julia, and knew that Julia wouldn't do anything with me without his sanction.

So I left him. I left the panties on the sofa, went upstairs and stood on the landing for a while, staring at the door of the bedroom where Julia was sleeping. I tried to hear her breathing, wondered if she might call to me, and if she did, what would I do?

The thought made me panic and I went into the spare room and went to bed. I lay there wide awake, thinking of what had happened, and took pleasure from the ache of my erection. But I did not touch it and did not give it relief.

Next morning when I awoke my prick was hard again. I held it and felt its tension. There was a knock at the door and Julia came in with a cup of tea. She wore a short nylon nightdress and her breasts hung in the scoop neckline as she bent to place the cup on the bedside table. She smelled of bed and sex and I almost came.

Later, much later, she told me Rick had made her come into my room dressed like that. He started fucking her when he woke up and broke off so she could bring me the cup of tea. It turned me on and it did the same for both of them because a few minutes later, when I got up to go to the bathroom, I could hear them doing it.

Their bedroom door was partly open and I could hear the springs of the bed, his grunts and her moans. I stayed on the landing listening to them and masturbated and this time I *did* come, unexpectedly. Although I tried to catch it in my hands, some of my spunk went onto the carpet and I rubbed it in with my bare foot so they wouldn't see.

I had a wash, got dressed and went downstairs quietly. But it was a while before they came down. We had a late breakfast and looked at the newspapers and it was a very ordinary domestic scene. We went for a drink at lunchtime and went home again for something to eat. The day was desultory. It was as if we were all waiting for something to happen.

It was a warm, sunny day in May and Rick decided we should go for an early-evening drink. He wore a T-shirt and jeans, as usual, and I wore the khaki slacks and shirt that I had worn in Africa.

Julia bathed and changed. When she came downstairs my mouth went dry. She wore a pink V-neck sweater and a floppy knee-length black skirt that had a floral pattern and that was made of flimsy material. It flicked as she walked. Her stockings were black, as were her high-heeled shoes. I thought she looked incredibly sexy.

We went to a country pub where, after a few drinks, Rick began to make veiled suggestions about how tempting Julia looked in black underwear.

There was a moment when we had leaned forward around the table where we were sitting because he wanted to whisper a comment, and he took hold of the 'V' of the sweater and pulled it open so I could look inside at her breasts in a black lace bra. I was embarrassed as well as aroused and I glanced around to see if anyone else had noticed.

When we left, it was still light. Rick drove to an isolated spot on a disused canal. It held murky water but the buildings alongside it were derelict. We walked along the canal bank. The breeze kept lifting Julia's skirt and I made an excuse to drop back so that I could catch a glimpse of the tops of her stockings and the contrasting white of her thighs.

Two men came out of one of the buildings. One was about sixty and small, the other a big chap of about thirty. They were rough-and-ready sort of blokes and could have been looking for scrap. We nodded hello to them as we passed. They stood and watched and I knew they would be looking at the way Julia's skirt kept lifting. I wondered if being here was such a good idea.

Lock gates that hadn't been opened for years formed a bridge across the canal. The top of the wooden gates was wide enough to walk on and there was a safety rail at waist height. Rick crossed and Julia hesitated.

'Come on,' he said.

She followed and, because she had to use both her hands on the rail, her skirt kept lifting unchecked in the breeze, showing her legs, her thighs above the stockings, the black suspender straps and even her tight black panties.

I was once more in a state of high arousal. The two men simply stood and stared. I followed Julia across and tried to position myself between her and them. Rick seemed unaware of my anxiety. They stood side by side in front of me and he put his arm around her waist, said something to her, dropped his hand and groped her bottom.

We walked a little way more and when I glanced back I was relieved to see the two men had gone. Rick now put his hand up her skirt and pulled her to him. They kissed and he moved her against his groin.

At last he turned and led the way back, holding her hand. I followed and watched the wind lift her skirt and felt my prick pushing against my trousers. We crossed the lock gates but instead of going to the car, Rick went into one of the empty buildings, taking Julia with him. I followed. The faithful lapdog.

Rick said, 'Kids use these buildings. They fuck in them.' He was staring at the wall. 'Look. They write stories. In this one, they all fucked the one girl.'

As he read, the arm that was round Julia's waist dropped over her buttocks and he moved her until she was standing in front of him. He held her by the hips and moved himself against her while they both read the story on the wall.

'Dirty little bastards,' he said, still reading. 'They've turned me on.'

He lifted her skirt and his hands moved over her buttocks. I remained by the door, watching them and watching the canal bank, on guard against intrusion. He pushed down her panties, exposed her bottom and mauled the soft flesh.

Now he unfastened his jeans, pushed them down over his hips and pressed his prick against her, holding her by the hips once more and rubbing himself against her.

My throat was dry and my erection fierce. I could masturbate without touching it, simply by tensing it in my trousers.

Rick dropped his right hand over her stomach and from its movement I guessed his fingers were at her vagina. They stayed in that position, and Julia's breathing became a little heavier. Then she came, shuddering in his arms.

There was an old table and he leaned back against it and turned her, pushing upon her shoulders. She crouched in front of him and took his prick in her mouth. He held her head and fucked her mouth while she held the base of his weapon to control the depth of his thrusts.

As he did it, he looked at me and smiled his piranha smile.

Last night he had done what he did to prove he could, but this was a show. He withdrew his prick and raised her to her feet. They changed places and he turned her so that she leaned forward over the table.

He stood behind her and raised the skirt to her waist, exposing the full length of those gorgeous black-nyloned legs. He pushed her panties further down until they were at mid-thigh, a thicker band of black nylon around the tops of her stockings, and he entered her from behind.

As he fucked her, he pushed up the sweater and the bra cups and groped her breasts. His hands roamed her body, from buttocks and thighs to breasts, taking their pleasure, and she simply stood, legs apart, bent forward at the waist, her mouth open and eyes closed.

I was engrossed in this scene but a movement outside caught my attention.

'Rick,' I said, urgently. 'Those two blokes are coming.'

His smiled widened.

'I'm not,' he said. 'Not yet.'

Julia turned her head. Her eyes opened and she stared at me. Her features were heavy and she licked her lips and again I could not understand her expression. What was I supposed to do? What did she expect me to do?

The two men got closer and I became more agitated but Rick did not vary his speed. Julia pressed her lips together and looked away.

I was standing in the doorway to the building but before they got that far the men first reached an empty window from which the glass had long since gone. They had been staring at me but now they looked into the room and what they saw made them stop. They watched Rick fucking Julia.

He ignored them but carried on running his hands over her as he pumped himself into her. The two men exchanged a look and the large one stepped forward to the doorway. He ignored me, it was as if I was not there, and I stepped into the room and out of his way. They entered and continued to watch in silence.

Rick now held Julia by the hips and bit into his bottom lip and his thrusts were measured with venom. Then he gripped her tight and came, his hips shaking against her as he emptied his spunk inside her.

He rested a moment and then stepped away, his prick limp in his hand. Julia stood upright and her skirt fell to cover her, and she turned to face the two men. Her eyes were wide, her mouth open and her expression was wild, but whether with fear or excitement, I could not tell.

The big young man stepped to her and pulled her against him. His left hand went beneath her skirt and felt her buttocks, his right groped her breasts and he stared down into her face with pure lust.

'Like it, do you?' he said.

His older friend stood behind Julia and placed both his hands on her thighs and moved them up beneath her skirt.

My erection throbbed almost uncontrollably in my trousers.

I wondered if Rick would produce a knife again as he had years ago and stop what was happening. But he was standing in a corner, his jeans now fastened, watching with almost detached interest as these two men pawed his wife.

Julia glanced in his direction but he said nothing and the men unfastened their trousers. The big one crouched and ripped her panties, an act of sudden violence that made her shudder and made me tremble. The nylon tore and the remnants of the panties now hung from one leg.

'I'm first,' he said, and pushed Julia backwards until she was leaning against the wall upon which teenagers had written their sexual exploits and fantasies.

The young fat giant faced her, his jeans low on his thighs, his hips and buttocks flabby. He pushed her legs apart, bent his knees and used a hand to guide his prick. He pushed and Julia yelled as he entered her and lifted her off her feet.

Her shoulders rested against the wall and he put his forearms beneath her legs and held her buttocks as he fucked her, his flabby flesh shaking. His older companion stood alongside, stroking his own erection and waiting his turn.

It did not take long. He slapped against her, lifting her on and off his tool at a steady pace, making her yell out. Then he came, holding himself tense and shedding his sperm inside her.

When he put her back on her feet she swayed unsteadily and the older man took hold of her and tried to kiss her. But she turned away her face and he licked her neck as his hands roamed over her body, feeling her buttocks and breasts and the swollen lips of her sex.

He pushed her down and she crouched in front of him and took his prick into her mouth and sucked as he ran his fingers through her hair and touched her face. Both men had been extremely aroused by the unexpectedness of the scene and the sudden availability of sex with a beautiful woman, and he, too, soon came. He held her head steady, thrust vigorously three times, and began to shake.

Julia gulped and swallowed and, when he pulled away, she licked her lips. Her eyes were dull: she sat on the floor and didn't seem to notice that her legs gaped and her skirt had slid high up her thighs.

The two men looked at Rick who stared back at them with the hint of a dangerous smile. They ignored me, and, without another word, they left.

Rick crossed the room and held out a hand which Julia took and he helped her to her feet. He brushed the dust and dirt from her skirt and his hand lingered over her buttocks. He put his mouth over hers and kissed her, his tongue digging between her lips as if he wanted to share the spunk she had swallowed.

The kiss ended and he said, 'When we get home. I'm going to fuck your brains out.'

Julia pulled the remnants of her panties from her foot and dropped them on the floor, and they left the building. I hesitated, picked up the ripped black undergarment, put it in my pocket, and followed.

Rick gave me the car keys and I drove while he and Julia sat in the back of the car. They kissed and groped and masturbated each other all the way back to their house as the night darkened and set in.

As soon as we were inside, he pushed her against the wall in the hallway, pulled up her skirt and groped her buttocks as he kissed her. I was still by the door, unable to pass, and saw that Julia was responding as fiercely. I had been about to turn on the hall light but no longer thought it would be an appropriate thing to do.

Their mouths broke apart and Rick said, 'Bed.'

My spirits immediately sank. The show was over. Maybe I could listen outside their bedroom door?

He pushed her towards the stairs and looked at me.

'You too, Brains.'

Me too?

What did he mean? I felt panic in case I was expected to lose my virginity. I mean, I wanted to lose my virginity but I was frightened I would make a fool of myself. It had been two years since I had seen them. They probably thought I had lost my virginity in Africa.

I followed, excited and frightened. Perhaps that was how Julia had felt when confronted by the two men: both excited and frightened. Rick pushed her into their bedroom and left the door open for me.

Once inside, he crossed to the window and pulled the curtains closed. The room was in deep shadow and I remained in the doorway, unsure of what my role was to be. He began to undress. He looked at Julia.

'Take them off,' he said.

Julia pulled the sweater over her head and dropped it on the floor. She was watching Rick. She had not looked at me, not acknowledged my presence. I felt I was slipping back into my non-role of silent witness.

Rick looked at me and said, 'And you, Brains. We're all going to bed.'

My blood pounded. Julia unclipped her bra and dropped that on the floor, too. I watched the sway of her breasts. My fingers were clumsy as they unbuttoned my shirt. I was glad it was dark. I wondered if I was meant to remove all my clothes.

She unfastened the waistband of the skirt, unzipped it and let it slip down her hips and pool at her feet. My erection lurched at the dim vision of her wearing only stockings, suspender belt and high heels.

Rick was naked. He pulled back the covers and Julia

leaned down to push off her shoes before climbing into bed.

'Everything,' he said to me, getting in next to her.

I sat on the edge of the bed to remove my shoes and socks. I unfastened my trousers and pushed them and my underpants off at the same time, and then slid beneath the covers.

Julia lay in the middle of the bed, Rick to her left and me to her right. They lay on their sides, face to face, kissing, arms and legs entwined. I lay on my side and watched in the dark. I was no longer the silent witness. I had become part of the movement of the bed, part of their smell, even though I was keeping my distance.

Her stockinged foot touched my leg and I shuddered. He rolled her onto her back and her arm lay flat on the bed between us. I could sense her hand inches from my erection.

Rick lay over her, sucking her breasts, a hand between her legs. His fingers must have entered her for she moaned and her head tilted back and her body arched. His arm moved rhythmically and she moaned louder. Then he lifted his hand from beneath the covers and held his fingers before her face.

'You're full of spunk,' he muttered. 'You're dripping with his spunk.'

He pushed his fingers into her mouth and she sucked them. Her right hand gripped the sheet of the bed, the back of her fingers brushing against my erection, and I pulled myself away the necessary fraction of an inch to break the contact.

Now Rick climbed upon her and pushed her legs apart, got himself into the right position, and pushed his prick into her. The whole situation was unreal. They continued to ignore me, even though he began to fuck her. I lay alongside them, my body as rigid as my erection, painfully attempting to keep myself from touching her, but it was impossible.

As he banged into her more wildly, her legs flopped and were flung wider and moved against me. She ignored the contact and I became bolder and no longer held myself away. I edged a fraction closer instead of in the opposite direction, and my thigh touched her thigh, my leg felt her nyloned leg, and my prick brushed against the heat of her flesh and the ruched silk of a suspender strap.

They fucked for a long time. They did not make love, but fucked, pure and simple, as if I was not there and she ignored all contacts with me. He raised himself above her on his arms and she raised her knees. She closed her eyes and came and he grinned like a triumphant wild man.

He got off her, turned her over onto her stomach, lay on her back and entered her again, this time from behind. Her head lay on the pillow, her face turned away from me, so that she was anonymous. Her arms were by her side and I became aware that my prick was against her hand which lay palm up. Without thinking, I rolled onto my stomach so that my prick lay in her hand, at the same time trapping her hand beneath me.

Rick fucked her and she lay unmoving, a passive recipient. His groin slapped against her buttocks. My thigh lay against her thigh, my leg against her stockinged leg and now my prick lay in her hand.

Again she ignored it. She had become a sexual accessory. Although I had trapped her hand I did not feel confident enough to move myself against it deliberately. But Rick's movements caused the mattress to move and caused me to move upon her hand.

Then Rick moved her again and changed positions. He laid her on her back and knelt by her head and I watched, from inches away, as Julia sucked his prick that was slick with her juices and the spunk of the other man. I watched as he wiped his glans across her face. I watched her with her mouth open, her tongue flicking. I watched her eagerness and her submissiveness.

He changed position again and I lay once more on my side. He turned Julia onto her side so that she faced me and he lay behind her and again entered her. Her body now shook to his thrusts, her breasts moving temptingly, her nipples so erect as to be close to bursting. Her eyes were closed and her mouth open and I inhaled her breath.

One of her arms was raised and her hand lay on the pillow between us, but the other was beneath the covers. It seemed it was chance that it came to rest around my erection. She did not grip my prick. Her hand simply lay curled around it and I moved my prick ever so slightly in and out of the tunnel of her fingers.

She was so close and yet still out of reach. I watched Rick's hands maul her breasts, then saw one hand dip down and disappear across her stomach. Her face changed when his fingers touched her vagina. That was a time when I knew nothing of the clitoris, but I knew that there must be a particularly sensitive spot down there known to his fingers.

He masturbated her with skill and I watched her expression change and knew she was approaching climax. Then it was upon her and she came. I felt the heat of her breath on my face and, at the moment of her orgasm, her hand tensed and gripped my prick and I also came.

Oh, the exquisite agony of the moment. Of being literally gripped in her climax. Of the embarrassment and the mind-blowing ecstasy as my spunk spurted up her arm and onto the bed. And as my bulging eyes regained their powers of perception, I saw Rick watching me from over her shoulder, saw his eyes in the dark and knew his grin was in place.

I closed my eyes in shame and lay on my stomach to cover the wet patch on the mattress. Then I heard him grunt and heave, and he came, too, causing Julia to press against me.

After his orgasm, our bodies untwined to seek comfort and, believe it or not, after all the frantic sexual activity, it was not long before they were asleep. It took me a little longer, the doubts again making me wonder whether or not I should sneak back to the spare bedroom, but then sleep overcame me as well.

Some time during the night, I was awakened by Rick fucking Julia once more. I pretended to be unconscious and watched their dim shapes through half-closed eyes in the dark. He lay on top of her and pounded her until he came but she did not respond. Submissive or asleep? When he finished he rolled off and was soon snoring again.

I must have gone back to sleep as well but when I next awoke it was with a large erection that was pressing against Julia. At first I thought it must be an erotic dream for my senses were still adrift in the dark. And then I realized I had curled up against Julia's back and that my erection lay along the groove of her delicious buttocks.

My hand was on her thigh and had been stroking her flesh, from the curve of her bottom along a suspender strap to the nylon of her stocking. I froze in terror and listened to the night sounds. Rick was snoring on her far side and her breathing was steady and deep. Thank goodness I had not disturbed her.

For a moment I considered the best way to break the contact but then realized that this stolen moment need not end like that. My erection pulsed against her softness which was slick from secretions and sex and sweat. She was asleep. What harm could it do?

I twitched my prick and stifled a moan at the pleasure. My palm roamed her flesh again, softly seeking curves and straps and nylon. I moved my hips ever so slightly and my prick moved in its silky slick bed.

This was too much. This was heady stuff. The danger of discovery and the sweetness of stolen sensations. I moved against her buttocks again and, with rising panic, knew I had lost control as my prick pulsed and spat my spunk against her softness.

The mixture of terror and pleasure was amazingly potent and the orgasm was deliciously intense. At last I eased myself away, worried briefly about the mess I had left upon her, and fell asleep.

I was awakened by Rick once more performing upon her body. She lay on her stomach and he lay upon her back. Her face was turned towards me and her eyes were open. She watched me as he fucked her and I held my stiff prick in my hand. He finished and rolled away. A moment later he got out of bed.

'Time to get up,' he said, and went to the bathroom.

Julia gave me a small, sleepy smile, blew me a kiss, and also got out of bed. She put on a dressing gown and went downstairs.

It was Monday morning and they both had to go to work. The arrangement we had made was that I would leave after my weekend visit, mid-morning. There was no reason for me to rise and face embarrassment.

Rick returned from the bathroom and got dressed and

downstairs I could hear a kettle boiling and smell bacon frying. I pretended to be asleep and he eventually left the room and went down for his breakfast.

Now I heard Julia go into the bathroom and listened to the water running as it filled a bath. I remained beneath the covers with the smells and the warmth and my hand slid over the sheet and found dried patches of secretions.

Julia finished in her ablutions and came into the bedroom. I would have liked to have watched her get dressed but dared not let her know I was awake.

'What time will you leave?' she said quietly, knowing full well I was awake.

'About ten,' I said, and pushed the covers down a few inches and looked at her.

She was in her underwear. White underwear and tan stockings and a white blouse. As I watched, she stepped into a skirt, pulled it to her waist, zipped it and hid the vision.

We exchanged a long look.

I said, 'If you ever need me, you know . . .'

'I know.' She smiled, came to the bed and bent down and kissed me on the forehead. 'Take care, Charlie,' she said, and left the bedroom.

A few minutes later, the front door opened and closed and they had gone. I was alone in their home and was filled with the knowledge that I could now be a different kind of voyeur. I rolled into the middle of the bed where Julia had lain and buried my face in the pillow and found her smell. I slid beneath the covers and down the bed and found that other smell, the aroma of sex.

The feeling of possession that I had at that time, of being in possession of the bed, the bedroom and their house, was all-consuming. It was so marvellous that afterwards

I actually considered breaking into the homes of young married couples when I knew they would be out so that I could recapture the experience. But I didn't: not out of decency, but out of cowardice.

I flung the bedclothes back and inspected the sheet for the stains of passion and lay against them and remembered how they had occurred. I got off the bed and opened the drawers of the dressing table until I found Julia's underwear and lifted the silky garments and suspender belts to my face.

Where were the black stockings and suspender belt she had been wearing, I wondered? I went into the bathroom and found them in a laundry basket and went back and lay on the bed, still naked, and inhaled the glorious aroma of Julia and sex.

My erection throbbed and I was tempted to masturbate but decided to extend the experience. I didn't wash for I wanted to keep the smells. I reluctantly put the stockings and suspender belt back in the laundry basket, dressed and packed my bag.

I left the covers pulled back so that when they returned home that evening they would see the evidence. I guessed the sight of it would be enough to make Rick throw her down upon the mattress and start again.

And that was it. I left the house and drove home, Julia's ripped black panties in my pocket and my erection full and waiting.

Chapter 15

A chauffeur in a limousine picked up Dr Tess Flanders for the drive to Charles Penn's country house. As they left London, she sat back in the soft leather seats and smiled at the opulence of cocktail cabinet, TV and video, CD player, and a terminal with fax, computer and telephone link.

It was an office, as well as an entertainment centre. She stroked the leather of the seats and wondered what sort of entertainment might have been carried out upon them.

As if all the on-board facilities were not enough, the chauffeur had also handed her a sealed package containing his employer's latest confessions.

Charles Penn was a strong and attractive man, she had decided, whom she was growing to like more with each meeting, despite his aberrations. Not that gaining enjoyment from watching others engaged in sex was an aberration.

Tess smiled at herself, this time. She had a habit of correcting even her own thoughts for the sake of accuracy.

Being a voyeur was not the problem, as she had explained to him. His *obsession* was the problem and she suspected that Tamara was another aspect of that obsession.

Apart from the difference in the ages of Penn and the girl, she could see other pitfalls into which his hopes could messily disappear without a trace. That is, if he was as serious about Tamara as he said he was, or as serious about her as he thought he was.

Sexual attraction often carried its own smokescreens and *aides d'amour*. It could inspire lust that lasted no longer than the act of congress and it could confuse individuals into believing desire was eternal love.

At the moment, Penn had not been persuaded to indulge his lust, even though that opportunity had been offered by Tamara to test whether or not it would survive the experience. The longer it went untested, Tess believed, the deeper would become his infatuation.

Penn, she felt, had discovered vulnerability as well as voyeurism in his formative teenage years, and ever since had been careful not to be vulnerable again. In business, he was formidable. In sexual matters, controlled. But he had hidden the emotion that was essential to the well-being of every human spirit beneath protective layers of reason, excuse, argument and self-deceit.

People too often got confused over priorities. Being a financial success in the City was fine – but it did not make you a better person.

Running a mortgage and a car and a job and a family were also fine. But they were not, in themselves, worthwhile unless the reason why they had been undertaken in the first place continued to be appreciated.

Too often, the pressure of keeping up the payments made people lose sight of the fact that they were working so hard because they loved someone. And if that premise did not stand up to analysis then the relationship concerned was in trouble.

As the song said, people who needed people were the luckiest people in the world. They needed to share emotions, share life. And that was basically Penn's problem. He

might be a great success in business but when it came
to love and emotion he was a failure. He was frightened
to confront life.

Tess leaned forward and poured herself a gin and tonic
to which she added ice from the icebox in the small
refrigerator. For now she would forget analysis. She
would enjoy the luxury of the limousine and the latest
chapter from Charles Penn. She opened the package and
noted the number of pages.

It seemed as if he was getting into the swing of
confession.

There was also a guest list, with potted biographies, that
had also been written by Penn. She read that first:

'Monty Radcliffe of Badger UK makes independent
television programmes. It is not widely known, but I
own a controlling share of the company through an
offshore investment portfolio, although Monty is MD.
He is thirty-eight, married, with three children. His wife
and family live in Provence and he visits occasionally. He
is overweight and has a fondness for young women (but
don't we all) and is a damn fine television producer and
film-maker, despite, in this instance, being totally pliable
to my wishes.

'He will be accompanied by Susan Crowther-Flook who
is twenty-five years old and is a public-relations executive
with Badger UK. She has been with the company for three
months, is a blonde English rose and is the current object
of Monty's desires. Another seduction through the misuse
of power, perhaps?

'Jamie Philpott, as you know, is a rock-and-roll singer
of fame and notoriety, and fronts the band Nadir. He is
worth financially slightly more than one million pounds
but should be wealthier. He has lost much of the vast

amount of money he has earned through bad advice, bad investment and bad behaviour. He has the potential, however, to continue making vast amounts from his music. His manager is attempting to negotiate a film contract for him to extend his career further.

'His manager is Delia Watling, aged forty-three, a very attractive dark-haired woman with a beguiling smile who can be deadly in business. She is single and has ambivalent sexual tastes, having no preference between male or female.

'She will be accompanied by her personal assistant Fiona Manderville, who is twenty-eight and who is sometimes required to sleep with her boss if no one else is available, and sometimes required to sleep with business contacts if it means swinging a deal. I warn you, Delia is a shark.

'Film producer-director Mark Trimm will be there. He's one of the new great British hopes whose debut feature film won an award at Cannes. The film, by the way, was *Goodnight*, a black comedy about collective suicide. He's twenty-seven, laid-back, and does not take very much seriously. I suspect *Goodnight* was part talent and part a joke.

'With him will be Liz Bizley, same age and disposition as Mark, who co-wrote *Goodnight* and who has already had success on television with drama scripts.

'Delia, of course, is hoping to discuss a project with them that might be suitable for Jamie.'

Tess counted down the names. With Penn and herself, that made a party of ten for a weekend that promised entertainment and discovery.

Now, with a frisson of excitement, she put down the list, picked up the manuscript and began to read.

* * *

The house was Georgian with its own grounds, stables, indoor and outdoor swimming pools, a games room with a bar that resembled that of a country pub, and twelve bedrooms.

Penn greeted Tess on her arrival and showed her to her first-floor en suite room with its views of rolling countryside.

'This is lovely,' she said.

'I take no credit,' he said. 'A design consultancy furnished the place.'

'To your taste and choice?'

'Well, yes.'

'Then you should take some credit, Charles. It's not like you to be modest.'

'Perhaps baring the soul is good for the soul.' He glanced at the package she had dropped on the bed. 'Have you read it?'

'Yes.'

'And?'

'And as usual you want instant appraisal and approval. I think you need to mature, Charles Penn.'

She smiled as she said it, but they both knew there was an element of truth in the statement.

Surprisingly, he said, 'You're probably right.'

Was this a breakthrough?

'Have the other guests arrived?' she said.

'Monty Radcliffe and his young lady, Susan, got here shortly before you. Mark Trimm and Liz Bizley . . . you read my guest list?'

'Yes.'

'Well, Mark and Liz are in the pool. Tamara's here. She's in her room. The others should be here within the hour.'

'What was Tamara's reaction when she heard Jamie Philpott would be here?' Tess asked.

Penn shrugged.

'She pulled a face and said she had been out with him once, but I wasn't to know that.'

'Ingenuous young thing.'

Maybe her sarcasm had been a bit heavy because Penn frowned at her. But really, Tamara could not be so naive as to believe Penn had not known about her past before he had arranged the weekend and invited Philpott. Tess wondered what interpretation Tamara had put upon it?

Penn said, 'And then she warmed to the idea and said it might be an opportunity to persuade him to appear on her television show.'

'It's already a show?'

'She's an optimist.'

'Of course.' Tess sensed Penn was a little tetchy. Maybe all this was coming together too soon. She smiled. 'So,' she said. 'Once everyone is here, what's the running order?'

'Meet in the library at six for drinks. Dinner at seven.'

'What time are charades?'

He smiled and his tetchiness went.

'We're already playing charades, Tess.'

When Penn left her, she inspected the bathroom. As she might have expected, the bath was a jacuzzi. Why not? she thought, and turned on the taps.

As the bath filled she wandered through the bedroom and noted the well-stocked drinks tray on a credenza, an elegant sideboard that hid a refrigerator stocked with champagne and Chablis.

Temptation, temptation. She could resist but she wondered about the other guests? Would some of them make it through dinner?

Tess removed her outer clothes as she walked around the large room and paused for a moment to stare out at the green Sussex countryside. Then she realized she was standing in front of the window in her underwear.

Good God, she thought, moving to one side. The sight might scare horses and young children, if any were out there. Then she caught sight of herself in a full-length mirror and got another shock.

The sighting was unexpected and, for a moment, she was a stranger and saw herself with a stranger's objective stare. She walked across the room until she was standing directly in front of the mirror and turned to look at her profile.

Not bad, she thought. A curvaceous body that had kept its shape, and so it should because of the exercise she took. And yet it had taken an unexpected glimpse of herself before she appreciated it.

Of course, the ivory-white underwear helped, as underwear invariably did. A cleavage bra, silk panties, a garter belt and the sheen of Lycra stockings should be de rigueur for ladies of a certain age who wished to retain their allure.

But when had she had last had the urge to be alluring? Until recently, she had been content to wear trouser suits and jeans. Until she had started seeing Charles Penn.

There, now the thought was out and it made her blush. Fortunately there was no professional conflict. Any help and advice she was giving Penn in her capacity as a sex therapist was unofficial. Besides, she would do her best for Penn with regard to his dilemma over Tamara. However, if it did not work out . . . who knew what might happen?

Her hand had strayed between her thighs and she shuddered at her own touch. Her blush deepened as she saw herself afresh in the mirror and turned away in embarrassment.

Penn's last chapter lay on the bed and she was wickedly tempted to sprawl there and read it again. Was it the eroticism of his words that aroused her, or the man himself? His vulnerability, perhaps?

The thought of being able to solve his problems by taking him to bed herself was appealing and arousing. She bit her lip and smiled at the ramblings of her mind. One glance at herself in a mirror in high heels and stockings and she was considering herself to be a femme fatale. Had Nancy Friday ever had this problem?

Tess walked into the bathroom, switched off the water and switched on the jacuzzi. She went back into the bedroom and paused again in front of the window. It was only five o'clock: sunshine was making the room warm and light and she was loath to draw the curtains.

The movement below was unexpected. A young man was on a path that was lined with shrubs. He had stopped to stare at her. Once more she moved to one side and now she did pull the cord that drew the curtains closed.

For a moment she remained leaning against the wall and reverted to analysis. The young man had been no Peeping Tom. The sighting had been by accident. This provided her with several questions bouncing around inside her head. Who was he? And what had he thought of her?

Being seen and watched wearing nothing but her underwear, even for such a short and unplanned time, had further aroused her. How long had it been since she had had a meaningful and sexually fulfilling relationship?

Here she was, a leading sex guru of the paperbacks, purporting to give advice to a millionaire with the sexual appetite of a satyr, getting turned on by being seen in her underwear by a young man.

No, more than that. By the thought that the sight might have turned on the young man, too.

Good God: now she analysed it, she had been in a state of semi-arousal since Penn's first confession in Majorca. Their conversations, the videos and his erotic writings had kept the tension mounting. No wonder she sympathized with the man. She had, in a way, acquired his condition.

She had become a voyeur of his sex life, had subsequently been aroused and had taken no steps to alleviate those feelings of arousal. Climbing into the limousine this afternoon had given her an erotic charge. Damn' near everything she saw or touched now had a sexual context.

Physician, heal thyself.

Tess laughed. She hoped the laughter would dilute her own dilemma. How could she retain her objectivity as a sex therapist when, if she scratched right down to the bottom line, what she really needed was a good fucking herself?

Wow. Now she had said it. Another shock. She stared at her reflection across the room that was now shaded from the sun. She had not grown two heads and her panties had not become wet with uncontrolled desire.

Why should she be any different to anybody else, she thought? Sexual desire, whether embraced or denied, fulfilled or frustrated, played a large part in the human condition.

She should not doubt herself. She could still do a professional job for Charles Penn.

Tess winked at her reflection.

And maybe, along the way, she could get her rocks off.

She went to the credenza, opened a half-bottle of Chablis

and toasted herself in the mirror. Now she removed the last of her clothes, topped up the glass of wine and took it with her to the jacuzzi.

What would the night hold, she wondered?

Chapter 16

Drinks before dinner for any gathering of strangers was usually a defensive affair. Strengths and weaknesses were unknown, likes and dislikes undiscovered. For some, alcohol was a necessary bolster to a lack of confidence, which meant that drinks after dinner could often provide unexpected consequences.

But, as Tess might have known, this was no ordinary gathering of strangers.

Of course, she had prior knowledge of motives and position, and she found her own role as observer (and there she went again, placing herself in comparison with Penn once more) interesting and entertaining.

Monty Radcliffe, the TV producer who had given Tamara such high hopes, obviously knew how to cruise through drinks at any time of the day or night, and drank champagne like a veteran. Penn had said he was overweight. Corpulent as a pig, thought Tess, with fleshy lips and several chins.

His companion, Susan double barrel, looked somewhat lost. As Penn had described, she was a blonde English rose but not of the delicate variety. Susan was rather a full hardy bloom from the shires with wide cornflower-blue eyes, large but perfectly formed white teeth, and a penchant for saying 'Gosh!' with an exclamation mark.

Tess noticed she was a full-breasted girl who filled the low-cut blue cocktail dress she wore, and she did not think

Susan had been chosen for the position of public relations executive on communication skills alone. She also drank champagne, but not as wisely or with the same seasoned aplomb as Monty.

Delia Watling, the manager of rock singer Jamie Philpott, was slim, dark and gothic in a black silk trouser suit, and nursed a glass of Chablis although she did not appear ever to drink from it. She was self-assured and missed nothing, including Tess watching her from the other side of the room.

When Tess smiled at being caught, she received in return an enigmatic pursing of the lips. Delia was, after all, a bisexual, according to Penn. Maybe Tess would be offered the chance to get her rocks off in a totally unconventional way.

Fiona, her personal assistant, had lustrous red hair in Renaissance ringlets and pale luminous skin. She was slim and had a full mouth. Her dress was crushed velvet and clung to her body: the effect was sensual until you got to her eyes. They showed nothing, neither amusement, interest or boredom. She had learned to mask her feelings totally. If the eyes were the windows of the soul then hers were shut.

Tess noticed that she was drinking vodka martinis at frequent intervals.

Jamie Philpott was both less and more than she had expected. Somehow she had thought a rock star who made an amphitheatre of girls scream and wet their knickers would have more charisma.

The charisma was definitely lacking and he looked as if he had been recruited from the streets of Paddington to even up the numbers. There was no denying he was good-looking, though not outrageously so. But what he did have, she was surprised to discover, was charm.

But the night was young and he might be less charming if he kept on drinking brandy and champagne with the same application, although so far he had been almost shy and delightful. He wore jeans, of course, and a denim shirt.

At the moment he was talking with the young British film-making duo of Mark Trimm and Liz Bizley. Trimm wore a baggy suit and an open-necked shirt and was of medium height, slim build and unremarkable appearance except for the liveliness of his face.

If Fiona's eyes were shut, Mark Trimm's were open for two-way business. He did not mind anyone taking a peep into his soul but his gaze warned he would do the same in return. He was amusing and witty and, as Penn had said, laid-back.

Liz Bizley had been a surprise. Tess, who was forever on her guard about making assumptions, had expected the screenwriter to be dowdy and possibly even pierced with nose rings. Her preconception had been fostered by Penn's description of their hit film, *Goodnight*, and somehow she had matched up the British underground arts movement with London Underground buskers.

But the young woman was no busker and had no strange body piercings that were apparent. Her hair was dark and cut short in a bob, she was attractive with an intelligent and enquiring oval face, and she wore a short sleeveless red dress and high-heeled shoes and, it appeared, very little else. The nipples of her breasts could clearly be seen through the material of the dress and she wore no stockings.

Her legs, arms and face were tanned and she wore little make-up except to highlight her eyes.

After all Tess had seen of Tamara in photographs and videos, the real thing could have been a disappointment. But, she had to admit, the girl *was* lovely, with a willowy body and a bright open face with amazing green eyes that encouraged everyone to fall in love with her. Now she could tell what Penn meant by Tamara's innocence, even after she had watched the videos.

Tamara wore a full-length lilac silk dress with shoulder straps that was about as substantial as an underslip, and no visible underwear.

At the moment, she was in conversation with Monty Radcliffe and Tess wonderd if the TV producer was fulfilling his contract by warning her, in confidence, of Penn's reputation.

Penn was with Tess and she had noticed that his power was such that no one dared join them unless by invitation – with the exception of Tamara who was the court butterfly and could go where she pleased.

'Is Monty doing the deed?' she said.

'Probably. I think he has other things on his mind for later.'

'Susan Gosh!'

'Exactly.'

'What a terrible judgement,' Tess said, immediately feeling guilty. 'Classifying the poor girl with a single word.'

'There are worse things.'

'Such as?'

'Going to bed with Monty.'

'Does she have a choice?'

They exchanged a look.

Penn said, 'There is always a choice.'

Their eyes remained linked for longer than was comfortable without embarrassment and she looked away. As one of Penn's best-selling authors her invitation to the gathering was more valid than that of most, but she suspected their friendship was becoming obvious to the guests for they had been talking together for some time.

'Perhaps . . .' she said.

'I think . . .' he said.

Tess turned her head back and caught him looking at her cleavage. She wore a simple black dress gathered at the waist that had a wrap-over top that often bulged and that she wore occasionally to be naughty. It had been quite a while since she had last worn it.

'I'm sorry,' he said.

'For God's sake don't blush.' She smiled and he laughed. 'Your guests wouldn't understand.'

'That's true. But I do apologize.'

'Don't. That's why I wear it. It confirms a truth long known but which I sometimes forget.'

'What's that?'

'That I'm a woman.'

'You are certainly that, dear lady.'

'And right on cue,' she said, diverting his attention with a nod, 'here comes your butterfly.'

Tamara joined them. She did not have a glass in her hand and had not so far accepted a drink. Clever girl, thought Tess, without malice. This was a gathering where it might pay to keep your head. Virginity for them all, she suspected, was long gone but sense and sensibility were still to be treasured.

They exchanged small talk until Penn excused himself.

Tess said, 'I'm so glad I was invited this weekend. I have a project, you see. And Charles said there could be just the right people here to help me.'

'A project?'

Tamara gazed at Tess with total commitment. She had closed the rest of the world out of their private conversation.

It was very flattering and Tess understood how it would impress Charles Penn.

'Yes, with my books. You know about my books?'

'Who doesn't? My friends were totally fractious and forsaken when they heard THE Dr Tess Flanders would be here.'

Fractious and forsaken? Tess laughed with pleasure despite herself.

'Well, that makes it easier for me to explain,' she said. 'I want to go a stage further than the printed word. I want to try to move into a video format. I know there are any number of so-called educational sex videos available, but they are done with about as much passion as a DIY manual on erecting a garden shed.'

Tamara laughed and Tess carried on.

'I want to illustrate the fantasy aspects of sex as a straightforward erotic aid. No pretence. Eroticism doesn't have to be full-frontal nudity and a prick like a piston. You know what I'm saying?'

At this, Tamara laughed out loud.

'I know exactly what you're saying.'

'Well, the point is, I'm looking for a freelance film-maker, video-maker, whatever, to talk it over with, discuss the possibilities. I mean, I had thought I might mention it to Monty but his appearance does not give me confidence.'

'Oh, he's very good,' said Tamara.

'I know he is. But he's legit. Mainstream. Besides, he doesn't look sexy. What I want is someone with sensitivity for the subject matter. Eroticism is a difficult art. Handled badly it can be banal, laughable, stupid. Handled correctly it can be superb.

'The Americans, I have to confess, are not in the running. The French are the masters, but the British have been known to produce real quality when they take it seriously. And I would be much happier making films with an Englishman than a Frenchman, seeing as I don't speak French.'

Tamara nodded and said, 'I see.'

Tess shrugged and tried to look up-front American.

'So I guess I thought I'd ask if you knew anybody. Or anybody who might know anybody? Charles says you have a way of putting people in touch with people.'

The girl flushed with pleasure.

'Yes, I do. And I think I might be able to help you. I have a very good friend, an old friend, who is a video film-maker. Alex Brown. He might be just the man you're looking for.'

'Great,' said Tess. 'Maybe sometime this weekend you can give me his number?'

'I can tell you right now,' she said, and did so.

Tess picked up her bag and from it took a small notepad.

'I never go anywhere without it,' she explained. She opened it and spoke as she wrote, 'Alex Brown, you say?'

'Yes.'

'And the number again?'

Tamara gave her the number and said, 'And give him my love and tell him I said he should help you.'

Tess smiled. 'I'll do that,' she said.

Charles Penn did not stint on alcohol of the finest quality and the majority of his guests succumbed to it in varying degrees. Wines changed with the courses, while champagne was available as an alternative.

Dinner was light, varied and mildly adventurous, and started with mushrooms with filo pastry, and moved onto fish soup with rouille, before main-course options of curried tofu stir-fry, Moroccan chicken with couscous, and chicken livers with currants and sherry.

Monty Radcliffe had all three main courses, Tess noted, and several guests sampled two. She chose the stir-fry and declined the dessert choices of passion fruit syllabub or summer trifle. It was no surprise when Monty again went for both.

He certainly believed in seduction on a full stomach.

The though made Tess shudder. He had had a full stomach before he had started eating.

After dinner, they retired to the games room and its atmosphere of an English pub with recorded music played on a jukebox. Tess found it pleasant although she guessed that as country house parties went, this was an unconventional move.

Jamie, who was getting noticeably drunker, played pool with Charles Penn. Tess had watched the singer's behaviour towards Tamara and noticed they had both been guarded to the point of politeness.

For the first time, Tess found herself alone for a moment and Mark Trimm joined her.

'It's the lady in the window,' he said, without pre-amble.

She had forgotten the incident and had had just enough to drink for it to no longer embarrass her.

'You must be the man in the shrubbery.'

'You make me sound like a Peeping Tom.'

'Were you?'

'I saw you by accident . . .'

Tess laughed and said, 'I've been called many things before but never an accident.'

Mark smiled and continued, 'But if you give me a time

when you are going to do it again I'll make sure I'll be back in the garden for a second showing. Then I will happily be a Peeping Tom.'

'I'm flattered.'

'I enjoyed it. *Will* there be a second show?'

'If it's by arrangement, it's no fun.'

'Who told you that?' he said.

'I'm a sex therapist. I know these things.'

'Well, I don't need therapy but I know what I like. An arrangement would suit me fine.'

'You keep on like this and you'll make me blush.'

'I don't think you blush too easily.'

He kept eye contact with her, all the time they were talking, and she read the sexual interest in his gaze. Maybe she should wear this dress more often. Maybe she should stand in front of windows in her underwear more often.

'Are you going to make a film with Jamie?' she said.

'What a subtle diversion,' he said, but answered her question. 'Maybe. His manager certainly wants it.'

'Has she made you an offer?' she said, with deliberate double meaning.

'I turned that one down. I had this vision of waking up with my body drained of blood.'

Tess laughed, and said, 'But the film might be on?'

'Yes. It's a definite possibility.' He glanced across the room towards where the singer was playing pool. 'Believe it or not, that long-haired lout is a chameleon. Put him on stage or the screen and he suddenly has presence.'

'You're a fan?'

'Not really. But he would be great box office.'

'A refreshing view,' she said. 'I thought you were an idealist.'

209

'I'm a working-class idealist. I like making money as well as movies.'

He was looking into the folds of her dress and Tess felt a pleasant tingle between her legs. She had been such a goddamn control freak for so long that she had forgotten the pleasures of flirting and sexual arousal.

'Enjoying the view?'

She was blatant on purpose.

He lifted his gaze and smiled broadly.

'Very much,' he said. 'I always think black underwear is so sophisticated.'

'On older women?' she taunted, half in self-mockery.

'On *beautiful* women,' he said, with a straight face. 'And you are a beautiful woman, Tess.' He shot a dismissive glance at the room. 'There's no one here to compare with you.'

She laughed and realized it was a defensive device to give herself time to think.

'Thank you, kind sir,' she said. 'You must tell me what you're drinking. I'll make it compulsory at every function I attend.'

He smiled to make her feel at ease.

'I'm only speaking the truth. Of course, you're a therapist and you'll probably put a different interpretation on what I say. You'll probably think, he's only saying that because he wants to get me into bed. And you know what? You'd be right.'

Tess placed her hand on his arm, leaned forward and kissed him on the cheek.

'That is the nicest proposition I've had in a long time,' she said.

'Do I take that as a rebuff?'

'There's a whole weekend ahead, Mark. Who knows?'

210

Liz Bizley and Fiona Mandeville joined them and talk turned once more to the possibility of a film project with Jamie. After a while, Tess was able to disengage and go in search of a bathroom.

The bar area was equipped with traditional lavatories for men and women, but Tess had seen the gothic Delia heading in that direction and so left the games room and went down the corridor to more conventional facilities.

It was quiet out here, away from the music and noise of the bar. The door of the cloakroom was partly open and she pushed it fully open, stepped inside, and closed it softly behind her. As she did so, she realized immediately she was not alone.

The cloakroom was T-shaped. The entrance foyer was the upright and the main area ran lengthways across the top. To the left was an enclosed lavatory cubicle and to the right was a wash basin, vanity mirror, and glass shelves with combs, brushes, scents and deodorants.

This foyer section was lined with coats that acted as soundproofing. The walls of the vanity area were mirrored.

Tess held her breath. The sounds she could hear were unmistakably those of sexual passion. She felt embarrassed and guilty at intruding even though she couldn't see anything. But she could if she peeped round the corner.

The excitement hit the pit of her stomach at the opportunity she had and at what she was about to do.

She took a step forward to get a better look in the angled mirrors and saw full-bloomed English rose Susan double-barrel was leaning over the vanity unit with the skirts of her blue dress up around her waist and her knickers down around her knees.

Jamie Philpott, rock singer and possible future film

star, was behind her with his trousers down, thrusting energetically into her.

The girl's underwear was a blue that matched her dress and the suspender straps were taut across fleshy white thighs that quivered to the shock of Jamie's attack. She gasped in time to each thrust, polite little gasps, that emerged as 'Oh, oh, oh'.

Tess stepped back among the coats and closed her eyes. A flush suffused her face and the desire between her legs that had been a pleasant irritation while she was flirting with Mark Trimm was now molten.

She had walked into this situation unwittingly but stayed because she had wanted to and had become trapped because she had succumbed to the overwhelming urge to watch.

The noises round the corner changed.

'Oh gosh!' said Susan.

'Down,' said Jamie. 'Go down.'

Bodies moved, clothes rustled, and Tess felt in danger of being discovered at any moment as the excitement intensified.

The two people round the corner settled into a new position.

'Mmmmm,' said Susan, and something plopped. 'I don't know if I should . . . mmmmm.'

'Just suck,' said Jamie, his voice impatient, his breathing ragged.

Tess identified the new sounds, stepped away from the coats and once more risked a look in the mirrors.

Susan was sitting on the floor with her back to the wall and her eyes closed, her fingers holding the base of Jamie's engorged penis which was in her mouth. He held her head in both hands and thrust almost as strongly as he had when he had been inside her vagina.

He was, and Tess acknowledged her choice of words, fucking Susan's mouth.

For a second, Tess was horrified but then she realized that Susan did not seem to object. The murmurs that still escaped her throat were ones of pleasure and encouragement.

'Come on, baby. Come on, baby,' he said. 'Oh yes, oh yes, oh yes, I'm coming, I'm coming . . .'

He gasped. His buttocks clenched, Susan gulped and her cheeks and mouth worked as she received his ejaculation. Tess slumped back among the hanging coats and composed herself. Now she had to make a move before she was discovered.

She opened the door silently and slipped outside, took several deep breaths, and then went back in, closing the door loudly behind her.

At the T-junction she stopped and feigned surprise.

'Oh,' Tess said. 'Excuse me.'

Jamie had just finished fastening his jeans but Susan was still sitting on the floor, her expression a little dazed, her lips a little too shiny to be natural.

'Gosh!' she said.

Tess went into the cubicle, closed the door, slumped in the corner to the carpeted floor and breathed a sigh of relief. Maybe later, when she was separated by time and distance from this place, she could write herself a letter and give herself advice and put it all in a new book.

But by God, it had been exciting.

Without being aware of what she had been doing, her hands had pulled back her skirt and her fingers were stroking herself through her panties and oh, it felt so good. She looked down at her legs that stretched before her, shapely and attractive in black stockings, sensual above the stocking tops where the arrowed straps of her garter belt stretched.

Subconsciously she compared her legs with the fleshy thighs of Susan Gosh! and was again swept with guilt: for judging the girl, for the comparison, for becoming a voyeur, for sitting here now, in a lavatory cubicle, touching herself.

But it did feel so good.

Later, she promised herself. Later when she was alone in her room she would forget she was a therapist and become a sexual person and give herself pleasure. But for now, she should sort herself out and get back to the party.

When she left the cubicle she was surprised to find Jamie still in the cloakroom. Ostensibly he was admiring himself in the mirror. He stepped to one side to allow her access to the vanity unit but, in effect, he was blocking the exit.

Tess stared into the mirror, pretending to check her makeup, and watched him watching her. His smile was self-assured. Why should it not be? He never had trouble with girls. They swooned at his feet or, in the case of the English rose, were pushed to the floor and obliged.

'I'm sorry if I interrupted something,' she said lightly.

'You didn't. We'd finished.'

'And so have I,' she said, turning from the mirror and facing him. Her body language said she expected him to move. He didn't.

He reached out with his right hand and stroked her cheek. The smell of the girl's vagina was on his fingers. The aroma was intoxicating.

'There's no need to hurry,' he said.

Tess still could not identify his charisma but she did feel his sexuality. Or perhaps it was the knowledge that he had just fucked another girl and come in her mouth that made her so aroused?

He stepped closer and put his arms around her and,

incredibly, he was kissing her. Her arms remained inert by her side but his tongue was in her mouth and his lips were masticating upon her lips. Equally incredibly, his penis was erect again and was pushing urgently against her abdomen.

For one moment she was on the verge of pushing back, wrapping her arms around him and letting whatever might happen just happen. But she realized the stupidity of the situation and the arrogance of the young man.

This was his choice, not hers. A purely tribal choice. He was not attempting to seduce her because he was madly attracted to her but because she was there and she was female and she was well, dammit, attractively fuckable.

Her anger overrode the dangerous desire that was making her damp between her legs. She put a hand between their bodies and took hold of his penis. He ended the kiss and leaned back and smiled at her. Despite everything, he was still very attractive.

'You want it, don't you?' he whispered.

She dropped her hand lower and cupped his balls and squeezed, just hard enough to remove the smile.

'It's very kind of you to offer, but actually, no, I *don't* want it. At least, not from you.'

Tess squeezed a little harder and he winced and removed his arms. She moved him away from the exit, smiled, and finally released her grip. He exhaled with relief.

'Sorry, Jamie,' she said. 'You're not my type.'

Chapter 17

The evening had started too early with too much drink for it to last very late, although Tess was amused to see that politeness – and the power factor – dictated that the guests waited for Penn to dismiss them rather than simply saying they were tired and going to bed.

She and Penn sat on high stools at the bar and talked. Most of the others had grouped themselves around a table and were engaged in a conversation that seemed to be only vibrant when Mark Trimm was leading it.

Away from the others, Jamie and Tamara were closely ensconced, although the singer now seemed affected by the drink he had consumed.

Penn said, 'Monty told Tamara.'

'Any reaction?'

'Not yet.'

'What did she say when he told her?'

'Not a lot. Apparently she just listened and thanked him for his concern.'

'A wise girl that keeps her own counsel.'

Penn poured her another glass of champagne as Tamara and Philpott crossed the room towards them.

Tamara said, 'Jamie's hungry. I noticed a kitchen behind the bar, Charles. Is there anything for a sandwich?'

'I'm not sure what there is. If he wants anything, call the servants.'

'I wouldn't dream of it,' she said. She dragged Philpott by the arm. He smiled at them drunkenly as he passed. 'I'll fix something.'

Tess watched them go behind the bar and through the open door into a well-lit kitchen area. She was aware that Penn was watching her.

'Have you enjoyed it, so far?' he said.

'It has been an experience I wouldn't have missed for the world.'

'For the quality of intellect?' he said, mockingly.

'For the propositions.'

His eyebrows rose.

'Propositions?'

'Mark made a very charming pass at me.'

'He did?'

'Yes, he did.'

Tess was pleased to see that Penn was confused about how to react.

'What did he say?'

'Well, it's a little complicated. It started when he saw me at my bedroom window.'

Penn gulped but tried to hide it and Tess suppressed a smile.

'At your bedroom window?'

'I was getting undressed and I didn't realize anyone was in the garden.' She shrugged. 'I was admiring the view and, unknown to me – at least, until I saw him – so was Mark.'

'He was looking at you in your underwear?'

'Yes. It was white underwear.' They exchanged a look that lasted a long time and she added, 'And tan stockings.'

Penn spoke at last, with feeling.

'The lucky swine,' he said and, this time, Tess did

smile. 'So he propositioned you and . . . you turned him down?'

'Not quite like that. Not as definite as that. I said there was a whole weekend ahead of us.' She fluttered her eyelashes at Penn. 'Who knows what might happen?'

Penn nodded, his face a mask.

He said, 'You said propositions. Plural.'

'Oh, yes. The second was much more direct. Jamie got me in the cloakroom.'

Penn's eyes widened.

'What did he do?'

'Well, what he did was have sex with Susan in the cloakroom. I walked in on them. Afterwards, when Susan had gone, he tried it on me with me.' She shook her head. 'No finesse.'

'What did he try?'

His thirst for detail was encouraging. She licked her lips, held his gaze and spoke in a low voice.

'He touched my face and I could smell Susan on his fingers. The smell of sex? The smell of her vagina?' Penn shuddered. 'He pulled me to him and kissed me. A real kiss. His tongue was in my throat. He had his erection back already. He pushed it against me. He was very confident and very sexy.'

Penn sucked for saliva and said, 'What happened?'

'I squeezed his balls and he let go.' Tess smiled at the apparent relief in Penn's face. 'Mind you, I must admit I was tempted.'

'You were tempted?'

He sounded shocked.

'Why not, Charles? The whole purpose of this weekend is a sexual investigation. The reason for our meetings has been sexual. You write some pretty steamy stuff, you know, and then I get caught by a twenty-seven-year-old voyeur who tells me I'm beautiful and wants to go to bed with me, and I walk in on a couple fucking in a cloakroom. And I'm not supposed to feel sexy?'

'I'm sorry,' he said. He shook his head helplessly. 'It sounds stupid but because of who you are and what you do, I thought you were above all this, this . . .'

'Fun?'

He laughed.

'For want of a better word.'

Tess placed a hand on his arm.

'I'm a woman, Charles, as well as a therapist. I enjoy sex. I enjoy fucking.' She chuckled and her eyes twinkled. 'And who knows? Mark has a nice sense of . . . fun.'

Penn tried to smile but it was not convincing.

'You always have me on the wrong foot,' he said.

'You're sitting down.'

'You I know what I mean.'

'I guess,' she said. 'By the way, I asked Tamara if she could recommend a man who made dirty movies.'

'You did what?'

'Not in those terms, but that's what it came down to. A guy I could collaborate with to turn my books into erotic films. She recommended Alex Brown.'

'Well, she's not wrong,' said Penn.

'No, but you might think she would be embarrassed by the liaison. Particularly as I talked about making erotic movies. If she was playing safe, his would be the last name she would mention.'

'I see what you mean. But I don't know what it means.'

'It means she has no guilty hang-up about the films she made. That, or she is so naive the thought they

they could be a threat might not have occurred to her. Either way, it means, as you keep saying, that she's an innocent. Guilt and sex don't seem to equate in her mind.'

'And that's good?'

'I think it's good and I think it's honest.' She looked round the room. 'Anyway. These folks are drooping, Charles. I think they're waiting for your blessing so they can go to bed.' She glanced at the group. 'Whose bed they each end up in could be interesting.'

Penn composed himself.

'One certainly is that Monty will be taking Susan back to his room.'

'Well,' said Tess, 'she's already had the main course. She might as well have the pudding.'

A plate fell and smashed in the kitchen. The main conversation stopped and Fiona Manderville, red Renaissance hair flying behind her, went immediately behind the bar and through the kitchen door.

'I think it's time for bed,' said Penn, to the room at large. 'Sleep it off and start again tomorrow. What about it, Monty? Feeling tired?'

'Just a bit, Charles.' The fat man yawned to show he was sleepy. 'Come on, Susan. We'll make a move. I'll walk you up.'

He made it sound as if he were offering a walk home from the prom but the girl decided she needed fortitude and downed a full glass of alcohol before getting up from her seat to go with him.

Mark Trimm and Liz Bizley also prepared to leave and Delia went behind the bar in search of her rock-and-roll client. As she entered the kitchen, Tamara came out and joined Penn and Tess.

'He's just drunk,' said Tamara. 'They know how to cope with him.'

Delia and Fiona now emerged, holding Philpott between them, negotiated the bar and said their goodnights as they left the room. He hung between them apparently incapable of speech.

Tess said, 'Where will he sleep tonight?' She said it almost to herself, not expecting an answer.

Tamara said, 'With Fiona.' She stared after them, and added, 'There is no malice in him, you know. It's just that sometimes he believes the legend. You know, the rock star thing? Especially when he's drunk or drugged. On occasions like this, Fiona is a pretty good minder.'

Penn said, 'She's an unusual minder.'

'Oh, she's good in bed, as well,' Tamara said, and smiled innocently. 'And that's important where Jamie's concerned. He wakes up in the night and wants satisfaction. Fiona will see to it. If she wasn't there, he would probably go looking for someone and then none of us would be safe.'

She smiled sweetly at Tess.

Tess said, 'Then bully for Fiona.' She got down from the stool. 'I'll say goodnight, too. See you both in the morning.'

'Goodnight, Tess,' said Penn.

'Goodnight,' said Tamara, taking a possessive step closer to her man.

Tess gained her room without incident and was happy there was a lock on the door. The last think she wanted was a drunken rock singer attempting to get into her bed.

She turned the key and stood for a moment with her back against the door, enjoying the privacy and the peace of the room. Even the light was an intrusion and she switched it off.

Earlier, her hormones had acted up and she had been as horny as hell. Now she was just tired. Was that because she was a woman of a certain age? Or was it because she didn't have a man?

Tess unzipped the dress, stepped out of it and threw it over a chair. With the electric light still off, she opened the curtains and let the moon shine in. The fields and distant woodland were clothed in silence and moonglow and, combined with the alcohol and a long eventful day, the view was as good as a sleeping pill.

She turned away and looked at her moonglow reflection in the mirror. In this light she could pose for *Playboy*, but even her cynicism could not dilute her pleasure that she really did look pretty damn' good in high heels and black underwear.

For a moment, she contemplated making love to this beautiful stranger in the mirror.

But what the hell, she thought. I'm too tired.

Tess kicked off the shoes but did not bother to remove anything else. She pulled back the covers, got into bed and was soon asleep.

Charles Penn was in the study next to his bedroom. This was unlike any normal study, although it had a conventional desk upon which was a personal computer, a fax and a telephone.

What made it different were the bank of television screens that filled one wall and the second desk, the video control desk at which he sat and through which he could monitor which screens were switched on and which were not, and, more importantly, the hidden cameras that were secreted in many of the rooms of the house.

He had never had to justify this study to anyone because

no one, apart from the technician who had installed it, knew about it. But after the times he had recently spent with Tess, he was beginning to think in terms of justification.

What could he say? He was a voyeur!

Penn did have certain rules when it came to observing the behaviour of guests. He did not have cameras located actually in any lavatories, for instance. For goodness, sake, just because he had a hobby it did not mean he was a pervert.

And one rule he had imposed upon himself at the start of this weekend was that he would not take visual advantage of Tess. He valued her friendship too much to do that. At least, he thought it was friendship.

He had been surprised at his own reaction tonight when she had told him she had been propositioned by Mark Trimm and the appalling Philpott. He had been even more taken aback when she intimated that Philpott might have inadvertently given her a sexual thrill and that she was still considering Trimm's offer.

Maybe he should make arrangements to ensure the second possibility did not come to pass.

Perhaps he had had power for too long. These days he expected and he assumed. If necessary, he demanded. He had even set out to capture Tamara as if tussling with a conglomerate for a takeover. His power had isolated him and made him take things for granted.

Tess he could not take for granted. That was one of the reasons he enjoyed his relationship with her. Another was that she was a beautiful woman and, for chrissakes, of course beautiful women had feelings and needs. He just didn't want them to be fulfilled by Philpott or Trimm.

He stared at the wall. A row of numbered screens flickered dimly: bedrooms with their occupants asleep. In only one room was there a light still on. In bed lay Tamara. She was reading a Catherine Cookson novel.

Penn pressed the keyboard in front of him and brought up, on the monitor screen on his desk, the interior of the cloakroom. The view was from a camera that was fixed above the door of the lavatory and whose lens looked towards the vanity unit rather than into the WC itself.

He pressed a rewind button, waited and pressed 'play'. He checked the time displayed on the screen and fast-forwarded. He found Philpott and Susan, the English rose.

Tess was right. Philpott had no finesse. He acted as if he was doing the girl a favour. What's more, the girl acted as if she thought she was the recipient of one.

Philpott kissed her for a whole five seconds before pulling up her skirts and turning her round. Penn watched with interest as the singer pulled down her knickers and pushed his fingers into her vagina. The girl was shapely, it was true, with an over-large arse that Philpott seemed to enjoy feeling.

Penn had not intended to arouse himself. He had been interested only in watching the encounter between Philpott and Tess, but he could not stop his erection growing as the singer pushed down his trousers and entered the girl from behind.

The power-broking millionaire stood up and undressed as he watched the screen. He removed all his clothing and was naked when he resumed his seat. He watched Philpott bang into the girl from behind, then withdraw and push her to the floor. He watched him push his penis, wet with her juices, into the girl's mouth and he watched her suck it until it disgorged sperm into her throat.

What Penn did not see, because of the restricted position

of the camera, was Tess sneaking a reflected glance in the mirrors from behind the coats.

Penn waited and, sure enough, Tess entered, apologized for her timing and went into the cubicle. The millionaire voyeur stroked his penis while he watched Philpott usher the girl away and then wait for Tess to emerge.

He turned up the sound and listened and watched the verbal exchange, anger flaring at the young man's insolence. Penn's erection stiffened at the sight of Philpott pushing himself against her, and he was relieved and amused when she took hold of his testicles and extricated herself from the situation.

For once, Penn had not wanted the scene to develop sexually in any way whatsoever. He had just wanted Tess to get out of there unscathed and unmolested. If he had been in the corridor outside at the time and had learned what had happened, he knew he would have punched the daylights out of the young shit on the spot.

His feelings for Tess surprised him again. Now he had discovered them it was as if he had removed the plug from a dam and was in danger of being carried away.

He was getting too intense. He needed to relax. He entered new instructions on the keyboard and the monitor screen blanked, the number upon it changed, and he rewound another tape. This time he knew exactly where to stop it and press 'play'.

The bedroom was Monty's. The light was on and the fat television producer was undressing. Sarah, with yet another drink in her hand, was sitting on the edge of the bed. Monty wore baggy white undershorts that flapped, a vest and his socks. He removed the vest, but it didn't improve his machismo.

This was theatre of the absurd and Penn shook his head.

Not the socks, Monty, he said to himself. Not the socks.

Monty removed the underpants. It still didn't help.

'Gosh!' said Susan.

The fat man reached below his stomach and found his penis. It looked like a finger. He massaged it lovingly and Susan drank whatever was in the glass in one gulp. She looked as if she was close to passing out but Penn guessed that wouldn't stop Monty who was now naked apart from his socks.

Penn continued to shake his head.

The socks, Monty, he said to himself. Give yourself a chance and take off your socks. But the advice was ignored.

'Now you,' Monty said. 'Take off the dress.'

Susan was unsteady when she got to her feet but she was a game girl. She unzipped the back of the dress and let it fall from her so that she was revealed in all her glory of overflowing blue brassiere, wide hips, taut suspender straps and impossibly small briefs.

'Oh, my God,' Monty said. 'You're beautiful.'

The girl perked up at the compliment. She smiled, reached behind her and unclipped the bra. The cups flew off, happy to be free. Her breasts were huge and literally outstanding, without the hint of a sag. Her nipples were large brown teats.

'Oh, Susan,' said Monty.

She responded to the reaction and turned her back on him and began to push down those small briefs. Her buttocks were large but shapely, her thighs full. When the garment was at her knees she smiled cheekily at Monty over her shoulder.

Susan dropped the briefs around her feet, stepped out

of them and staggered slightly, causing her flesh to quiver. There was a lot of her but it was all in proportion. She had an hourglass figure, but it was for a twenty-four-hour clock.

Monty seemed overcome by the bountifulness of his good fortune.

'You're gorgeous, darling,' he said. 'Absolutely bloody gorgeous.'

He moved towards her and they grappled. They fumbled together and she fell back onto the bed and he scrambled after her. He reached for the light switch and the room became dark but Penn watched the shadows and listened to the soundtrack.

Monty grunted and was energetic. He made a lot of nuzzling noises. Before long, Susan began to snore gently but it was a long time before Monty finished and did the same.

The activities Penn had watched had been mildly inspirational but he could not get Tess out of his mind. He switched desks and booted up the computer.

He would write another chapter of his experiences with Julia and Rick. He told himself that he was learning more about himself with each confession, each revelation. Like it or not, he was evaluating the incidents and his motives. He was convinced the key to his future lay in his past.

Besides, he wanted to complete another chapter as a present to Tess. She had admitted her own sexual feelings and had made her own confession by saying his erotic writing had affected her. A few more pages might turn up the flame of her passion.

He glanced up at the bank of screens and saw that Tamara was still reading.

How would she like to read his confessions, he wondered? She would find them a little different to Catherine Cookson.

His gaze lingered on the television image of the beautiful young woman and he felt a surge of love and desire.

Was it possible for a man to love two women at the same time?

Or was his attraction to Tamara locked in his past? Was he attempting to embrace youthful beauty because he was getting old? Was he looking for another conquest, another domination?

He looked back at the blank computer screen and felt the urge to write and, with it, the usual anticipation in his genitals.

Penn's fingers moved to the keyboard and he began.

Chapter 18

Charles Penn's story

I suspected we had reached a culmination in our odd three-way relationship the weekend I spent with Rick and Julia. At the back of my mind, I suppose, I realized nothing would be the same again between us. I did not know it would be the last time I would ever see Rick.

Six weeks after that amazing weekend, Julia telephoned me to say he had left her. He had packed a bag, climbed onto his motorcycle and gone.

'Perhaps he'll come back,' I said.

'I don't think so. He said he was going for good.'

Once more I was in a dilemma. Should I visit and offer support and perhaps something else, or should I wait to see if he returned? I wanted to ask if it was my fault, but dared not.

Julia let me off the hook by saying she would call again in a week if there was any news.

'I need time to think, Charlie,' she said. 'But I remember what you said. If I need you . . . ?'

'I still mean it, Julia. Just call.'

The next time she telephoned was to tell me Rick had been killed in a motorcycle accident in Scotland. Her parents were travelling to be with her and my presence was not immediately required.

I went to the funeral, which was a small affair, but drove home again afterwards. Julia was still in the care of her parents, but I knew she would eventually call. She did, three weeks later.

She was back at her own home, the home she had shared with Rick. Remarkably, for someone who aspired to be one of the wild ones, he had been well insured. Julia would be the beneficiary of several thousand pounds and she was keeping the house, at least for the time being.

'Charles,' she said, 'I need you.'

My days as 'Charlie' and 'Brains' were over. She only ever called me Charles after that.

I drove there, not knowing if I would be staying a few hours or a few days. It was odd, seeing her on her own. It felt as though a part of us was missing. Rick had always been the motivator and the instigator, whether it had been in conversation, the direction of Julia's life, or sex.

But his absence had a liberating affect upon Julia. We sat in the front room on a rainy afternoon and talked. And this time, she took control.

She wore that same flimsy black skirt with the floral pattern she had worn at the canal. The same pink V-neck sweater, black stockings and high heels. I thought she was the most alluring woman I had ever seen and I kept casting what I thought were surreptitious glances at her legs.

'Marrying Rick was a mistake,' she said. 'I know that now. I was so young when I met him, so impressionable. He took me over.' She shrugged. 'I did everything he said. Everything.' She lowered her eyes and I looked at her legs. 'You know what I mean.'

'Yes,' I said.

'Well, with you, it didn't seem wrong. You were a good friend. More than a friend. I knew how you felt about me, and I think, even then, I was a little bit in love with you.'

Her revelation shook me so much I looked up from her legs and into her face. She raised her eyes and smiled at me.

I said, 'I was always in love with you.'

'I know. Which was why, when Rick wanted me to do things, I didn't mind because I thought I was giving you something. You know, giving you some kind of pleasure.'

'You did,' I confessed.

'And because we never did it, make love I mean, somehow that kept our love pure.' Her eyes were as big and as innocent as those of the sixteen-year-old I remembered in her school uniform. 'Does that make sense?' she added, wistfully.

'Yes,' I said.

I would have agreed to anything. I wondered if she still had the school uniform.

'It's strange, Charles, but when you went away and Rick and I got married, the excitement seemed to go out of our relationship. Rick was in a rut and didn't like his job, didn't like the house. I think he no longer liked me.'

'No. Not that,' I said, fervently.

'Then when you came back, he changed. He changed after your first phone call.' She blushed and looked down at her hands in her lap before steeling herself to raise her eyes and meet mine. 'The physical side of our marriage hadn't been very good until then. But when you called and he knew you were coming to see us, just the thought excited him.'

'Excited him?' I prompted.

Julia nodded. 'That night we made love, passionately.' Her blush deepened. 'No, not love. It wasn't making love.

It was more basic than that. It was just doing it. You know what I mean. I can't say the word, but you can.'

I gulped and said, 'Fucking.'

'Yes,' she said. 'That.'

'I'm sorry.'

'No, don't be. Women have appetites, you know, as well as men. And we hadn't done anything for a long time. It's probably terrible for me to admit it, but I enjoyed it. I mean, we all need to relieve our tensions, don't we?'

'Of course.'

'That weekend,' she said, 'Rick seemed to want to go as far as he could. There was no arguing with him when he was in that mood.' She gave me a tight smile. 'In a way, it was quite a relief. When he took charge I didn't have to make any decisions. I just did what he said, even if what he said was shocking. It was his decision, not mine.' She nibbled her bottom lip. 'If anybody was guilty it was him, not me.' She shook her head helplessly. 'Do you know what I mean?'

'Yes,' I said. 'I know exactly what you mean.'

I did, too. I had got used to letting him dictate the sexual action with Julia, both when I had been a witness and when I had been involved. He had accepted the responsibility for the three of us. I had been released from all decisions and all guilt. All I had had to do was be there. Now Julia was saying the same thing.

'That weekend,' she said, 'it seemed like he was possessed. In a way, it was catching. I hope you don't think too badly of me, Charles, for what happened with those two men?'

'Of course not, Julia.'

Just hearing her refer to it made my trousers throb.

'I mean, once they had seen what Rick was doing to me, I couldn't avoid it, could I?'

'No, you couldn't.'

'There was no point resisting, was there?'

'No.'

'So I had to let them do what they did to me, didn't I?'

I thought my trousers might explode but I nodded.

'You had to.'

'The fat one.' She shuddered. 'His belly was so flabby. When he pushed it against me . . .' I wanted to touch myself but dared not. 'When he pushed my legs open and put it in me. Put it inside me . . .'

Julia was not making strict grammatical sense. I remember thinking that at the time. But her words were more powerful than those of Hemingway.

'Yes?' I said.

'He was so strong,' she said, not looking at me, her eyes lowered. I stared at her knees that had drifted apart with the drama of the telling and I was trying to pierce the shadows beneath the skirt. 'So strong. He was big, too. His . . . you know, you can say it, I can't . . .'

'His prick.'

'Yes, his . . . prick . . . was big.'

Julia shuddered and I shuddered. I didn't think I could take much more.

'He was a big man,' I said.

'When he came . . . when he came inside me . . . he shook so much I thought he might damage me. Oooh.' She pressed her knees together momentarily and then crossed her legs. 'He was very powerful when he came. Inside me, I mean.' Her skirt gaped at the side and I could see the top of her stocking. 'He flooded me.'

I said, 'It wasn't your fault, Julia.'

'I know.' She looked up at me, her face red, and flashed

a smile. 'It was Rick's fault. Rick's decision. All I had to do was let it happen.' She shuddered again and her eyes closed. 'It was a glorious freedom, you know. A glorious freedom.'

'I know,' I said softly, and she opened her eyes and stared at me.

'Yes, I think you do,' she said.

'That day, I did nothing to stop it,' I said. 'I let Rick make the decision. I didn't interfere. I felt the freedom, too. A different kind of freedom. I don't know what you thought, never did know what you thought. Maybe you thought I was weird. But I loved you, I always will love you, and watching other people do those things to you seemed to make that love stronger.'

(Note to Tess: now that I am writing this with the benefit of hindsight, the passing years and our several chats, I can see that Julia and I were talking a fair percentage of claptrap. We wanted to delude ourselves. Or at least, give ourselves reasons to continue playing games.)

Julia smiled at me.

'I never thought you were weird, Charles. I thought you were loyal. And I was pleased that weekend that, for once, you too were able to get at least some satisfaction.'

'It was incredible,' I said, and momentarily lowered my gaze, for now I was blushing.

'You came twice,' she said. I looked up again and saw that she was smiling shyly. How had she known about the second time? I thought she had been asleep. 'I enjoyed it when you came,' she said.

I gulped and said, 'So did I.'

My erection had become painful and perhaps it showed in my face.

'Are you all right, Charles?' she said. 'You don't look comfortable.'

'I'm not,' I said.

'Why . . . ?' She stopped what she had been about to say and realization dawned. 'I'm sorry,' she said, and raised her hand to her mouth. 'How thoughtless of me. I've caused you to become aroused, haven't I?'

I was surprised she knew, but I nodded.

'It's my fault,' I said.

'No, it isn't. I should have known. Rick knew. When the three of us were together? He used to tell me afterwards that he could see it in your face, how aroused you were, how uncomfortable it could be. I'm sorry, Charles. Do you want to go to the bathroom or something?'

'Yes, I think I should,' I said.

Julia smiled and thoughtfully diverted her eyes as I got to my feet and limped from the room to go upstairs to the bathroom. I unfastened my trousers, gave my erection its freedom and breathed a sigh of relief. I bathed it in cold water but it wouldn't go down. There was a knock on the door.

'Are you all right, Charles?'

'Yes. Fine.'

I repackaged my prick more comfortably, fastened my trousers and opened the door. Julia was on the landing.

'It's my fault,' she said, and stepped closer to me. Her hand found the bulge in my trousers. 'I think perhaps it's time we took care of it properly.'

She was very close although the only point of contact was her hand on my erection. I thought she had never looked so beautiful and I could have remained standing there, admiring her for a long time, except I realized she was waiting to be kissed. So I kissed her.

Julia came into my arms and our mouths opened and our tongues met. My prick was now pressing against her body.

When the kiss broke, she said, 'Come on,' and led me into the bedroom. The curtains were closed, the bed covers were pulled down and the white-sheeted mattress waited for us. She lay down on the bed and pulled me with her. We kissed again.

'Undress me,' she whispered. 'Touch me. Do anything you want to me. Everything you ever dreamed.'

What a wonderful invitation and, at first, it was a wonderful experience. I pushed up her sweater and she raised her arms so that I could pull it over her head and throw it to the floor. My mouth went down over her skin and I pulled down her bra cups and tasted her breasts.

As I sucked, I ran my hand up her leg, beneath the skirt, my palm sliding from stocking to warm flesh to soft buttock. This was heaven.

Her bra came away and then the skirt. When she pulled at my shirt I ripped it off and felt her naked breasts against my chest as we kissed. My hands went into her panties and felt the soft globes of her bottom.

'Take them off,' she murmured, her breath ragged.

I pulled her panties down her legs and off over her feet. But when I lay against her again and my hand began to move towards her vagina I panicked. My erection began to wane.

'What's wrong?' she said, but I didn't know how to tell her. She held my head in her hands and gazed into my face. 'You've never done it, have you?' she said.

'No,' I confessed.

She kissed me tenderly and I thought I saw a new excitement in her eyes.

'Then I'll teach you,' she said. Her hand tugged at my trousers. 'Take them off.'

I rolled to the edge of the bed, pulled off my shoes and socks and remembered the last time I had done this and how Rick had fucked her while I lay alongside: my erection returned. I pushed off my trousers and underpants and rolled back onto the bed alongside her.

Julia took my hand and placed it on her vagina.

'Feel it,' she said. 'Touch it. Explore it.'

She let me do exactly that while we kissed, my prick pressing against her thigh: I discovered how the lips of her sex parted, I found the wetness inside and I pushed a finger into her.

After a while, she guided my fingers so that I explored the full dimensions and complexities of the folds of flesh that guarded that hot greedy mouth between her legs.

'There,' she said, pressing one of my fingers at the apex of her sex. She rubbed herself against my finger and moaned. 'Just there.'

I had found her clitoris and realized this was the spot that Rick had massaged to make her come. I was determined to do the same. Julia repositioned my fingers when they strayed but her response was gratifying. Her breathing shortened and she curled against me and yelled out and orgasmed, shuddering on my hand.

My prick still throbbed and my urgency still pulsed but it took her a few moments to recover. She kissed me and then guided my head downwards.

'Down there,' she whispered.

Willingly I slid down her body, lay between her legs and gazed upon her open sex for the first time. It was my intention to use my mouth on her but she held my head away and touched herself.

'Watch,' she whispered.

I watched her fingers work, how they rolled and rubbed the clitoris, and how she held it while pushing three fingers of her other hand inside her vagina. I listened to the noises and inhaled her smell and watched and learned as she brought herself to orgasm.

Now she allowed me to offer my ministrations. My fingers slid inside her and emerged wet, and I held apart the lips of her sex, gazed at the pink interior, smelled that glorious aroma and, without a second thought, covered her vagina with my mouth and made love to her.

My enthusiasm seemed to please her and she writhed beneath my suckings and lickings. Then she guided me again to her clitoris and I began to learn the art of cunnilingus and to relish the glorious feel of soft flesh above black nylon.

Julia came again and then pulled me up to lie against her. She took hold of my stiff prick and said, 'Your turn, Charles.'

She guided me on top of her and opened her legs so that my prick lay between her thighs. I could feel the heat of her wet furnace.

'Put it in,' she whispered.

I reached between us and tried to guide it but my inexperience made me clumsy. Her hands joined mine and by example she showed me how to part the folds of flesh and guide the head of my penis into her tunnel.

The glans went in and I gasped at the heat.

'Push it in,' she said.

I hardly dared. It felt as if it would be consumed by fire. It also felt on the brink of coming, so I sank it inside her and cried out and was consumed. I came and came and probably passed out.

The Voyeur

When my senses returned, I was still lying upon her and she was holding me in her arms and cooing to me like a baby. My prick had softened but was still inside her.

'I'm sorry,' I said.

'It was fantastic,' she said. 'It's always quick the first time.'

Eventually I slid from her body and lay alongside her. I wondered how long it would be before my erection returned. I needn't have worried. Julia now slid down the bed and took hold of my flaccid penis that glistened with her juices, put it into her mouth and sucked.

Memories of that other night in this very bed came back, of how she had sucked her husband's prick. Earlier memories of how she had sucked the prick of the elderly man in that derelict shed by the canal. My erection returned.

She slid back up the bed, kissed me and said, 'Now do it again.'

I got back on top of her. This time I fitted it into her vagina myself and was able to enjoy the experience without exploding. God, but it was exquisite. Because of Julia I had kept myself away from other women. What had I been missing?

We fucked and she came. I turned her over and fucked her from behind, reaching round to find her clitoris, and she came again and so did I, sinking against the softness of her bottom.

Julia pulled the covers over us and we slept for a little while. I awoke because she was sucking my prick. We fucked and sucked again and she had three more orgasms but I was back in control of mine. She was insatiable and when I began to tire she told me of the things Rick had made her do, relived the times I had been there and told me of others when I hadn't.

My jealousy fuelled my desire once more and I continued to fuck her with vigour.

'No secrets,' she kept saying. 'We must have no secrets. You must do everthing.'

Eventually she rolled onto her stomach and when I climbed upon her back she moved her buttocks and directed me to another entry point.

'You must do it there as well,' she said. 'He did. So must you.'

The entry into her anus was more difficult. But I was now familiar with her body and, in truth, I did want to do everything her husband had done, as a way of staking my claim.

We managed it and here was a new delight for this grip was tighter and more intense.

'Fuck me,' she whispered, and I did and came that way, inside her.

Call us hasty, but we were married within a month. I had all those pent-up years of sexual frustration to shed and she remained insatiable.

The wedding was quiet: the neighbours did not approve of the speed with which Julia had found someone new but we were unconcerned. We had a full sex life to keep us occupied except, pretty soon, we didn't.

Now we were married, there was no danger, no excitement. I found I had to use memories of the past to get an erection. Then I began to fantasize about taking Julia to the canal again and finding two men to fuck her. But I found that fantasy was a remedy with a short lifespan unless it was put into practice.

I think we both began to panic that we had made a huge mistake, for now the mystery had gone: I had got used to her shy and innocent glances and had experienced her insatiable appetite for sex.

We still declared our love and we slept in each other's arms but I was finding it increasingly difficult to perform the act. The turning point came when we were invited to a fancy-dress party by someone at the bank where Julia worked. That was the time when I discovered that Julia really did still have her old school uniform.

I was watching television in the living room one evening when she came downstairs and held it up. She had been looking for something to wear to the party.

'What do you think?' she said.

'Oh, yes,' I said.

She noticed the tone of my voice.

'I'd better try it on,' she said.

Julia went back upstairs and I wondered what I had let myself in for. The idea of her in the uniform had been appealing. She would be adopting a different persona, she would be sweet sixteen again and I could take advantage of her. But could I? Would I be able to?

She came back downstairs and into the room and my prick stiffened. The gymslip was navy blue and was short. She wore a white blouse beneath it and a school tie, and black stockings and flat shoes.

'Well?' she said.

'You look lovely,' I said.

Julia stood in front of me and I hesitated about putting my hand up her skirt. If I committed myself would I be able to deliver?

'I was wearing this when I met Rick,' she said, in a low voice. 'I was wearing this when he . . . did it to me the first time.' She licked her lips. 'When he fucked me for the first time.'

My hand slid up her skirt and went above her stockings onto her flesh.

'How old were you?' I asked, a tremble in my voice.

'Just sixteen,' she said. 'Let's go upstairs. I'll tell you what he made me do.'

We went upstairs and Julia told me what he had made her do and how he had fucked her and I became a voyeur by proxy. But it worked and I fucked her.

Afterwards, I sensed this had been a one-off. I could not survive on memories and stories. I realized that unless we found some way of maintaining the excitement our marriage was doomed. We found the excitement at the party.

Julia wore her school uniform with her hair in bunches, and I went as a vicar, a look which was easy enough to achieve by wearing a black T-shirt and a loose white collar the wrong way round beneath an ordinary suit. Needless to say, it was Julia's outfit that evoked most comment and interest.

The party was held in a large detached house with French windows at the back that opened into an extensive conservatory. Our relationship had become fragile and she had rather a lot to drink in a short time. It almost seemed as if she were flirting with other men on purpose and I watched as she danced with one after the other of them.

She took delight in flicking up her skirt to show the tops of her stockings, or spinning so that the pleated gymslip flared. The men were laughing but I could read their expressions. I found myself getting excited.

When I danced with her she pushed herself against me.

'You're hard,' she said.

'And you're a naughty girl.'

'I can be naughtier.'

Later, as the party progressed and the lights got dimmer, I watched her smooching with a young man as they danced. Watched his hands touch her bottom and pull her closer against him. Later still, I noticed them slip away together. I followed them into the room at the rear of the house. This was quieter and darker, and another couple were already occupying a settee.

'Sorry,' I murmured, and noticed the French windows closing as Julia and her conquest went into the conservatory.

My pulse was racing as I went through the house and into the kitchen. Two men and a woman were pouring beer and joking.

'More beer, vicar?' one of them said, and they all laughed.

'No, thanks,' I said. 'I need some fresh air.'

They nodded in understanding, and I went out of the door and round the back of the house in the darkness. It was almost autumn but I didn't feel the cold. I removed the white collar from around my neck and pushed it into a pocket as I approached the conservatory.

There were dim lights inside that gave it an unearthly glow. The lights also allowed me to see Julia and the man. Her back was against the locked glass-panelled door that led into the garden and he was in her arms. They were kissing and her hips were moving, even writhing, against him. I melted into the shadows alongside and crouched to watch, separated only by a panel of glass.

His hands moved over her buttocks, down over the pleats of the gymslip, and beneath the skirt. His palms caressed the backs of her thighs, partly on the stocking tops and partly on her flesh, and then he lifted his hands, sweeping up the skirt as he gripped her black-pantied bottom.

It was all happening at eye level beyond glass that was so thin I could hear them gasping and grunting in each other's arms. His hands went up to the waist of her panties and his left slid inside and pushed down the nylon material as it cupped her flesh. His right hand also went inside them at the front and I could tell from her gasp and the way she pivoted that he was delving at her vagina.

'No, no,' she muttered. 'You mustn't.'

'But you want it,' he said.

She squirmed against his fingers and squealed and put her hands between their bodies as if to fend him off.

'My husband might find us,' she said.

'No, he won't. Not in here.' The man gasped and Julia yelped. 'Oh, but you are so wet,' he said.

I could hear his fingers working between her legs.

'No,' she said, but it was a denial without much conviction.

'You need to come,' he whispered. 'Let me make you come.'

Julia gave up the fight and allowed him to do what he wanted. Her arms went around his neck and they kissed as he masturbated her with his right hand, while his left pulled and groped at her buttocks.

Their mouths broke apart and she began to gasp as she shuddered against him, hanging from his neck.

'Did you enjoy it?' he said.

'Yes.'

'Then my turn. Quick. Before your husband comes.'

He did not know how true were the words he spoke. I crouched there in the shadows with my prick stiff in my trousers. I had not felt this level of excitement since Julia had taken my virginity, since Rick had fucked her while I lay alongside them in the bed, since he had fucked her in the wood as I supported her in my arms.

I heard him unzip his trousers and saw Julia put her hands between them but that was not enough for him. He put his hands on her shoulders and pushed her down.

'Suck it,' he said.

'No,' she whispered. 'Not here.'

'Suck it!'

He was taking no argument and she sank beneath the pressure. They half-turned so that I could see her crouched in front of him, his prick held in her hands. He held her head and pulled it forward impatiently: she opened her mouth, accepted his prick and sucked.

The man held her head in place, his hips moving backwards and forwards. As he fucked her mouth, I crouched inches away, watching, and almost came in the dark. But I controlled myself and admired her technique, the very same technique she used on me, watching her cheeks hollow and bulge and her fingers working the base of his shaft.

It was not long before he came and she swallowed repeatedly, seemingly greedy for his spunk. When his limp little prick slid from between her lips she licked the corners of her mouth like a satisfied cat.

He helped her to her feet and said, 'We'd better go. My wife will wonder where I've been.'

All his assurance had been shed with his spunk.

'You go first,' she said. 'I'll follow in a few minutes.'

I heard him go quickly through the conservatory and the other door open and close. Julia turned and stared into the night: slowly she dipped her gaze, stared down at me and smiled knowingly.

She unlocked the door against which she had been leaning.

'Come in,' she whispered. 'You'll get cold.'

I went inside and she locked the door behind me. She

leaned back against it, as she had with the man she had just fellated, and I put my arms around her. I looked into her face that looked so innocent yet which, I knew, held so much sensual desire.

We kissed and I pushed my tongue in her mouth and imagined it was still slick with the man's sperm. I remembered Rick doing the same thing, and my hands went beneath the skirt of her gymslip and into her panties and she pushed herself against my iron prick.

When our mouths parted she said, 'Did you like it?'

'Yes.'

'I knew you would.'

We kissed some more, yet even as I mauled at her and pushed my fingers between her legs I knew that what I had seen was not enough, that I wanted more. I rubbed her clitoris and she orgasmed quickly on my fingers and I breathed in her breath that carried the smell of alcohol and sex.

She knew me. I think she knew me better than I knew myself.

'Shall we go back to the party?' she said.

The party lasted another hour before people began to leave and those who remained were either extremely drunk or amorous or sometimes both.

Julia had been dancing with another young man. He was small and dark and although they had moved very closely together and had kissed he had been aware of my presence and had not attempted to go too far towards indecency. She introduced him to me as Jonathon.

'I said we'd give Jonathon a lift home,' she said, with a smile. 'That's okay, isn't it, Charles? Jonathon lives quite near us.'

'That's fine,' I said. 'Are we ready to go now?'

Julia got in the back of the car with Jonathon and I drove. I sensed he was nervous.

'It's all right, Jonathon,' I said. 'I'm a good driver and I haven't had much to drink.'

'He's been saving himself,' said Julia, with an intoxicated giggle.

Jonathon laughed, still nervous.

'It's all right,' he said. 'I'm not worried.'

I suddenly realized that it was in my power to put him at his ease and to control what happened.

'You two should cuddle up,' I said. 'It takes this heater ages to work. Give him a goodnight kiss, Julia. It won't be long before we're there.'

'My lord and master,' she said. And then, more softly to the young man. 'Kiss me, Jonathon. We must do what he tells us to.'

They kissed and I watched from time to time in the mirror. After an initial reluctance, Jonathon was won over and returned Julia's kisses. Her hand reached between his legs and his went beneath her skirt.

My erection was back and stronger than ever. I stroked it in my trousers as I drove.

I parked in the drive of our house and only when the engine stopped did they break apart.

'Coming in for a coffee, Jonathon?'

'Well, I don't know . . .'

'Of course you are,' said Julia.

We went inside, into the front room where I had sat and watched while Rick had fucked and sodomized Julia that first weekend. The front room was planned to her mother's design, with its nice, respectable decorations and ornaments. The front room where respectability was about to be defied again.

Jonathon sat on the settee and I got a bottle of wine from the kitchen. When I returned with it, Julia was next to him. She broke away from him and left him looking guilty.

I poured the wine and we sipped and made small talk for a few minutes. Julia sat low in the settee next to him and stretched her legs out. Because the skirt was short, the darker welts at the top of her stockings could be seen.

'Did the girls look like that when you were at school, Jonathon?' I said.

He shook his head, looking down at her legs.

'Not nearly so beautiful.'

Julia said, 'What a lovely thing to say.'

She leaned over to kiss him. The skirt slid a little higher and now a suspender tab could be seen.

'My wife does have nice legs, doesn't she?' I said.

'Yes.'

'Show him, Julia. Show Jonathon your legs.'

Her eyes widened and she gave me her innocent look.

'Should I?' she said.

'Yes,' I said. 'Lift your skirt and show Jonathon your legs.'

Julia slid up the pleated skirt of the gymslip, revealing her flesh above the stocking tops and the black suspender straps. Jonathon stared and licked his lips. His face was flushed and he had no idea in what he was involved, as naive as I had been when Rick had put on that first show for me.

'All the way, Julia,' I said, and she pulled the skirt up around her hips so that the tight V of her black panties could also be seen. 'You can touch if you want, Jonathon,' I said, and he glanced at me, startled. 'Touch her.'

He put his right hand on her knee and slid it slowly

upwards across the nylon stocking. When his palm reached her flesh he paused and looked at me.

'Go on,' I urged gently.

His palm crossed onto her skin and Julia closed her eyes and bit her lip and turned her head away, as if embarrassed by what was happening. He hesitated.

'Touch her between her legs, Jonathon,' I said. 'Feel how wet she is.'

The young man dipped his fingers between her thighs. Julia gasped softly.

'Open your legs, Julia,' I said. 'Let Jonathon touch you.'

Her thighs opened and his fingers slid onto the black nylon of her panties. She moaned.

'She's wet, isn't she?' I said.

'Yes,' he murmured.

'You naughty girl,' I said. 'Wetting your knickers. And getting Jonathon stiff in his trousers. You are stiff, aren't you, Jonathon?'

'Yes,' he said, helplessly.

'Stand up, Julia.' I gave my voice added authority, and she stood up. 'Take off the gymslip.'

After all that had happened so far this evening, she still managed to look shocked and glanced shamefacedly at Jonathon.

'Must I?' she said.

'Yes. Do it.'

Her fingers unfastened the buttons at the waistband and then those at the shoulders and let the gymslip slip slowly down her body. She held it by the straps as it pooled at her feet. Now she was just wearing a white blouse and a tie over her underwear. The blouse only reached her hips and her delicious legs were fully revealed.

I pointed at the gymslip and motioned for her to discard it. She stepped out of it and laid it to one side.

'And now the panties,' I said.

Her hand went to her mouth and she gasped, a picture of innocence-in-pigtails about to be ravished.

'My panties?'

'Take them off,' I said.

She licked her lips, her face pink, hooked her thumbs into the waistband of the panties and slid them down. Jonathon gulped as he watched their removal. She had to bend forward to step out of them and his mouth dropped open as he stared at her naked bottom.

I held out my hand and she stepped forward and dropped the panties into it.

'Now I think it's time you apologized to Jonathon for leading him on and giving him an erection.'

'I'm sorry, Jonathon,' she mumbled, without looking at him.

He shook his head. He was beyond speech.

'That's not good enough, Julia,' I said. 'His prick is uncomfortable in his trousers. Kneel down and get it out.'

'What?' he said, and his hand went to his crotch.

'It's all right, Jonathon,' I said. 'She made you stiff so it is only fair she does something about it. Kneel,' I said to Julia.

She knelt in front of him and parted his legs. My own erection was throbbing with anticipation.

'Take it out,' I said, enjoying the feeling of being totally in control.

Julia unfastened the young man's trousers. At first he made a token resistance and then he slumped back on the settee, utterly bewildered by the turn of events. I got up from my chair and went and sat next to him on the settee. He was still nervous but his prick was huge.

She held it in both hands and gazed up with those big eyes at me.

'Suck it,' I said.

Her mouth opened and the tip of her tongue ran around her lips.

'Must I?' she whispered.

'Suck,' I said.

Jonathon shuddered, his eyes fixed on this beautiful creature between his legs. She licked her lips again, dipped her head and took his prick in her mouth.

He groaned as his head fell back and his eyes closed. Her head moved up and down upon his prick and I slid off the settee to kneel on the floor next to her so that I could watch more closely.

Julia was an expert at sucking cock and an expert at lewd behaviour calculated to send me wild. She held Jonathon's prick by the base and lifted her lips from it, her mouth slack and open, saliva glistening on her teeth, and rubbed the glans across her face with calculation. And all the time those big innocent eyes were fixed on mine.

I knelt and watched as she resumed sucking and I ran my hand up her leg, over her thigh and across her buttocks. I reached around and dipped my fingers into her vagina which was open and wet. I pushed my thumb inside her and she contracted around it as I reached between her legs with my fingers, found her clitoris and rubbed it gently.

She groaned and moved her hips. Her eyes closed and her little-girl act was forgotten for the moment as she concentrated and came, shaking, while all the time the young man's prick was buried in her throat.

When her eyes opened again I removed my fingers, raised

them to my mouth and, while she watched, sucked them clean as an offering to her depravity. Then I got up, went back to my chair and revived myself with the perfume of her panties.

Jonathon's eyes were open but they were glazed.

'I think my wife needs fucking, Jonathon,' I said.

'What?'

'Julia?' I said.

'Mmmm?'

She raised her head from its work and waited.

'Ask Jonathon to fuck you.'

'Must I, Charles?'

'Yes. You must.'

'Must I say the word?'

'Yes.'

She looked up at the young man and said, in a tremulous voice, 'Please. Will you . . . fuck me?'

He raised his startled gaze from her face and stared at me for guidance.

'Don't disappoint her, Jonathon. Say you will.'

Jonathon looked back into her face and said, 'All right.' He stroked her cheek tenderly. 'If you want me to.' He was still unsure whether she was a willing partner in the proceedings.

'I think from behind, Jonathon,' I said. 'Just as she is, actually.'

Julia sat back on her haunches and Jonathon moved his legs. She leaned back onto the settee, her face in the cushions, her arms spread, her buttocks raised. He knelt behind her, his trousers loose and around his hips. He hesitated a moment and looked over his shoulder at me.

'Are you sure?' he said.

'Totally.'

He reached between Julia and himself, adjusted his position, and pushed forward. His gasp declared his entry and he held her hips as his head tilted back again.

'Oh, my God,' he muttered, and began to thrust with short desperate strokes. 'Oh, my God.'

His body convulsed forward over her back and he came inside her. When his twitches stopped he slumped backwards and, for a moment, sat on the carpet, still bewildered. Julia did not move.

Now that his sexual needs had been dealt with, he seemed to become more aware of, and embarrassed by, the situation. He knelt up and fastened his trousers. He glanced at me with a nervous smile.

'You can let yourself out,' I said, calm and in control.

'What? Oh, yes.'

He got to his feet and hesitated as if unsure whether or not to say goodnight, for I was ignoring him and staring at Julia who was still kneeling in front of the settee with her buttocks in the air.

As he got to the door, he said, 'Goodnight,' but I did not answer. I listened to the front door slam shut behind him.

I dropped to my knees from my chair and unfastened my trousers. My prick was huge and firm and throbbing. I shuffled across the carpet to Julia and, without ceremony, pushed it deep into her vagina.

'Oh, yes,' she murmured, her sex muscles tightening around it. 'Oh yes, fuck me.'

And I did, with great pleasure and enjoyment and control. I fucked her until she whimpered and came again. I laid her on the carpet, knelt over her head, pushed my prick into her mouth and she sucked and bucked and moaned. And I then lay upon her, put my mouth to her sex and sucked her in return, tasting her juices and another man's semen as she came wildly.

Finally, I turned her once more and laid her upon the settee, her face pressed against the back cushions, her body spreadeagled against them, and I sodomized her in memory of Rick. She screamed and cried out and scrabbled with her fingers at her vagina to give herself one last orgasm and I came upon her shudders.

(I've enjoyed writing this, Tess, but it is very arousing and very draining. Am I getting there? Am I ridding myself of Julia? Or have I invented a new form of voyeurism?)

Chapter 19

Tamara stayed in bed the next morning. Jamie Philpott went horse riding with Susan, who was remarkably perky after a night in Monty Radcliffe's bed. Monty was not feeling quite so bright. He disappeared to the library with a pot of coffee and the morning newspapers.

Mark Trimm was called back to London by an urgent telephone call, Liz and Fiona retired to the swimming pool, and gothic Delia went with them to observe.

Tess opted for a walk on her own. Penn took the latest instalment of his manuscript to her room before she went. She held his gaze as she accepted it.

'Will it turn me on?' she said, without guile.

'I sincerely hope so.'

'You know, one of these days I may just spontaneously combust.' He laughed and she smiled. 'Maybe I should take Mark up on his offer when I get back.'

'Mark had to leave,' Penn said. 'Urgent business.'

Tess raised an eyebrow.

'How unfortunate.'

'Yes. Isn't it?'

'Then I shall see you later,' she said, but without inflection, and closed the door before she could see the smile on his face.

Penn went back to his study. He thought that today he might try a small test. A two-way test, one that would measure both Tamara's willingness to, perhaps, love and obey, and the nature of his own feelings towards the girl.

He watched the television screens. At the swimming pool, Fiona was for once actually showing signs of life. Left alone together, she and Liz, the attractive writer, had become friendly.

Alone together? Where was the gothic Delia?

He found her entering Tamara's bedroom. He transferred the image to his desk monitor and turned up the sound. Tamara was propped up in bed watching an American chat show on television, the sort where dysfunctional families tell all about incest and cross-dressing while the host feigns interest and gets them to divulge that extra revelation.

The drapes were still closed across the windows and the television screen gave the room a changing rainbow glow.

Delia said, 'God, what a bore.'

The woman crossed to the bed. She wore black trousers and a black sweater and carried a black satchel, which she dropped on the floor. She lay upon the bed alongside the girl.

Tamara said, 'Who looked after Jamie?'

'Both of us. When he woke up, Fiona gave him a blow job.'

'He's just a child, really.'

'For a child he has a rather large appendage between his legs. You may remember, he has the urge to stick it into anything that is warm and wet.'

'I remember.'

'You sound as if you miss him?'

'I do. But he's so unpredictable. One day he'll grow up.'

They watched television in silence for a while. Then Penn noticed that Delia was watching Tamara rather than the screen. She was staring at her breasts which were barely contained in a wispy white silk nightdress.

Delia touched Tamara's shoulder and ran her fingers down her arm. Tamara did not stop watching television. The older woman slipped the nightdress from the girl's shoulder, baring her breasts, and cupped one. Tamara sighed.

The woman turned her head, leaned forward and kissed the girl's neck. Tamara's eyes closed.

'You shouldn't,' she said.

Delia had rolled onto her side and leaned over the girl. 'Shut up,' she said.

The girl whimpered and the black-haired woman kissed the lissome girl on the lips, holding her head between her hands. When she lifted her mouth away, Delia looked like a vampire.

'Please, don't,' said Tamara.

'You will do as I say, slut.'

Delia got off the bed and pulled the sweater over her head. She wore no bra and her breasts were small and round with pert nipples. She dropped the sweater on the carpet as she walked back to the bedroom door, which she locked. Now she unfastened the trousers and removed them and her shoes.

Her body carried no excess weight and her legs were firm as well as shapely, her buttocks tight and round and accentuated by a black thong.

As she strode back to the bed, Tamara whimpered again and closed her eyes. She stretched her arms above her head as if they had been tied there. Delia stripped back the bedclothes to reveal the girl. The nightdress only reached her hips and she wore nothing else.

Delia pushed the thong from around her waist and let

it drop to her feet. She stepped out of it and climbed onto the bed.

'No,' whispered Tamara.

'Shut up, slut. You will do as you're told.'

Penn watched in detached surprise as Delia had sex with Tamara. The girl continued with her mild vocal objections even though this caused Delia to turn her over and spank her delightful bottom quite fiercely.

The older woman was a sexual artist and built up both her own and Tamara's sexual tensions, holding them at a high peak for a long time before allowing orgasms to quench them. She sucked Tamara's vagina, she pinched and slapped her body, she kissed her mouth and suctioned at her breasts, and she demanded much the same in return, pushing the girl's head between her legs and exhorting her to suck.

For Penn, this was an unexpected morning matinée and he enjoyed it, with his trousers open and his erection pulsating.

At last, Delia guided and encouraged Tamara to a climax as they lay in a final clinch, their vaginas rubbing against each other.

The girl's head tilted back as she stifled a gasp of ecstasy. Delia's eyes flickered and she allowed herself also to slip over the edge. The two entwined bodies clung together and shook and slowly, as the spasms of orgasm died away, they rolled apart upon the bed.

They did not move for several minutes. The television was still on and the chat show continued.

Tamara said, 'Do you want some tea?'

Delia sat up and stretched.

'No. I think it's going to be a long day. I need something stronger.'

She got up, went to the drinks on top of the credenza and poured a gin and tonic that was heavy on the gin, adding ice from the refrigerator beneath. She brought the drink back to the bed, unselfconscious about her nudity, and picked up the satchel along the way.

Delia put the drink on the bedside table and sat on the bed. From the satchel she took a bottle of pills, spilled two into her palm and offered them to Tamara.

'No, thanks,' said the girl, now sitting up to stare, once more, at the television.

The woman popped them into her mouth and washed them down with gin and tonic. She put the bottle back in the bag and stared at the television.

'Jamie has gone riding,' she said, in a disinterested voice. 'With that large girl. Susan the tooth fairy.'

'Oh, yes.' Tamara's reply was equally without interest. 'She seems a nice girl.'

The silence stretched for a while, and then Delia said, 'I wonder if he's fucked her yet?'

'Probably,' said Tamara, as if their half-hour of passion had never happened.

'I hope,' said Delia, 'they didn't give him a mare to ride.' Tamara laughed and the woman added, 'If they did, that could be next on his list.'

Penn switched off the monitor and the image from Tamara's bedroom was transferred to one of the screens on the wall without the sound.

Tamara continued to amaze him. Perhaps her innocence was genuine, after all. She did not have a harsh word to say about Philpott and was even pleasant about Susan, the girl with whom he had gone riding, when, perhaps, another ex-girlfriend might have found something even slightly critical to say. He and Tess had, after all.

There was a delightful vulnerability about her, and yet he remembered the bondage video. Of course she had been vulnerable in that, but her enjoyment had been obvious from her orgasms. Or had the orgasms been forced from her? Imposed upon her?

He had a sudden thought and keyed in the transfer of another camera location onto his monitor, rewound the tape to a specific time, and played it.

This camera was in the kitchen behind the bar. He fast-forwarded it for a few seconds and, when Tamara came into view, played it at normal speed. She was leading Philpott by the arm the previous night. Penn turned up the sound.

Almost as soon as Philpott had staggered out of sight of the people in the bar, he seemed to sober up. He took hold of Tamara, pushed her back against a wall, wrapped his arms around her and began to kiss her.

Her hands pushed against him and when her mouth broke free, she said, in a whisper, 'No, Jamie. Don't spoil it.'

'Shush,' whispered Philpott in return. His hands were pulling at her dress. The thin material bunched around his wrists as he lifted it up her legs. 'You want it. I know you want it. You always want it.'

The dress was around her waist and she buried her face in his shoulder as his fingers went between her legs. She gasped as his fingers entered her and her head tilted back again.

'Jamie. Don't. Not here.'

Then her eyes closed and she bit her lip as his fingers worked in her vagina. His movements were quick, hurried but assured. The murmur of conversation from the other room could be heard on the soundtrack.

Penn quivered and gripped his penis. He could even

make out the voices of Tess and himself. Laughter. The pouring of champagne.

On screen, Philpott unfastened his jeans and pushed them down his thighs. He spread Tamara's legs and Penn remembered what Tess had called her. A butterfly. She looked like a butterfly now, helpless against the wall and about to be impaled as Philpott manoeuvered to enter her.

The denim-clad singer pushed and Tamara gasped as his penis went into her. She clasped her hands around his neck and he held her legs as he thrust. Her eyes were closed and she continued to bite her bottom lip.

Philpott changed his grip on her. He put his hands beneath her knees and held her by the buttocks so that she was almost bent double and her legs dangled over his arms. This was not a technique that was practised on the spur of the moment. Penn guessed they had done it this way many times before.

Tamara's face showed tense concentration and Philpott seemed to be close to coming when Fiona entered the room. She hesitated, cast a quick look behind her, and stepped inside. Tamara turned her head, her eyes wide with panic at the intrusion, but relief showed in her expression.

Fiona said, 'For God's sake hurry up.'

Philpott grinned and said, 'Just coming.'

He ejaculated into Tamara who once more closed her eyes, bit her lip, and concentrated just enough to orgasm also.

The singer lowered her to her feet and staggered backward across the kitchen. He knocked a plate from a work surface and it smashed on the floor.

Tamara's dress had dropped into place and she took several deep breaths. Fiona went to Philpott and helped him fasten his trousers. As she was doing so, Delia

Phillip Mason

came into the room. She took one look, and her face
tightened.

'For once, Jamie,' she said, 'just for fucking once, why
can't you behave?'

Philpott, trousers fastened, was happy to adopt his mantle
of drunkenness again. He gave a clenched-fist salute and
said, 'Rock and roll.'

Delia said, 'For fuck's sake let's get him to bed.'

Tamara left the kitchen to join Penn and Tess, and
Philpott put his arms around the two remaining women
who led him out with a great show of incapacity on
Philpott's part.

Penn switched off the tape. He shook his head. Again.
It seemed like he was always shaking his head these days.
Indecision was something he had not entertained for thirty
years and now it was back. He could play word games
for ever about Tamara. It was time for the real games
to begin.

Penn took Tamara for a drive that afternoon. The sun
shone, the day was hot and she wore a pink miniskirt and
a loose white T-shirt with no bra beneath it, white ankle
socks and white Reeboks.

He thought they might be mistaken for uncle and niece,
rather than potential bride and groom.

He drove them in an open-topped Porsche to a country
pub by a river where they sat outside beneath an umbrella
and watched the ducks. He had a glass of wine and she
had a tonic water.

'You don't drink,' he said. 'I mean, ever. I've noticed.
A glass of wine can last all night.'

'I like to know what's going on.'

'How about drugs?'

264

'I don't do drugs. I find unadulterated life quite exhilarating enough.'

'You must have one weakness.' He smiled. 'How about sex?'

Tamara smiled and looked back at the ducks in the river.

'My offer still stands,' she said.

'I don't mean that. Is sex your weakness?'

'I like sex.' She turned her gaze back to him. 'Anyone who doesn't is a fool or a liar.'

Penn said, 'Has Monty warned you about me?'

'Yes.'

This time she did not look away.

'Were you shocked?'

'I'm still here.'

He nodded.

'Sex is my passion,' he said. 'But not just casual sex, or sex for the sake of it. I enjoy controlled and directed sex. I like to command, Tamara. I like to dominate.'

He smiled and sipped the wine.

'Maybe,' he said, 'that was the attraction when I first saw you. Your innocence. Innocence that needed to be led down the many and varied paths of sensual experience. Innocence that could survive all sexual impositions.'

Tamara still stared into his eyes with that intensity that made him feel like the only person in the world.

'Am I making any sense?' he asked.

'Yes,' she said.

'Are you easily led?' he asked, softly.

'In some ways.'

They sat in silence for a while and then he said, 'Let's take a walk.'

A path ran by the side of the river and they followed
it. They passed anglers sitting on the bank, and a young
family also out for a stroll. Penn stopped at a stile that led
to another path that ran away from the river.

'This way,' he said.

He helped her over the style and took the opportunity to
look up the miniskirt. Beneath it she wore a white cotton
thong. Her body smelled of a delicate moisturizing oil. He
followed, taking her hand, and they walked away from
people and the sounds of the river and were soon enclosed
by silence.

The official footpath turned to the right. But running
straight on through heavy undergrowth and trees was a
track that was much less well used. A hand-painted sign
said: No Entry.

'Feeling adventurous?' Penn said.

Tamara's wide eyes stared into the undergrowth and she
wet her lips with her tongue.

'Whatever you say,' she said.

They walked down the private path and within a hundred
yards were lost to the world.

'This is just an ordinary piece of English countryside,' he
said, 'and yet, after what we have been talking about, to
me it reeks of sexual possibility. Can you feel it, Tamara?
Can you feel the tension?'

'Yes.'

'We have removed ourselves from civilization. From
society's rules. The only rules are the ones we choose to
make. The ones *I* choose to make. The only rules are my
rules, Tamara.'

Her fingers fluttered in his. He could sense her pulse.
The trees and high shrubbery had cut out any breeze and
the heat was oppressive. Even the birds seemed to have

stopped singing and the only sound was the crunch of their shoes on the track.

He stopped and turned her to face him. She gazed at him with those big green eyes, trusting, fearful and hopeful. He could feel her quiver as he traced the contours of her beautiful face with his fingers.

'Remove your skirt,' he said.

For a fraction of a second she hesitated, and then her hands went to the elasticated waistband of the skirt. She pushed it down her legs and stepped out of it. He held out his hand and she gave it to him.

'Imagine, Tamara,' he said, in a low voice. 'We could meet anyone along this path. A gang of youths looking for sport. A man walking his dog. Men with sex on their mind.'

The girl was biting the inside of her bottom lip which made her look even younger and more vulnerable.

'Walk ahead,' he said.

Tamara walked in front of him and he followed, three or four paces behind. His erection throbbed and he straightened it in his trousers. She was a vision of utter delight.

The white T-shirt ended at her waist and the thong accentuated the curves of the cheeks of her bottom, which quivered as she walked. Her legs were long and willowy in the ankle socks and white shoes.

Ahead the undergrowth thinned and there were half-derelict buildings in a clearing. Sunshine splashed on the overgrown cobbles of a yard. From somewhere came the sound of someone chopping wood.

Tamara stopped at the edge of the yard and Penn came alongside her: his hand stroked down from her waist and over her buttocks.

'Don't be shy,' he said. 'Over there.' He pointed across the yard to an open doorway. 'Let's explore.'

He waited so that she walked ahead of him once more and the sound of chopping stopped. A young man with an axe straightened from his work away to their right and stared at them. He was bare-chested. Tamara kept on walking and went into the building Penn had indicated.

Bales of straw filled most of it and a wooden staircase led up to an open loft. Meat hooks, chains and old ropes hung from the ceiling beams. Sunshine that came through the door and windows from which the glass had long since gone lightened the gloom.

Tamara turned to face him and Penn dropped her skirt that he had been carrying on a bale of straw. He picked up a length of thin rope and tested its strength.

'Take off the T-shirt,' he said, without emotion.

She obeyed and dropped it on top of the shirt, revealing her small and beautiful breasts with their pink tips. He didn't look but was intent upon weaving the rope until he had created two interconnecting cuffs with a loop above them.

He said, 'This is called a true-lover's knot. Put your hands through the cuffs.'

Again she obeyed. He held the loop and pulled the two ends of the rope that dangled below: the cuffs tightened around her wrists. He reached above his head, and hung the loop over an iron hook in the ceiling beam.

Tamara's arms were stretched above her, the cuffs held in place by their own tension. Her slim body was shaking slightly, her breasts high and quivering, the nipples erect.

He moved behind her and felt her buttocks. He held her hips and pushed himself against her.

'Feel that?' he said, in a low urgent voice. 'You made my prick go hard, you naughty girl. Walking around like that.'

As he rubbed his erection against the softness of her buttocks, his hands went up her body and over her breasts. She was whimpering softly.

'What shall I do with you, you naughty girl?'

His right hand now slid down across her flat stomach and his fingers pushed beneath the front of the thong that she still wore. He delved down the curve of her abdomen and through the silkiness of her pubic hair and found the channel of her vagina.

'Oh, Tamara. You're wet.' His fingers pushed and delved and she gave a little cry and swung on the rope. 'You're so very wet.'

His fingers plied her open sex, penetrating her and releasing more moisture. He used it to oil her clitoris which he rolled. He gripped her buttocks with his left hand, digging in his fingernails, as he masturbated her.

'You naughty, naughty girl,' he whispered in her ear. 'You want to come, don't you? You want to come.'

She was gasping and murmuring but making no sense.

'If you come, I'll have to punish you, Tamara. I'll have to mark that pretty bottom of yours with the end of a rope.' His fingernails dug into her soft flesh and his other hand worked with urgency at her sex. 'Do you hear?'

Her head fell back and she cried out and shook upon the rope as she came.

Penn held her for a moment until she regained the strength to stand on her own feet. He moved away and found another piece of rope. He swished it through the air experimentally.

Tamara's eyes were glazed and her face was heavy with lust as she watched. Her hips twisted and contracted in anticipation. He went behind her, swished it again, and then hit her across the buttocks with it, not hard, but enough to leave a mark.

Phillip Mason

'Ah, ah!' she shouted, and writhed upon the rope.

He hit her again, and again she cried out, and he gave her half a dozen strokes before he stopped. He was sweating and his erection throbbed with a dull persistence.

'Tamara,' he said. 'You have an admirer.'

The young man who had been wielding the axe was staring in through the window. He was perhaps eighteen and his eyes were wide as they stared at the young woman's body.

'What's going on?' he said.

'My niece has been provocative,' Penn said. 'She enjoys showing her body to men and arousing them. I am giving her the spanking she deserves.'

The young man moved to the doorway. He was about six feet in height, well-built and tanned. He wore only jeans and work boots. He had left his axe behind.

'Are you all right, miss?' he said.

'All right?' said Penn. 'Of course she is all right. She is so all right she is on the verge of permanent sexual orgasm.' The man glanced at him. 'Look for yourself,' Penn invited. 'Pull down, if you will, those flimsy panties she is wearing and see the state of her vagina.'

For a moment, the man looked at him as if Penn was mad. But the millionaire said, 'Do it!'

The young man stepped forward and knelt in front of Tamara.

'Inspect the contours of the garment,' Penn said. 'Put your hands upon her and inspect the garment. It was made for provocation.'

The youth put his hands on her hips and slowly slid them around so that they covered her buttocks. His face was very close to her vagina.

'Remove the garment,' Penn urged, and the young man tugged the thong from around her waist and pulled it down

270

over her hips. It slipped down her legs to her knees. 'Take it off,' Penn said.

He lifted her feet, removed the thong and discarded it. His hands went back to her hips, his eyes staring at her pubic hair and her Venus mons.

'Open her vagina,' Penn said, in a low voice. 'See how swollen is her clitoris. See how wet are her membranes. See how she wants sex.'

The youth put his thumbs to Tamara's vagina and opened the lips of her sex to reveal the wet pinkness within. His breath caressed it and the girl moaned and the strength seemed to leave her legs.

'Kiss her,' Penn said softly. 'Give her what she desires. Use your mouth upon her.'

He needed no second bidding, but leaned forward, his tongue already searching, and buried his face in her sex. Tamara twisted on the rope and cried out loudly. He slurped noisily at her and she yelled and groaned.

Penn stepped behind her once more. The youth was holding her by the hips and thighs as he used his mouth. Penn swished the rope and hit her across the buttocks. Her cries became wilder and his strokes became harsher, until she gave one last yell of finality, shook as never before and expired into ecstasy upon the rope.

Now Penn released her from her bonds and laid her on a thick bed of straw that covered part of the floor. The young man waited, crouching by her side.

'Has she made you stiff?' Penn asked.

The young man nodded.

'Hear that, Tamara? You've made his prick go stiff. I think you should do something about it. Don't you?' She stared at him but did not seem capable of speech. 'I

271

think you should suck his prick, you naughty little girl.'
He glanced at the youth. 'Put it in her mouth.'

Penn knelt by her head in the straw and the young man
gulped, unfastened his jeans, and released a large erection.
He looked once more for confirmation and Penn nodded:
he knelt over the girl's face.

'In your mouth, Tamara,' Penn said. Her mouth opened
and accepted the prick. 'And suck.'

Tamara sucked and Penn sat back on his haunches and
watched: her long slim body stretched upon the straw, naked
but for shoes and socks, and the young man crouching by
her head. A young man who suddenly gasped and came
into her mouth.

As he fell back to sprawl in the straw, Penn noticed an
older man standing in the doorway. He wore cords and
check shirt and carried a shotgun, safely broken open, in
the crook of his arm.

Penn heard Tamara gasp as she also saw the new-
comer.

'Who are they?' said the man.

'I found them here, Mr Shaw,' said the young man,
struggling to his feet and fastening his trousers.

'Get back to work,' said Shaw.

The young man disappeared through the doorway. Shaw
stared at them. Tamara had placed her hands daintily across
her breasts and vagina.

'Well?' said Shaw.

Penn said, 'My niece enjoys sex. I was just about to invite
that young man to fuck her, but he came too soon.'

Shaw stared at Tamara's body. Penn got to his feet and
took hold of one of her arms.

'Stand up, Tamara. Show the gentleman your wares.'

She got to her feet but was unsteady. Penn stroked her

flesh, ostensibly to brush away stray pieces of straw. He made her breasts and buttocks quiver.

'Isn't she beautiful?' he said.

He ran his fingers through her hair and, without warning, pulled her to him and kissed her deeply. His tongue probed her mouth and her body responded and pressed against him.

Penn broke the kiss and gently pushed her away. He looked at the man with gun.

'Perhaps you'd like to fuck her?' he said.

Shaw put the gun on the floor and stepped forward. He ran his hands over Tamara's body, feeling her softness, his fingers inspecting her vagina. Her eyes flickered as if ready to close.

'She's ready for it,' said Shaw.

Without further ado, he turned her and bent her over a bale of straw. Standing close behind her, he unfastened his trousers, pushed them down, and guided a short but thick penis between her legs. He slid it along her vaginal crease, found the opening and pushed it inside. Tamara groaned and her arms stretched wide across the bale.

Shaw held her by the hips and pounded her with only his own pleasure in mind. Even so, Tamara's moans gained in volume and became a wail and she came. The unexpectedness of her climax tipped the man into his and he emptied his sperm inside her.

He was breathless when he stepped away and said nothing as he fastened his trousers and retrieved his gun. Just before he left, he spoke.

'It's private land, this,' he said, and then he was gone.

Penn laid Tamara on the straw and stretched out with her, holding her in his arms, stroking the hair from her face, and shushing her as if she were a baby.

For a short while she drifted into exhaustion, if not sleep.

She was a beautiful child with an innocence that might last for ever. A delicious butterfly. Tess had called her that and she had been right. A delicious butterfly who would enhance any collection.

But did he want to remain trapped in a world of controlled experiments for the rest of his life? Did he want to be a curator or a lover?

When she stirred, he helped her dress and led her from the building. No one was about and they crossed the yard hand in hand.

A main road was surprisingly nearby and parked near the gate into the courtyard was the Porsche. Tamara did not ask how it had got there. Penn helped her climb into the car and they drove back to the house.

Chapter 20

Tess was on the terrace enjoying peace, quiet, her own company and English tea with delicate salad sandwiches when Charles Penn found her late that afternoon.

'You look relaxed,' he said, joining her.

'I am.'

A servant appeared carrying a tray with a fresh pot of tea and a cup and saucer. Penn poured his own.

'Did you read it?' he asked.

'Of course. Fascinating and horny, as ever.'

'Good. I have one more piece to write and then it's over.'

'Over?'

He stared into her eyes and said, 'I think so. I think I've come a long way. I think you've been a great help.'

'Thank you. Still no charge.'

Penn smiled and said, 'There may be no charge but there may be consequences.'

Tess returned his smile. 'There are always consequences,' she said. She sensed there were things he did not wish to discuss right at this moment, things he was maybe saving for later. 'I've been talking to Jamie,' she said.

'The wild man of rock?'

'He's not as objectionable as he would like people to believe. Believe it or not, he is very fond of Tamara. Won't have a word said against her.'

Penn said, 'Last night he had her against a wall in the kitchen while we talked in the bar.'

Tess had not known this had occurred but it did not surprise her and she could not help but smile.

'Well, they *are* very old friends,' she said. 'He knows the arrangement between you and Tamara and I suppose it was bravado that made him do it. He presumably didn't think you would find out. That apart, he told me he would do nothing to upset or spoil any future Tamara might choose with you.'

Penn held her stare and said, 'He said something else, didn't he? What else did he say?'

'He said you were old enough to be her grandfather, but that was her choice.'

For a moment, Penn looked as if he might have apoplexy. But the anger subsided and he burst out laughing.

'He's damn' right, too.' He shook his head. 'She is a lovely girl, Tess.'

'I know. I called Alex Brown – the video maker? – and had a long chat with him. He says the same thing. He said she had what he called a quality of innocence.' She paused. 'And an insatiable sexual appetite. It's a great combination.'

'You've been busy.'

'Something else, I discovered, about an attribute I admire. You know how Tamara gives you all her attention when you talk to her? How her eyes drink you in and she ignores everyone around, as if you are the centre of the universe?'

'Yes.'

'She's short-sighted.'

He guffawed.

Tess said, 'All in all, Tamara is a beautiful free spirit,

open to virtually any sexual suggestion, who feels no guilt, enjoys the pleasure, and has no malice. Your arrangement? It was undoubtedly made in good faith.

'You might have been wearing blinkers, but she wasn't. I think she expects that eventually you will decide you don't really love her. If that happens, she will allow you to withdraw with grace and you will remain friends.

'Until then, she is perfectly content to remain part of the arrangement you made. She is happy to be within your influence. She obviously enjoys sex games and domination. But as well as enjoying them, she understands them. She understands her innocence and knows how to use it.

'But let me assure you on one point. I honestly believe she likes you, Charles. Probably even loves you. But then, she does love a lot of people.'

Penn shook his head and remembered it was a habit he meant to break. But he kept finding himself trying to understand situations he had previously ignored. Or maybe he had never been in such situations, with such people, before.

He said, 'I know I've had my fair share of experiences, but even I'm a little shocked by the way these young people indulge their sexual appetites. I mean, Philpott, last night, for instance. He has his way with Susan in the cloakroom, tries it on with you, has Tamara in the kitchen, and then goes to bed with Fiona.'

Tess said, 'He's a rock star. That's what he's supposed to do. And be honest, if you'd had the chance at his age, wouldn't you have done the same?'

'I suppose so,' said Penn.

'It's a different world from what you're used to, Charles. The arts, film, video, rock and roll. They don't meticulously plan events or remain in control. They take their kicks when and where they find them. It's not a bad philosophy.

'One of these days, you will have stayed celibate for six months in some carefully contrived devious plot, and an hour before you are due to blow your gasket and enjoy the release, you'll get knocked down by a fifty-seven bus.'

He laughed and an old joke came to mind.

'They'd never get the coffin lid down,' he said.

Tess grinned, and said, 'But you see what I mean? Take it when you can, because it may not be there forever.'

They drank tea and Penn eventually said, 'I took Tamara out this afternoon. A sort of test run.'

He said it diffidently and although he obviously wanted to share the information did not seem to know how to go about doing so.

Tess said, 'That's sounds a little cold and clinical.'

'I suppose that's the way I set it up. And I did set it up. Planned the lot, choreographed it. Even practised tying knots.'

'You perfectionist, you.' She let the smile on her face lapse because he wanted to be serious. 'How did it go?'

'Perfectly. She was a willing victim and, oh my God, so innocent. I'll show you the video.'

'You had it filmed?'

'Of course. Hidden cameras. Tamara didn't know it was planned. She might have suspected, but she couldn't know. I didn't want the situation to lose its element of danger for her.'

Tess said, 'What happened?'

'I tied her up naked in an old barn and beat her with a rope. A controlled beating, of course.'

'Of course.'

'And a farmer and his labourer both had their way with her.'

'And did she enjoy the experience?'

'Very much.'

'And did you?'

He gazed into his teacup, as if trying to read the leaves.

'Yes,' he said, but sounded doubtful.

'But?'

'But it left me feeling empty.'

'Did you have sex with Tamara, Charles?'

'No.' He paused, as if trying to understand his own feelings. 'I enjoyed the game. She really is a beautiful girl. But I didn't want to. Afterwards, I . . . cuddled her.'

He looked at her with a nonplussed expression.

Tess felt as if she were talking across an abyss into which she might fall, but she asked the question anyway.

'Is it love?' she said.

His eyes held her gaze and he shook his head slowly.

'No. I have great affection for her, but I'm not in love with her. I never could be.' He smiled. 'I'm old enough to be her grandfather,' he said.

The abyss closed and Tess was still there. Just the other side of the table. She smiled warmly.

'Well, that's one aspect of the problem resolved. But what about the other? Are you still happy being an obsessive voyeur? Or are you ready for a more emotionally fulfilling sexual experience?'

Penn said, 'You almost make it sound like an offer, Tess.'

'Maybe it's make-your-mind-up time, Charles. I hear Mark is coming back this evening.'

He grinned, and said, 'I know. I arranged it.'

'For me?'

Tess was genuinely shocked.

'No. For Delia and Jamie. I believe in happy endings. Mark was called up to town to discuss a firm offer to back a film project featuring Jamie Philpott. I set it up, through an intermediary, so he doesn't know of my involvement. Mark is coming back tonight to break the good news. Maybe, for once, even Delia will smile.'

Tess said, 'Why are you backing the movie? Is this a sudden whim?'

'I never do anything on a sudden whim, you know that.' He shrugged. 'Maybe I should. Maybe I will. No, this is based on sound business practice. Mark is a hot new director. His current film has won an award at Cannes, and is a cult hit not just here but in the States.

'The ragamuffin Mr Philpott, for some reason that I don't understand, appears to ignite youthful passions on both sides of the pond. He is at his most potent right now. He has also already taken a screen test and the results were admirable.

'There is a risk, as there is always a risk in any business venture, but even a bad movie will have box office potential simply on the names of Mark and Jamie. And if it is a good movie, I stand to make an awful lot of money.'

Tess said, 'And I thought this weekend was for sexual adventure.'

'It still is.'

'You have something else planned?'

'Tamara is to get her TV show. Monty will announce that tonight, as well. One of the regions has commissioned it on the strength of the advance tapes and guest list. She is rather good in front of a camera, as it happens. Those big eyes? And her brain is not as fluffy as some would think.

She may be a free spirit when it comes to sex, but she is an ambitious free spirit.'

Tess said, 'One of the regions? This wouldn't be the franchise in which you are a major shareholder, would it?'

He smiled.

'Of course. But I don't back losers. She has the potential to make it a success and I shall make sure she has the best people around her. Jamie Philpott and Mark Trimm will be on the first show, talking about the film they are to make together. That will ensure the show gets networked from the start.'

She laughed and now she shook her head.

'You amaze me,' she said. 'You create happy endings and make money as well. What have you got lined up for me?'

Tess regretted making the flippant remark as soon as she said it. Penn looked at his watch.

'I'll tell you, and then I have things to do before tonight. I have that last chapter to write. Remember?'

And then he told her.

Everyone met in the library for drinks before dinner and this time even Delia was smiling. They gathered together like old friends and congratulated each other on the news that Mark Trimm had brought from London.

Even Jamie seemed prepared to behave like a responsible adult, but then, he hadn't really started drinking yet.

A motorcycle messenger arrived on cue with a package for Monty and he was able to make his own announcement.

He grabbed Tamara and gave her a hug and a kiss on the cheek.

'You're in, darling,' he said. He held up a cassette and waved a piece of paper as if he had just returned from Munich with a peace deal. The gathering waited expectantly. 'Tamara has her own show called . . . *Tamara*.' They cheered. 'We go into production ASAP.

'Listen, listen. Jake Peabody at ITB says, and I quote, "Loved the rough cut. Where'd you find her? She's a gem. Network slot guaranteed." '

Tamara appeared to be stunned.

'I thought we had to do a pilot first,' she said.

Monty beamed and said, 'What we had was so good I went with that. And it worked.'

Penn said, 'Then let's see it, Monty.'

He pointed to a TV and VCR at the end of the room and Monty switched on the set and played the video.

The twenty-minute film started with state-of-the-art graphics that showed a montage of day-in-the-life shots of Tamara at her flat, catching taxis, dining out, entering nightclubs, all spliced together with an authoritative voice-over that placed her firmly at the centre of a capital that seemed the glitziest and hippest in the world.

Short segments that had been shot on location at the Tower of London, on the open-top deck of a tour bus, looking across the Thames at the the headquarters of MI6, and wandering through Portobello Road market were segued into a pacy sequence during which Tamara made witty and cogent comments as well as looking winsomely beautiful.

A face-to-face ten-minute interview with the male star of a West End show also worked remarkably well, with the star appearing to be totally captivated by her, and it ended on the club scene with celebrities drinking champagne at her table, while she revealed amusing snippets of show business gossip.

The final credits rolled with the same panache as they had opened.

Tess said, 'Swinging London, all over again.'

Delia said, 'The voice-over. That wasn't Paul from the RSC, was it, Monty?'

'It was,' the fat producer said with glee.

'Good God. He doesn't come cheap,' Delia commented.

'I called in a favour,' Monty said.

Tess glanced at Penn but he was showing no emotion.

Tamara was being congratulated but she, too, was looking at Penn, with a knowing smile. She left the others to go and kiss him on the cheek.

'Thank you, Charles,' she whispered.

A servant entered the room and handed Penn a portable telephone, and the rest of them quietened down while he took the call. He raised the telephone towards Tess, she took it from him and they left the room briefly.

Glances were exchanged and eyebrows raised in curiosity. A few moments later, Penn re-entered the room.

'I'm sorry,' he said. 'That was the police. Tess's apartment has apparently been burgled. It's nothing to be alarmed about, just one of those damned inconveniences. But obviously, she feels she needs to go back to town immediately and check on what's missing.'

There were murmurs of sympathy.

He continued, 'It's not a nice thing to happen to anyone, particularly an American friend, and I'm sure you'll understand why I've insisted on taking Tess back myself.'

'Here, here,' said Monty.

'Please, continue celebrating,' Penn said. 'Apart from this minor misfortune, it seems to have been a weekend that has brought most of us success.'

Tamara said, 'Will you be back, Charles?'

'Oh, yes. Later tonight. We'll see you for breakfast. Oh, and by the way, Jamie, there are more videos in the cupboard by the machine. Some of yours, a copy of *Goodnight*, plus some amusing out-takes. You didn't know I had that, did you, Mark? And if anyone wants a night at the movies, there's a bootleg of the new Ralph Fiennes.

'Please. Enjoy yourselves, and I'll see you in the morning.'

Before he could take his leave, Tamara approached him and held his arm. She kissed him again on the cheek.

'Thank you, Charles. For everything.' She smiled, her eyes huge as they stared into his. 'And goodbye,' she said softly.

'Goodbye, Tamara.'

He patted her hand and finally left.

Tess was waiting for him in the hall.

'Okay?' she said.

'Of course.'

They left the house and the chauffeur and limousine were waiting. The chauffeur drove them to a country restaurant twenty minutes away. They went into the bar and sat at a table and a waiter took their order for drinks. A moment later, the young woman who was the restaurant manager welcomed them.

'Mr Penn, madam. Delighted to see you,' she said, handing them menus. 'I'll send the wine waiter. Your table is ready whenever you are. There's no rush. Enjoy your drinks.'

When she left them, Tess smiled at Penn and said, 'You are a devious devil, Charles.'

'And you are looking particularly beautiful tonight, Tess.'

Actually, she felt quite good. She wore a little black number with a designer label that she had felt had been an extravagance when she bought it but which she now thought had been worth every penny. Black stockings and high-heeled shoes and, yes, matching underwear. She felt wicked, sophisticated and beautiful, too.

Penn looked at his watch.

'They will have found the blue movies by now. I wonder if they will watch them before or after dinner?'

They dined in leisurely fashion and drank Krug champagne. They talked about everything and anything except the party they had left behind and the subject that was uppermost on both their minds.

Shortly before midnight, they climbed into the back of the limousine and were driven back to the house, sitting carefully apart from each other.

As they got closer to the house, Penn called ahead on the telephone and was assured by what he heard.

'They have all gone to bed,' he told Tess.

Even so, the car stopped at the rear of the house and a servant let them in through French windows. Penn led the way upstairs.

He led her into his bedroom and switched on the light. On the bed were the pages of his manuscript. She picked it up.

'Last chapter?' she said.

'Yes.'

'Do I read it now?'

'If you're not too tired.'

'I'm not tired.' She sat in a low and very comfortable armchair and flipped the pages between thumb and forefinger. 'Ten minutes,' she said.

'Drink?' He held up a bottle of Bollinger.

'Yes. If this is the last chapter, it deserves champagne.'

He opened the bottle and she began to read.

Chapter 21

Charles Penn's story

Marriage to Julia was not a success. We continued to cling to each other in bed but, without extraneous stimulation, our sexual relationship was non-existent. Then even the cuddles became less frequent.

I began to suspect that perhaps all we had, all we had ever had, was a sexual tension that needed a third party to bring it to life.

Rick was still with us in spirit for when we did involve someone else in our games I remained the outsider for much of the time. I was the witness, as I had been in our youth, although I now got to fuck Julia at the conclusion.

But that's enough of soul-searching and philosophy for the moment, Tess. At least until I finish this. It's odd, but my prick is rising in anticipation at the memories I am about to unleash and relate, even though there is probably something else among them that I am about to confront.

However, here goes.

We no longer fucked except when we found a game to play with someone. In between times, I gained enjoyment as a voyeur from watching my wife. I watched her dress and undress, I watched her cross her legs carelessly, I watched her in the bathroom, I watched her climbing stairs.

I remembered other times and other men and imagined

new strangers doing things to her, watching her as I did, and masturbating over her and fucking her. This gave me erections that I nurtured but which I did not handle to a sexual culmination. In other words, I kept it rock-hard in my trousers for hours at a time and did not come.

We were on holiday in Marbella. It was out of season but the weather was hot and Julia was beautiful. She had acquired a delightful tan. We only had two more nights before we were due to fly home when a coach brought new arrivals: a professional football team from England who were on a training-and-relaxation break. It was no surprise that the players showed an interest in my wife.

The first night they were there, we both noticed the way they stared at her and cast envious glances. She gave small flirtatious smiles in return: my prick stiffened at the possibilities.

I said to her that she had a whole team of admirers and she laughed. We talked about them and she indicated one in particular whom she thought was attractive, a tall, blond-haired man called Rod, who happened to be a well-known England international.

Our marriage had been limping along like a lame pet that its owner did not have the heart to put down. The change of scenery and stimulation from being on holiday had helped. It had created diversions for us. But it was only with the arrival of these footballers that we had once more become a couple.

And even then not a couple in a marital sense, but partners in crime, as it were, locked in our own world and responding to the stimuli of an audience of strangers, some of whom we might snare and involve in our own dark games.

We stayed by the pool the next day and I enjoyed the way these fit young men stared at her shapely body in the bikini she wore. Two or three became friendly and came to sit with us, although I knew it was not my sparkling conversation that interested them but getting a closer look at her bosom and buttocks.

This Julia encouraged, unfastening the bikini bra strap to stop from getting tan lines on her back so that when she moved from a position of lying face down she had to be careful not to expose her breasts. She had to hold the skimpy material in place with both hands. The threat of her making a mistake was exciting and, on one or two occasions, she purposely showed more than she should have.

Julia also encouraged our new friends to massage sun cream into her body. At first it was only her shoulders but, as the mood became more intimate, she allowed one to smooth the cream into her thighs and the small of her back.

That night, as we got ready for dinner, I recognized the pulse of excitement that surged in my veins, and I watched as she dressed. She wore tiny white net panties and a white bra beneath a short figure-hugging pink T-shirt dress, and matching high-heeled sling-back sandals.

Her skin glowed from ten days in the sun and I could tell by the controlled way she conducted herself, and the pulse of a tell-tale nerve in her throat, that she, too, was aware of what the night might hold.

We had a drink in the bar before dinner, and Rod and two of his friends joined us. When she sat and crossed her legs, I saw the white V of her panties and I was sure Rod had seen it also. The conversation was light and friendly and when we eventually went into dinner, we went our separate ways to our separate tables.

It was our last night on holiday and we drank a decent Spanish champagne (and yes, Tess, there was such a thing, even back then). Afterwards, we went back to the bar and Rod joined us again.

There was a disco attached to the hotel, and it was natural that we should gravitate in that direction. The noise made it impossible to talk but it gave Rod the chance to dance with Julia and, once out of sight of me amidst the throng, he would be able to touch her.

We went back into the bar at eleven. The football players were supposed to be on a midnight curfew and we had planned to go to bed early because our flight was first thing in the morning. We had also planned to go to bed early because we did not expect to go to sleep immediately.

As we sat and talked at the bar, the other two footballers who had been with us earlier, Jimmy and Frank, also left the disco and joined us.

Julia was either tipsy or pretending to be, and when we eventually got up to go to our room I suggested they join us for a nightcap. She had had a pretty good idea I would be inviting Rod, but I could tell by the way she stiffened that she had not been expecting me to invite all three.

They accepted immediately and behaved themselves in the lift, with Rod being a gentleman by steadying her when she apparently lost her balance, without taking any advantage. In fact, they had all become rather quiet as we walked down the corridor to our room.

I opened the door and we went in I pulled back the curtains and opened the door to the balcony. I switched on only a table lamp. The music from the disco drifted up to us on the still night air. Julia seemed unsure of herself and went to the bathroom and I handed out bottles of beer and poured her a glass of wine.

Rod stood by the window and Frank and Jimmy sat on the double bed.

'You're lucky,' Rod said. 'You have a beautiful wife.'

I smiled because it was such an obvious ploy.

'Yes. She is beautiful,' I agreed. 'A good fuck, too.'

They were shocked by my bluntness, which had been deliberate.

Julia came back into the room and I put my arm around her and pulled her to me and gave her an open-mouthed kiss. My erection pressed against her and I held her around the waist with my left hand while my right went over her buttocks. I groped her so that our audience could watch our intimacy and become infected by it.

Our mouths broke apart. She laid her hands on my arms, and stared into my eyes and I could see the question in her gaze. She was asking did I really want this to happen? I smiled and nodded and kissed her again. She let me kiss her but did not respond. The three men did not speak. They watched.

When we broke apart, she picked up the glass of wine and drank it in two long gulps. She put down the glass and I refilled it.

'I don't think we need that light, Frank,' I said.

He leaned over and switched off the table lamp. Now the room was lit only by the moon. My blood was pounding in time to the music that came from the disco below where people were dancing and becoming intoxicated. Yet they would never get the feeling of intoxication that I knew we were all experiencing at that moment.

'Take off the dress,' I said to Julia, in a low voice that they all heard.

Julia looked at me and licked her lips. We were at the point where the game could be stopped. All she had to do was refuse. She knew this. We all did. We all knew that if she obeyed and removed the dress that she was agreeing to anything that might follow.

Jimmy drank from the bottle of beer he held but in doing so his eyes never left her.

I returned her stare but this time without a smile. This time my gaze commanded obedience. It said that all the games we had played before had led to this one. It said this was inevitable.

Julia reached down to the hem of the dress and lifted it to her waist, and the three men's eyes went to her tiny tight white net panties.

She and I still stared at each other and she took a deep breath, as if making a decision, changed her grip and pulled the T-shirt dress over her head. She dropped it on the floor, her body glowing in the darkness, the whiteness of the underwear emphasizing her availability.

They had seen her that afternoon in a bikini but this was different. That had been in a public place where rules of decency and social behaviour had to be obeyed and, besides, she had then been wearing a bikini. Now she was in her underwear, her bra and panties and high heels.

She picked up the glass and drained the contents again. When she put it down, I reached out and pulled her to me and we kissed again and I tasted the wine on her lips and felt her tremble.

After we kissed, I turned her in my arms so that she faced the three men and so that her buttocks pressed against my erection.

'Rod said you are beautiful,' I said. 'He's right, Julia. You are beautiful.'

At first I held her by the hips and moved her against my prick. She was deliciously soft and the tension in the room was rising even higher. Here was a young woman being

offered to three strangers by her husband. A young woman
who quivered and four men who were dry-lipped. Four
men with stiffened instruments of sex that were waiting to
be released from their trousers and plunged into her.

I unclipped her brassiere and slipped the straps from
her shoulders. She let it fall from her arms and drop to
the floor. My palms slid around the front of her body to
caress her breasts and I kissed the nape of her neck. She
tilted her head back against me.

My right hand now slid down her body and my fingers
went into her panties and pushed through the pubic bush
to her vagina. I watched them watching my hand. They
had become a totally captive audience. I pushed fingers
inside her and she gasped.

'She's wet,' I said, softly. 'I think she wants fucking.'

I removed my hand from her panties and stepped back,
away from her. Rod was the first to react. He came across
the room and took her in his arms and kissed her and she
put her arms around his neck and kissed him back. At first
the embrace was gentle but then his hands went down over
her buttocks, pushing into the briefs to find her flesh, and
the material tore.

Frank muttered a curse, got up from the bed and pulled
off his shirt. Jimmy looked at me.

'All of us?' he said.

I nodded and he got up and also began to undress. As
they were only wearing polo shirts and slacks it did not
take them long.

Rod was still kissing her but his tenderness had gone and
he was mauling her body. Her buttocks and breasts showed
white against her tan. She gasped again as he pushed fingers
inside her.

Then Frank, his lean, athletic frame naked, was behind

Phillip Mason

her and his stiff prick was against her buttocks and his
hands felt around her body for her breasts. Rod let go of
her and Jimmy replaced him at her front. Jimmy kissed
and mauled her with the same intensity.

They laid her on the bed as Rod hurriedly pulled off his
clothes and the torn briefs were ripped from her legs and
the shoes fell from her feet. She was murmuring and gasping
but we both knew she was beyond anyone's help now. They
would only leave her alone when they had finished.

Jimmy lay between her legs and sucked her vagina and
Frank lay alongside her and sucked and groped her breasts.
Rod watched for a moment, massaging his giant prick in
his right hand, and then touched Jimmy on the shoulder.

'She wants a prick up her, not a tongue,' he said.

Both Jimmy and Frank moved and Rod climbed between
her legs and fitted his prick into the mouth of her vagina.
He held himself above her and held the tip of his glans in
position but without pushing it inside.

'You want it, don't you?' he said. He moved it, stirring her
juices with it, and she moaned, but I couldn't tell whether
it was desire or despair. 'You do, don't you? You want a
good fucking?'

'Yes,' she said, because she knew that was what he wanted
to hear. That that was what *I* wanted to hear.

'Ask for it,' he said.

'Fuck me.' She moved her hips against him and I detected
a change in her attitude. 'Fuck me, you bastard.'

And do you know, I think it was me she was calling
'bastard', and not the man between her legs.

Rod sank his prick into her with a thrust that made her
gasp loudly and caused her legs to spread further and rise
so that she clung to his waist with her feet.

He did what she had demanded. He fucked her with fierce

strokes and without thought for any pleasure he may have been able to give to her, and he came quite quickly. No sooner had he finished than Frank was kneeling by her head and turning her face to his groin.

Julia rolled onto her side and took his weapon in her mouth. She held it round the base and began to suck and Jimmy pushed her all the way over onto her stomach. In the dim light, the white globes of her buttocks glowed.

He lay on top of her and pushed apart her legs with his knees. He knelt up and fitted himself into her from behind. He gasped and began his exertions. His muscular buttocks rose and fell in a frantic rhythm and soon he too orgasmed inside her.

Jimmy rolled from her and Frank now pushed her back onto her side. He was fucking her face with almost as much commitment as his friends had fucked her vagina. He lay down the bed, alongside her body so that he could grope her flesh as his hips pumped. She maintained her grip on the base of his prick and sucked and rubbed and masturbated. He made a strange noise in his throat as he came and she swallowed his spunk.

She flopped on her back, her mouth open, gasping for air, her legs apart, her hips twitching. The three men sprawled around her.

I felt totally calm and detached and yet my erection was so strong and upright against my stomach. I sipped a glass of wine and stepped closer to the bed. She had become wild with the wildness of the confrontation and was still wild even though they had been temporarily drained.

'You didn't come, did you, Julia?' I said.

Her tongue licked her lips again. Our eyes were exchanging messages.

'No,' she said.

'Do it to yourself. Make yourself come. Show them how.'

Her hands slowly slid across her body and went to that gaping gash between her legs. Her touch was hesitant at first but then her fingers rolled her clitoris and her eyes closed and she groaned and her thighs pressed together and her hips rose from the bed.

Julia's hands became more demanding, more penetrative, more expressive. Fingers slid inside her and emerged covered in the spunk of the two men who had just fucked her. As she continued masturbating with one hand, she raised the one that was wet with sperm to her face and sucked it clean.

It was as if she had become oblivious to us all, and perhaps she had. If she had intended her exhibition to incite them she achieved total success.

The three naked men had become transfixed watching this beautiful young woman giving herself pleasure with such abandonment. They sat around the edges of the bed watching and masturbating their growing erections.

Her left hand felt her breasts, mauling them as wantonly as the men had mauled them, tweaking at her nipples, while the right worked furiously at her clitoris. Then both hands were at her sex, fingers pushing inside while others rolled that demanding lovebud. Her breathing became laboured, her body tensed, and she climaxed loudly.

For a while, a strange silence fell on the bedroom and once more I became aware of the beat of the music from that place of normality on the ground floor.

It was as if inside that room we were all one, caught up in an unstoppable ritual of sex, that we were all victims in the grip of lustful compulsion, as if the beat was the pulse of our blood that made our sexual organs throb and our ears pound.

Then Julia herself broke the tension by groaning, spreading her legs and lifting her vagina. She parted the lips of her sex with her right hand, making an offering, a temptation. The men did not disappoint her.

All three slithered around her on the bed, licking her, feeling her, rubbing themselves against her, and, eventually, fucking her. I remained standing fully dressed at the foot of the bed, sipping the wine and watching the changing tableaux of naked flesh.

They alternated around her body, first one pushing his prick down her throat while another pushed it up her vagina and the third rubbed his across her face or against her buttocks or her breasts.

Inevitably, they sodomized her. Jimmy was the first as she lay on her side to suck Rod. Her body trembled and she groaned but she did not make any protest.

'Oh God, but that's nice,' he muttered.

'You haven't?' said Frank.

'I have.'

Frank immediately moved to her front and they attempted that wet-dream fantasy of all males of three-way penetration. By now she was completely pliable to their desires and bathed in lubricating sweat and sexual juices and they moved her without compassion until they achieved their ends.

Jimmy sodomized her while Frank fucked her and Rod knelt over her face with his prick in her mouth. If there was a moment when my control might have cracked it was then. But I remained the distant voyeur, the silent witness, and sipped the wine and felt my life concentrated in the pulse of my erection against my stomach.

The enormity of what they were doing meant it was not sustainable. Jimmy came first, probably because of the tightness of the passage, and his paroxysms caused Frank to ejaculate in her vagina.

Rod pushed them away, laid Julia on her stomach and took Jimmy's place. He lifted her hips, held his prick in one hand and rubbed it along the crease of her buttocks, found the entry and pushed it home with a deep grunt.

He held her hips, took several deep breaths without moving and then began to thrust. After only a short time, he came again.

His friends had already dressed and were standing sheepishly by the door when he rolled away. Julia lay spreadeagled on the bed and did not move. Rod quickly pulled on his clothes and looked down at Julia and then at me, the shadow at the feast. I toasted him with the wine.

It's strange to relate, Tess, but I felt superior and ashamed both at the same time. My toast was more bravado than anything.

He nodded and they left.

And then?

Well, I may have had remorse and I have already spoken of the shame. But I also had a raging erection.

I slowly removed my clothes, all the time watching her ghost body on the bed. She did not move but lay face down, spreadeagled and silent.

When I was naked, I stretched the moment even longer and stood and masturbated for a while. Then I knelt at the foot of the bed, in homage as well as to obtain a closer look, and continued to work my prick with my hand.

Finally, I slid onto the bed and began to lick my way up her legs, her thighs, her body. I snaked my way alongside her and kissed her as if she were a stranger and she returned my kisses with the same intensity and dispassion.

Then I fucked her in every conceivable way, wallowing

in the spunk of three strangers whom we would never see again, with my brain drowning in the depravity of what they had done and what I had engineered.

That night, dear Tess, as you might already have guessed, marked the end of anything Julia and I had ever had together. The next day, we treated each other with normality and courtesy and travelled back to England and to the house we shared.

Once there, we lapsed into a silence that lasted for several days. We did not exchange recriminations, we did not mourn for what we had lost, but neither did we still have friendship. If we had anything left, it was a strange sort of mutual tolerance.

I left one day while she was at work, leaving a note upon the dressing table. I said if she wished to instigate divorce proceedings I would give her every assistance and would, for that purpose, remain in touch with her.

At the time, I was unable to put into words, or even ideas, the reasons why our relationship had fallen apart. And for years afterwards, I chose not to examine them too closely because I felt the real reasons might be embarrassing.

Instead, as the years passed, I kept this image of Julia in my mind as she had been when I first knew her as a schoolgirl. She became my icon of innocence. My first love whom I had wooed and lost.

In retrospect, I suppose our relationship had always been unsustainable. Any relationship founded in such a fashion had to be flawed. There was no basis for the true love I had always believed I had for Julia.

True love?

The whole extended episode has led me to avoid true love ever since, which is why my life has been filled, instead, with sexual vignettes.

In these, at least, I have become the master of the charade. I have raised what I do to an art form and, I tell myself (or is this just another self-deception?) I have delivered sexual liberation to many frustrated young women in need.

Perhaps my reputation had become a magnet, or even a challenge, for some females. But I have never been short of beautiful creatures who, for whatever reason, wished to subjugate themselves to my desire, to my will, to my plans and to my instruction.

Like Julia, and, yes, like Tamara, there is a percentage of young women who are happy to forfeit free will and accept subjugation in their search for total sexual experience.

Occasionally, this can turn into obsession, but usually it is an outlet that can live quite happily alongside normal relationships and a normal way of life.

I do not know if that would have been possible with Julia for, I now accept, I was the obsessive. Even if I had wooed and won my icon without either of us ever having known or being influenced by Rick, I doubt if our relationship would have worked.

For at that time, I was in love with the idea of love. I was an adolescent who was probably incapable of love and I realize now that I never really did love Julia, and that she never loved me.

(Hindsight is a wonderful thing!)

We met under strange circumstances from which we could never escape. When Rick died, he left a vacuum into which we were sucked. The best that can be said is that we used each other. At the end, we did not even like each other. It was not that our relationship got too intense, but that it got too empty.

And so, over the following years, I concentrated on being a success in business, which I achieved. But I avoided the reality and humanity of the genuine sexual experience that is based in love.

Instead I elevated my status as observer and gave myself a master's degree. I became a Master of Control. An aesthete manipulator with a rod of iron; a staff of insignia with which I would anoint my disciples at the end of their course, a staff that inevitably rose again for the next supplicant and to the next challenge.

Perhaps, after a lifetime of indulgence with submissives, I was attracted to Tamara because I subconsciously recognized the same traits in her. I was not wrong.

But would it be right for a self-confessed obsessive to become involved with her in a long-term relationship? Of course not. The free spirit that is Tamara is better equipped than I was at her age to enjoy sex, love and human relationships in all their wild variety.

During our several meetings, Tess, you have read my confessions and listened, like Solomon, to my justifications. You have made me think deeper than how to stage the next game and made me examine my motives.

You have, without my noticing, prompted me to shed the layers of pretence within which I had hidden my emotions for years. You have caused me to confront myself and I discovered I was rather sad.

However, I also discovered that I valued your forthright friendship and, once my blinkers had been removed, that it was more than friendship.

You are a beautiful woman, Tess, and I only came to fully appreciate it when I felt a surge of such jealousy that I wanted to give a certain rock-and-roll singer the thrashing of his life. If that seems like an old-fashioned sort of thing to say, then it is probably because I am old-fashioned.

Good God, I'm old enough to be Tamara's grandfather.

Anyway, to get back on track for the final time, this is my last epistle, dear Tess.

I have enjoyed writing them and I hope you have enjoyed reading them. I have never been this open with anyone before, not even myself, and I doubt if I could have finally found maturity with anyone but you as my therapist.

PS: Does it breach the Hippocratic oath if I say I love you?

Chapter 22

Penn watched Tess uneasily, trying to gauge her reaction. She finally put down the typescript.

She said, 'You have a hell of a way with words, Charles Penn.'

'Maybe I should go into publishing.'

'You think you've finally got it all out of your system?'

'I think so.' He was disappointed she had not immediately responded to his declaration of love. Perhaps she was trying to save him from further embarrassment? 'I realized that as far as Julia was concerned, I had been in love with an image rather than reality.'

'Exactly,' she said.

'I had been fooling myself. Young girls were easier to manipulate. There were no complications.' He shrugged. 'Hell, I suppose in a way I was living life in a sweet shop.'

He emptied his glass and refilled it with wine.

'Except that eventually you start to notice the customers are so much younger than you are.' He smiled at Tess. 'You're the first person I've been able to talk to, really talk to, for years.' He laughed. 'I enjoyed being with you so much that I became blinkered again.'

'Blinkered?' she said.

'I equated you with friendship. A real friendship. For me sex was something else entirely. Christ, the two have never gone together before in my experience. It was a shock when I realized that I was very much attracted to you.'

Penn stood in the middle of the room, feeling like a naughty schoolboy.

'Go on,' Tess said.

'I suddenly realized how beautiful you are, what a sexually attractive woman you are.' He gulped wine. 'How I would very much like to make love with you. And then I panicked, because I thought being a friend might exclude the other.'

He turned away, embarrassed, and went back to the wine bottle.

Tess said, 'You've finally got Tamara out of your system?'

'Yes. I suppose I was looking for an excuse to have a proper relationship at last, but I had become locked into this Lolita complex. Thank goodness I met you and you straightened me out.'

'You straightened yourself out, Charles.'

'That's not true. You were the impetus and the stimulus.'

'There you go again. This time you make me sound like a hi-fi system.'

They both laughed and then he became serious.

'I also meant what I wrote, Dr Flanders. Do many of your patients fall in love with you?'

Tess still smiled, but sympathetically.

'It is an occupational hazard,' she said, evenly. 'What makes it unusual in this case is for the therapist to fall in love with the patient.'

For a moment, what she said did not make sense.

'You mean?' he said, and for once he was lost for words.

'Yes, you lummox. I love you, too.'

Tess remained sitting in the armchair and he remained standing in the middle of the room.

He said, 'Shouldn't we kiss?'

She got to her feet and he put down his wine glass and they went into each other's arms. The kiss was delicious and deep and arousing.

When their mouths broke apart, her voice was not quite even.

She said huskily, 'As well as love, I do have a rather uncontrollable urge to rip your clothes off and fuck you.'

'That's mutual,' he said. 'But first, there's something I want to show you.'

'That is not an original line,' she said.

He gently disengaged and said, 'I still have confessions to make.'

Tess watched him with a mixture of desire and curiosity. He opened the door that led into his study and indicated she should enter. They both went inside.

The study was dark. Light from the bedroom was reflected on the bank of screens on the opposite wall, none of which were active. Penn keyed instructions into his desk terminal and his monitor screen came to life. It showed the cloakroom and Jamie Philpott with Susan, the English rose.

Tess gasped.

'What is this?' she said.

She guessed exactly what it was, and felt the lurch of her stomach as she realized she might herself be discovered as a voyeur in the cloakroom.

'I had the house fitted with cameras.'

He flicked switches and the bank of screens came to life although the bedrooms were in darkness and their occupants asleep.

'All the rooms?' she said.

Tess remembered standing in front of the mirror in her underwear, touching herself.

'All but yours, Tess. There was no way I could watch you uninvited. The others?' He waved an arm at the screens. 'They spend their lives being watched. But not you.'

The monitor showed Philpott taking the girl from behind and Tess realized from the angle of the camera that she was safe. Now she began to take a fuller interest in what was on the screen. As she had discovered at the time, watching was quite a turn-on.

'Charles Penn, you are totally amoral,' she said, leaning over the desk to stare at the monitor.

'I'm a voyeur,' he said.

Tess glanced over her shoulder and fixed him with a look.

'And what about me? Will you want to watch me being fucked?'

'Only by me, in a mirror.' He shrugged. 'Or maybe on a very private video that is for our eyes only.'

Tess turned back to watch the screen. Penn moved behind her and she could feel his erection against her and his hands rested on her hips.

God, but it had been a long time.

Philpott came in the girl's mouth and Tess found herself licking her own lips. Her vagina felt on fire.

'Watch,' said Penn.

She watched herself come into shot for the first time and go into the cubicle. She watched the girl leave and herself re-emerge and Philpott make his play. When he kissed her, Penn gripped her hips fiercely.

'I may still thrash him,' he said.

She straightened and turned.

'But not until the morning,' she said.

They embraced again but this time with all the passion of lust. They mauled each other, their mouths slobbered against each other. Unwilling to release each other, they staggered from the study and into the bedroom where he threw her on the bed.

Penn switched off the light and began to rip off his clothes. On the bed, Tess unzipped the dress, pulled it over her head and dropped it on the carpet but removed no more.

She lay back and waited, her pale and curvaceous body crossed by the straps of her black underwear, her legs encased in shining black Lycra stockings to mid-thigh, her vagina covered by high-cut black silk panties to make her legs look longer.

He cursed as he struggled with the final items of his clothing. His eyes drank her in. Her eyes fixed on his erection: it was huge. He had not said anything in his confessions about its size but it looked monstrous and she moaned and stretched a hand towards it.

His body was muscular and lean. He was a powerful man who had practised the art of maintaining his erection for days at a time.

Yes, please, thought Tess.

Finally, he was naked and he leapt upon the bed and upon her. Their mouths fused together and his hands were strong and demanding as they explored the valleys, vales and peaks of her body.

His prick lay against her vagina and she whimpered and thrust against it.

'Fuck me, Charles. Fuck me. For God's sake, fuck me!'

He ripped the panties as if they were gossamer and his

fingers went between her legs and found her vagina wet and open and she almost swooned. Her lips were parted and she rolled her head from side to side.

'Please, please,' she said.

At last, that monstrous weapon was at her portals. He held it between the lips of her sex, guided it, eased it inside for the first few inches and made her gasp and moan. And then she could wait no longer, and thrust against him and dug her long nails into his buttocks as she demanded it all and now.

He sank it into her and she screamed and held him and raked him with her nails and shouted. He responded with a furious assault that drove her mind into oblivion as she came, and came, and came.

When her senses returned, he had removed her bra and the remnants of her panties and was sucking at her vagina. She came again, deliriously and helplessly.

His mouth was still locked onto her sex when she recovered and she had to prise it away and bring him up the bed to her. She kissed him and caressed his penis and found it still huge and still strong.

'You are amazing,' she whispered. 'But you must come too. Fuck me, Charles, and come inside me, and I'll suck you back to full strength. Come on, Charles. Do it.'

He slid on top of her again and fitted his weapon inside her and resumed his powerful rhythm that was once more taking her to the heights. But this time she did not want to go over them without him.

'Come on, Charles. Fuck me. Let it go,' she whispered in his ear as he pounded above her. The tension shook his arms. 'Fuck me,' she whispered. 'Fill me with your spunk. Do it, do it. Fuck me . . . aaah.'

At last, he came and spurted inside her with a massive

shudder and she orgasmed with him as they rocked in the closest of embraces.

As the aftermath washed them with tranquillity, he held her in his arms. They lay silent for a long time.

Tess eventually said, 'I've never had a multiple orgasm before. You gave me two.' She kissed his chest. 'And I want more.'

He said, 'You are the sexiest woman I have ever known, Tess Flanders. I don't believe it, but I think I'm getting another erection.'

'Good,' she said.

She slipped down the bed and caressed his penis with her breasts before taking hold of it, manipulating it, putting it into her mouth and sucking it. Within a short time, it had regained its strength and size.

Tess slid back up the bed and straddled him. She lay on top of him with his penis nicely trapped beneath her.

'I want you to fuck me every way possible,' she said.

'I intend to.'

They kissed and he lifted her and fitted his penis inside her and she rode him, her breasts swinging above his face, and they continued to make love and fuck for a very long time.

Charles Penn had slept with Tess only one night and yet his first reaction, when he awoke at dawn's early light, was to reach out for her. She wasn't there.

He sat up in bed and saw the door to the study was open. He could hear the buzz of electronics. He got out of bed, walked across the carpet naked and looked into the darkened room.

Tess, wearing one of his silk dressing gowns, was sitting at the control desk but the monitor was blank.

'Good morning,' he said.

She turned her head and smiled at him.

'Hi,' she said.

'What are you doing?'

'Just checking.'

'I thought you didn't approve.'

'I don't but . . .'

'But?'

'But this is all here and so am I and I thought it might be useful – professionally speaking, of course . . .'

'Of course.'

'To observe objectively before we actually do pull the plug.'

'We're going to pull the plug?'

'Oh yes, Charles. We have to.'

'But for now?'

'Well. For now, can you show me how to work the damn' thing? I would very much like to see what happened when they found the blue movies.'

He chuckled and leaned over her, switched on the monitor on the desk, and tapped instructions into the keyboard.

Tess said, 'It's as easy as that?'

'As easy as that.'

The monitor showed the library. It was empty and in darkness. He hit the rewind, stopped it, and pressed 'play'. His guests were sitting around, their eyes glued to the television. They were agitated. Jamie Philpott was so agitated he had Fiona's hands in his lap moving over the bulge in his trousers.

Tess said, 'They found them.'

Penn said, 'Shall I go forward a while? To the bedrooms?'

'Why not?' she said.

He tapped in new instructions.

'We'll try Tamara's room first,' he said.

The monitor showed an empty bedroom. He fast-forwarded but it remained empty. He tapped new instructions.

'Jamie's,' he said.

That too, was empty, and remained so on fast forward. He tried again.

'Delia's.'

This time the bedroom, and the bed, was occupied. Delia was naked and lying between the legs of another woman.

Tess said in surprise, 'It's Liz. And my God, she's enjoying it.'

They watched awhile. Penn turned up the sound and they learned that Liz was very vocal when she had an orgasm. Delia slid up the bed into her arms and kissed the girl passionately and Tess recognized her as another predator. But, she had to admit, a very attractive and sexy predator.

Penn said, 'Another?'

'Yes.'

This time the monitor showed Monty's room. The bed was filled with flesh. The corpulent producer and Jamie Philpott were both engaged in sexual activities with Susan at the same time and, from her reaction, she was loving every minute of it.

Monty still had his socks on and Jamie appeared to be besotted with the girl's amazing breasts.

Tess said, 'You know, I think Jamie may have at last found true love.'

Again, they watched awhile, for the action was extremely physical and sexual. It was raw and potent, even with socks on.

Penn said, 'That leaves Tamara, Fiona and Mark. Do you think they could be . . .?'

They were. The screen showed the interior of Mark's bedroom and here the action was much more laid-back and sensual. Mark sprawled on the bed, smoking what appeared to be a joint, and watched Tamara and Fiona make love together.

Penn was close behind Tess and he put a hand on her shoulder and she put hers over it.

'No regrets?' she said, as they watched the beautiful free spirit with the green eyes slowly writhing in pleasure at the touch of another woman's tongue.

'None,' he said. 'I need a woman, not a girl.'

Tess got up and turned to face him. The silk dressing gown opened and she pressed her naked body against his and felt his erection against her thigh.

'And I need a man,' she said. 'Right now.'

She began to lead him back to the bedroom but he paused, leaned over the control desk, flicked a switch – and all the screens went blank.

That's okay, thought Tess. I know how to switch them back on again.